TIBOR FISCHER

HOW

TO

RULE

THE

WORLD

corsair

CORSAIR

First published in the UK in 2018 by Corsair

1 3 5 7 9 10 8 6 4 2

Copyright © Tibor Fischer, 2018

The moral right of the author has been asserted.

A CIP catalogue record for this book
is available from the British Library.

ISBN: 978-1-4721-5365-4
ISBN: 978-1-4721-5364-7

Typeset in Perpetua by Hewer Text UK Ltd, Edinburgh
Printed and bound in Great Britain by Clays Ltd, St Ives plc

Papers used by Corsair are from well-managed forests
and other responsible sources.

Corsair
An imprint of
Little, Brown Book Group
Carmelite House
50 Victoria Embankment
London EC4Y 0DZ

An Hachette UK Company
www.hachette.co.uk

www.littlebrown.co.uk

For my Godmother

'This history is called Jaya. It should be heard by those desirous of victory. A king by hearing it may bring the whole world under subjection and conquer all his foes.'

The Mahabharata

TOOTING SEPTEMBER

'Don't you remember me?' asks the man on my doorstep.

He's my age. Worn jeans and a brown T-shirt. Maybe he has no money, maybe he's a trillionaire. That's London. You're a trillionaire, you can do what you want. You're right and everyone else, or everyone else without a trillion, and that is just about everyone else, is wrong. You wear a faded brown T-shirt with a small hole in it, because. Because you can.

It's unlikely that a trillionaire would be on my doorstep. And there's a ring in his words that suggests a South London chancer who drives a Porsche. But an old Porsche, not a vintage Porsche, a knackered one with rust, with no insurance and his two kids crouched in the back with the final demands under their feet, the tank half-full because he can't afford to fill it. The sort of chancer who's been driven to extinction by five-to-a-room Lithuanians and khatted-up Somalis who have picked up the challenge of assault, light-fingeredness and non-payment on the fringes of our capital.

'No,' I reply.

'You don't remember me?' He's smiling, but there's an edge, as if I owe him money or didn't return his lawnmower twenty years ago. Someone from school? Work? Tangiers? Aldershot? The Three Kings? No, it's no use, I don't remember, and I can't be bothered with this. Whatever this is.

'No.'

I wanted to take in my home for a last time, as I picked up the last box, before I dropped off the keys. To say goodbye. Have a moment to wallow in some quality self-pity. Whoever this caller is, if he'd turned up ten minutes later, I'd have been gone.

'Take a good look,' he insists. 'Sure you don't remember me?'

'No.' It always annoys me when someone refuses to understand no. No. It's simple, it's so short. I'm saying no because I mean no. I'm not playing hard to get. I push myself to add, 'Sorry.'

'You don't have a clue, do you?'

'No.'

'Good,' he says and knocks me out.

BANGKOK
OCTOBER

I don't want to be in this room.

Travelling a lot narrows the mind. You want your usual hotel in Bangkok (or Beirut or Baghdad), because they have a proper pool, or because it's close to the airport, or because they stock a good orange juice in the minibar, or because you know how to work the shower. No time is wasted finding out which floor serves breakfast, how exactly you get your coffee (do you hunt down a waiter or will they hunt you?) and which switch actually switches off the bedside lamp.

You want to be the ruler of the air-conditioning and to know the tasty items on the room-service menu. Thought-saving stuff to make the trip as smooth as possible, so that when the unsmooth stuff arrives, you have plenty of boot to deal with it. I should have known when I couldn't get into my favourite hotel in Bangkok, this would be very unsmooth.

I don't want to be in this room. I haven't wanted to be here for the last two hours, but they're making me wait. Standard stuff. Whatever's going to happen could have happened two hours ago, but they're demonstrating who-the-boss, as if they need to. I'm the distraught foreigner in the police station on an uncomfortable chair.

The Thais are a cheerful, hospitable bunch, until they aren't. You can get robbed, cheated and put on an uncomfortable chair.

I've bribed policemen in four continents, and it's about the etiquette. You can get it wrong: bribing too little; bribing too much (yes, you can); bribing too openly; bribing not bribingly enough; bribing too slowly; bribing too fast. Why can't they just hand you a guide? Hula Hoops, cigarettes, a leather jacket (a good one) and, naturally, cash have all worked their magic.

The chief comes in. He has the face of a man who could order a massacre. A puppy-hammering face.

'Call me Mike,' he says. His name is not Mike. I can see his name displayed on the door, a centipede-long name. He has decided, not unreasonably, that as a benighted farang I can't pronounce his name. It's courteous. Or insulting. Take your pick.

'He's mad as fuck, your friend.' Now Massacre Mike's showing off his use of the vernacular.

'He's not exactly my friend.'

'We all have the mad-as-fuck friend. Part of karma.' Mike's wondering whether he needs to explain karma to this white dumbo in front of him.

'Do you like paperwork?' he continues.

I assume no is the correct answer and say so.

'I don't like paperwork and I like the British Embassy's summer parties. Can you get Mr Stern out of the country immediately?'

Mr Stern. When was the last time anyone called him 'Mr Stern'? Wilhelm Stern, Villy the Violent Vegan. Widely known in the Vizz as 'that nutter', 'nutter number one' or most commonly as 'Semtex'. Surely the most fired, the most arrested, the most deported, the most black-eyed camera--man in the world? Can I get Semtex out of Thailand immediately?

8

'Yes.'

There's a part of me that says I should ask for a few days' grace to do our job. To fix things. That's your job as a producer, as a director, as the prime pusher, to ask for the impossible. To push. To push all day. To push as far as you can. The impossible doesn't turn up every day, but it's your job to ask. And ask again. To ask so often that you can't really remember what it is you're asking. You don't ask, you don't get.

It's too hot and I'm too tired to ask, because I'm faced with real impossibility. It's not allowed. If I had tried to organise such complete failure I wouldn't have succeeded. No human is capable of this level of intricacy.

I realise, to my horror, that I'm not losing my fight, my boot, my head-buttery, my what-are-you-looking-at? I *have* lost my fight. That I'd like someone to cover me with soil. Money and honey, fame, pleasure, these are the goals of youth; peace is what you go for in the end. To be Otanes.

'Any problem on the way to the airport, you both go to j-ai-l.' The way Massacre Mike sings 'jail' is unusually alarming. All the truly frightening people I've met have been like that: calm, unarmed, terrifying. Correction: the most frightening – those at the top of the terror tree – aren't calm, they're even jovial, they're comedians. The top Chechen I met, who scared me so much I almost fainted, looked like the village idiot and chuckled non-stop. Because it's funny. Because it is.

All the scarred types who glower and strain to be thuggish, they're always small-time. Like the Krays, who glowered in their photos but snivelled like little girls in jail.

'Thanks, Mike.' I attempt to fake my share in this cordiality. Massacre Mike mentions his cousin has an excellent seafood restaurant round the corner. I consider mentioning my cousin is big in seafood too, but I don't need to bond any more.

He adds: 'I am coming to London in a month. I enjoy expensive restaurants.'

I give him my card. Over the years I've found giving someone my card is almost a guarantee that you will never hear from the recipient, especially if you do want to hear from the recipient; but if Mike wants, I will take him to a restaurant, because I am not doing anything to displease this man. It's not an unreasonable deal.

We shake hands. Mike's hand is massive. It's a hand that's done a lot of manual labour. Digging shallow graves, for instance. Or deep ones. My hand is a wilted dandelion slammed on by a car door.

And I can't help feeling this isn't just about Semtex. This is about the oodh. Aka the jinko. Aka the gaharu. The agarwood, if you prefer.

Normally I wouldn't have brought Semtex on a job like this. Headies. It's basically pointless. More than pointless, exceedingly imprudent, as Herbie would have said.

We're nearly all self-shooting directors these days, but I like to have extra firepower. Especially in enemy territory. I like to have a cameraman who, if something unexpected kicks off, can handle it. And handle it well. I've felt that since that evening, long ago, when I spotted a senior government minister rutting in a car park in Richmond with a well-known popular entertainer. This was decades before everyone's phone had a camera. I was with a competent cameraman, but by the time he had fussed over the set-up, the action was over. You want someone like Semtex, who can lens at the drop of a hat, blindfolded.

Semtex did that once. We were filming a parade by the French Foreign Legion (the only part of the French military that actually fights because it's full of Germans). 'This is insulting,' he raged. 'Why am I here? Why are you doing this to me? A bunch of twats trooping past? You don't need a cameraman, you need a tripod. You're taking the piss, aren't you? I could do this blindfold.' So he did. It wasn't his best work, but still better than most.

What might be my last bit of luck got me this oodh commission from Johxn. Luck is finite, only a fool would think otherwise. No one gets it all. No one. Maybe some get a little more than others. That's hard to call. But no one gets it all. The real problem is guessing how much luck is left.

You get a reputation. For some reason I'm the man who's sent to riots, dangerous foreign shitholes. Organised crime in unorganised states. Any city with kids twirling automatic weapons. Revolutions.

My very first foreign job as an assistant cameraman: the January Events in Vilnius back in '91 when Lithuania broke away from the Soviet Union. I'd been told to disappear with our footage, so it couldn't be seized by anyone with a gun. I'd been drinking, heavily, in the bar of the Writers' Union.

I hate history. Unless it's being made, I suppose, but then it's not really history. I hate history, but a staggering brunette, possibly the second most beautiful woman I've ever talked to, invited me back to her place to discuss Baltic history. We all know what that means.

Or maybe she did want to discuss border violations and treaties, stranger things have happened. But my bladder was bursting with Lithuanian beer. So I went for a piss first. I nosedived on the dark stairs down to the toilet and broke my arm. As I writhed in pain, someone said: 'You're lucky. Those stairs have killed

11

more than the Soviets.' The cameraman I was assisting was shot dead the next day while I was on a flight home.

So how do you total it up? Lucky? Unlucky? I told my Uncle Joe and he just laughed, as he laughed at all my scrapes, because his position was, not unreasonably, as long as you're alive you have nothing to complain about.

I told everyone that I broke my arm falling down the stairs. It took me a while to figure out no one believed me. 'We heard,' is what everyone said to me.

There's always tax. Even if it's not marked on the bill. You pay. You always pay. I did Afghanistan. It was a miracle I survived that (that anyone did). And I was wounded. Badly. Not a bullet, not shrapnel. No, a dumb American journalist spilled boiling coffee onto my family jewels. I would have preferred a small-calibre bullet in the leg. At least you can brag about that later and show the scar when you're drunk.

♏

'Someone has to do oodh,' Johxn had said to me. 'I wanted Edison to do it, but he's been arrested, and Jack's busy too. Milly's lost her passport. You just can't get anyone good these days. Where's all the talent gone? Can you think of anyone good? A real pukka fucker?'

Years ago I might have been offended by Johxn's comments, but you do become numb. Sensation just dies off. I might have been offended that he was phoning me to ask for a recommendation rather than to offer me the work.

Years ago I might have been offended that he laughed when I suggested I could do it, but you have to fight through the laughter. It was the fourth time I volunteered myself that he agreed. It wasn't any slick sales talk on my part; it was 12.30. Johxn needed lunch.

'Oh, and whatever you do, don't use Semtex,' Johxn added. 'The legals insist on that.'

'Wouldn't dream of it.'

Oodh was something I hadn't come across. But I got the commission to do a doc about oodh, aka agarwood, aka jinko, basically bits of smelly wood that can be worth more than gold or mountain-fresh cocaine, that are big in Asia and the Middle East as incense, smoky bling, medicine. They're tree-scabs. Aquilaria trees have to be infected to produce oodh, and because it's hard to get and ultra-expensive, of course traders are lying, stealing, cheating and killing over it.

Semtex and me had just done an interview in a shitty suburb of Bangkok with a snitch who had liberally ratted out many Thai dignitaries and military types. It had taken months, a research trip, money to arrange. I dislike interviewees who are blacked out, fuzzy or voice-changed because with that cover, you can say anything. You can have your next-door neighbour or mum claim to be Osama bin Laden.

When I see that, I'm very sceptical because I know what lying, cheating shits work in the Vizz. I know because I've worked with them. I believed our snitch, because he was petrified and knew his nuts were on the line. So why blab? This is what fascinates me. Almost everyone will do just about anything to get on screen, even if they're blacked out and even if they risk getting killed. There's a terrible need to be noticed.

The bean-spiller was almost our last interview; we only had one more to do in the afternoon. So we had time for lunch. If you insulted Semtex, or did something traditionally provocative like pour a beer all over him, he'd probably look hurt and put on an air of noble forbearance. But . . .

m

I bid farewell to Massacre Mike and have a big seafood blowout in his cousin's restaurant round the corner, which I enjoy more than I thought I would, because this might be the last time I'm in Bangkok. I'm unlikely to get any more work, and I doubt if I'll ever want to spend any of my own money on travel, partly because I have no money, and if I did have some I wouldn't waste it on travel. It's that last-supper kick.

In my twenties I spent most of my time on the road. I lived out of a rucksack, and enjoyed it. Up and down Britain. All over Europe. China. Japan. The States. What I want now is not travel but a large house, somewhere sunny, that I'll only leave for twenty-minute walks, while I edit the *Magnum*. Friends can visit.

By the time I've finished dealing with the succulent octopus (which of course reminds me of Jim) and returned to the police station, Semtex has been produced from the cells. His almost complete lack of remorse is grating. He gives me a dirty look (80 per cent sulk, 10 per cent rage, 8 per cent bewilderment, 2 per cent contrition) as he's released, as if it was me that got us into trouble.

The silence is stony as we collect our gear (what's left of it at our hotel) and go to the airport. 'This will be reflected in my invoice,' is all Semtex says. I'm past any sort of concern. How do you tell the difference between fatigue, not caring and Zen? Or is Zen merely deluxe apathy? Apathy with great PR?

Honestly, if you actually provoke Semtex, you're less likely to have trouble with him. I've pulled him off a number of waiters and taxi drivers who said something inflammatory like, 'Good evening' or, 'May I help you?' Edison owed Semtex two weeks' money (and as far as I know still does), and we were all waiting for Semtex to flatten his nose, but

14

nothing happened. No, it's unfortunate serving staff who get the worst of Semtex, and there are many places that don't understand vegetarians, let alone vegans. I remember Semtex biting one waiter in Seoul because he suggested a boiled egg.

And in addition to any misunderstandings because of his diet, there's also Semtex's habit of altering menus in places that serve meat. Very often he'll just scribble an addendum in pen, but sometimes he will go the whole hog and take away a menu to forge it and return the fake copies for distribution.

Well-tortured lamb in a fuchsia jus. Slowly strangled swan with a vervania stuffing. Mashed porcine hopes on a bed of Moabite. Blinded, then boiled alive, locally sourced kitten. He'll savour the ensuing outrage, or out-of-work actors struggling to explain what Moabite is.

He used to live in Brighton but he was barred from so many places for affray or menu-tampering that he had to move to Heathrow, which he claims is better for travel and he doesn't mind the noise. On light shoots he can actually walk to the airport in twenty minutes.

It's not just waiters that get a close-up of his knuckles; Semtex is no respecter of rank or power. 'I don't care if you are the Chief Constable of Manchester, I'm still going to thump you,' he declared, right before doing that, on camera, in the middle of an interview. You can see why he doesn't get hired much these days, and why he's often unavailable for work for months at a time.

Airside, as we have two large hours to wait, Semtex defuses the lack of conversation by wandering off to the shops and the duty-free. I've already got my presents for the family; I picked up some dried durian, the king of fruits, at the hotel for the wife and some longan honey for my son. Luke loves honey on toast for breakfast.

15

Shop when you can. I wasn't in the army long, but that's what I learned. Do it when you can, because you might not always be able to do it. I'm not in the mood to buy a newspaper; I stare into space, wondering whether I can come up with some way of nicing up the situation.

A group of four men are shoving each other about, and as soon as I realise they're British, I get as far away as possible. Inevitably, they follow me to the other side of the lounge. Every nation has its loudmouths, those whose ideacaves harbour no life, but nothing is as bad as the British stag party. Except the British stag party abroad. I move back to the other side of the lounge, but I can hear them. Once we brought timekeeping, engineering and gunboat justice to the world, now we transport arse-baring, plastic breasts and howls.

One, wearing a T-shirt that says, 'Let's not bother with words or feelings', is holding onto his cock. Not a quick confirmation or reorganisation, not a showy scratch, he's clinging onto his cock as if it's a winning lottery ticket. He's late twenties, he's not drunk, he's in the middle of a crowded airport, and he's waddling around like a two-year-old. Why is he at my airport? Why is he on my planet?

To make sure I'm not being over-judgemental, I time him to verify that it's not some underwear crisis. I count to twenty and he's still squeezing away as if fighting a stubborn tube of toothpaste. I'm just old enough to remember when travel was sufficiently pricey to discourage the mindless from exotic locations.

Finally, the cock-clutcher lets go. He now picks at his arse while discussing the purchase of aftershave. Alarmingly, he grabs a bottle of my usual brand. Should he purchase it, I will never be able to wear it again. Fortunately, he returns it to the display. I like it, my wife likes it, but fortunately my wife has no idea why that's the one I always buy.

The arse-scratcher looks familiar. I'd assumed because he's the identikit stag oaf, but I do know him.

I recognise his ski-lodge eyebrows. He's Luke's teacher. Teachers are the first in a long procession you encounter in life, to feed you flannel. First teachers, then colleagues, doctors, ironmongers, sailing instructors, insurance salesmen, swimming coaches, bankers, boiler repairmen, mechanics, microsuctionists, postmen, tree-surgeons, dry-cleaners who fob you off, and then finally you end up back with the teachers as they hand you flannel about your son, and you wonder whether your parents fell for it.

At the parents' evening, he had cheerfully assured us that everything was fine. It was the cheap but effective tactic of telling hearers what they want to hear.

What do you teach your child? I suppose all of us would like our children to be honest, friendly and helpful, even though those are the worst qualities to have. The Allower doesn't favour decent people.

The best tactic is to lie, cheat and stamp on the faces of those around you. If you're punctual, you'll wait. If you're loyal, you'll be betrayed. If you're generous, you'll be swindled. If you help others, you'll be slapped by their ingratitude. If you work hard, you'll be tired. If you don't steal, you'll be poor. But you can't want that for your child.

You want your son to be a loyal friend, a defender of the weak, a helper of old ladies, but that gets you bugger all. To be liked, to be popular, to be respected, these qualities don't pay well. I suppose the solution is to behave with family and friends (although friends are tricky) and war with everyone else.

17

You want your son to be happy, but you don't want him to be a blando, someone who progresses quietly without obstacles. That means a bit of grit. You want him to see darkness. Once is enough. In an ideally controlled and not-too-unpleasant way. A brief, judicious application of hardship. I doubt anyone who hasn't tasted shit can be worth knowing.

My fight is really extinguished. I try to think of Bongo Herman, and how he manfully fought the bass, but it's no use. I see a discarded copy of *El Pais* two seats down. My Spanish was never much good and since I haven't used it that hasn't helped, but I reach over. If I opened the newspaper to see a headline stating there was an international petition to have me publicly executed, it wouldn't surprise me.

The oodh project is kaput, I'm at an airport surrounded by cock-clutchers who are forming our youth and dangerous headcases, and on top of all that, Herbie is dead. I yearn to lie down on the ground and curl up into a ball.

El Pais runs an article about a place called Göbekli Tepe in Turkey. If I understand the article correctly it's some religious site that's older than Stonehenge, which I always thought was as old as it gets; before that human aspiration was clubbing everything with a sabre-tooth's leg-bone. But Göbekli Tepe is *much* older than Stonehenge. Older than anything man-made apart from those cave paintings.

It's the most important archaeological site in the world, it says. The textbooks will have to be rewritten.

I love it when the experts have to put on the dunce's hat. Göbekli Tepe has great stone figures, mega megalith action that was buried for thousands of years until some Kurdish shepherd noticed something sticking out of a mound in the middle of total nowhere, and a German came and dug it up.

It's possibly the Garden of Eden. Because according to the Bible, Eden was between the Euphrates and the Tigris.

Why haven't I heard about this? Why don't British newspapers write about stuff like this? All they write about is the arses of women from Essex or Los Angeles. And if Göbekli Tepe was the Garden of Eden, why was it buried? Because it didn't get dusty and overgrown. It was buried. Buried very carefully and very heavily. By whom and why?

It's curious that there's any civilisation at all. There's no need for it. We could still be comfortable in the trees. Gorillas have pretty good lives. Such draining work, civilisation.

Göbekli Tepe sounds extraordinary, but stones get too much credit sometimes. Why are ancient civilisations revered as if they knew something? As if they had a secret message? Some last, lasting truth? No they didn't. They knew fuck all. That's why they're gone. If they were so clever why aren't they still here? If they had been so profoundly pally with the universe, trustees of the hush-hush, why are they the dust under my shoe? I notice I'm actually mouthing 'they knew fuck all'.

I rustle up some snaps of Göbekli Tepe. It's a little disappointing when you look at it. Like meeting any hero. T-shaped slabs of stone in pairs, so maybe man and woman. Or not. They and the encircling slabs have reliefs of animals that could be just about anything you'd want them to be: pigs? Foxes? Lizards? Vultures? And which could mean anything you'd want them to.

But Göbekli is a good bet because people are fascinated by the old, because they do think there is ancient wisdom. There's just the slight problem that slabs of stone don't make great entertainment.

'This is all your fault, you know.' Semtex returns with two bags of some Royal-approved handicrafts made by Hill

Tribes. The Royals are big in Thailand, and the military comes second.

'It is my fault,' I say.

'It is your fault, star,' Semtex insists, mistaking my admission for sarcasm. But it is my fault. There can be a serious downside to being a cameraman – you have to climb into sewers, crawl into eerie spaces, hang out of speeding trains – but the fussing, the putting something in front of the camera is down to the director.

At the restaurant, it had been my job to ask the waiter about the quickest meal, so we could lunch fast and get back to work, and it would have been my job, after twenty minutes, to sternly enquire where our food was. It had been a bad morning. Our first interviewee hadn't turned up. Our second interviewee didn't speak English, but thought he did. There's nothing you can do about people. Then our oodh whistle-blower had worried that he wasn't blacked out enough, even though he had his back to the camera.

One thing that my cynicism ('Bax, why are you so cynical?') and my pessimism ('Bax, how can you be such a pessimist?') help me with is organisation. I expect everything to go wrong. So I apply belts and braces, and tape. I triple check. I give everyone maps, running orders and phone numbers. Information is spunked everywhere. But you still depend on others. You can't dodge. Your debacle is waiting for you, enjoying a coffee.

The content is my problem. Whether there's an interviewee or not, Semtex gets paid. On shoots, Semtex and I have sometimes sat in restaurants fuming for an hour or more, waiting for our food, despite a long speech to the staff about how quickly we need to eat, and the promise of a huge tip.

But this time Semtex lost it, after only twenty minutes he

steamed into the kitchen, screaming, 'It's only a stir-fry,' destroying ancestral crockery, shoving aside two protesting waiters and biting another, surely poor form for a vegan. Then the noodle chef floored him with one punch.

There are a number of cities in which, if forced to, I could imagine starting a fight: Iowa City, Braunschweig, any French city (the French are so easy to beat up, even the Germans are bored by it). Bangkok isn't one of them. And Semtex isn't young. He's hitting forty and your reflexes simply aren't the same. In any fight, speed comes first. Second and third. It takes all the medals. It doesn't matter how much torque you can deliver from your wrist. Or how much you can bench-press or how dirty you're planning to be.

The noodle chef was effortless: his centre of gravity was perfect. That's how you could tell he was really good, he didn't actually move, he waited for Semtex to enter the cross hairs. Pow. I couldn't see the punch, it was that fast. And back to the noodles.

I'd say Semtex got off lightly with concussion and a night in the cells. Our doc was buggered because by the time I was soft soaping the police, all our kit had been stolen. All the interviews, our session with the snitch, the camera. Convenient for many oodh-profiteers. A very convenient theft. We don't have the budget to do it all again and in any case, our snitch's gone to hide in a swamp in the border region.

But it *is* my fault, because I hired Semtex in the face of many nays. It would have been much cheaper and easier and altogether more doc-completing to have used a local. I've gambled again, and lost again. Correction: 'gambling' is too glamorous, soldier-of-fortune, devil-may-care a term. A gambler courageously shows the finger to the forces of destiny. I've merely fucked up again.

21

'If we were doing Roger Crab. We wouldn't be here,' Semtex sulks.

'We wouldn't.'

He's never forgiven me for the Hermit of Uxbridge: Roger Crab. Roger Crab, dockleaf-devourer, vegan idol, wonderment and probably the most irritating man of the seventeenth century. A hermit, largely because he was hated by his family, his neighbours and anyone he came into contact with. He was sentenced to death by his own side in the Civil War.

It's the horses-for-courses thing. Semtex is a great with a camera, but he has no idea what makes a good doc, and also lacks the arse-licking and swindling skills necessary to sell a proposal for a doc. He's been pestering me for years to pitch Roger Crab, the drawback being there is nothing to film, outside of Uxbridge High Street and a woodcut of Crab. It's bereft of visuals and there is nothing more to say about Crab other than he was a viciously preachy vegan and everyone hated him. Every so often Semtex brings him up, and every so often I reply I'm mulling it over.

'Is it true you killed all those people?' Semtex asks me in a loud, airport-wide voice.

'I don't want to talk about it,' I say. Because I don't.

'What did happen exactly,' Semtex continues in his loudest voice, 'when you killed those people?'

'I'm not talking about it. You're not irritating when you try to be, you're only irritating when you're yourself.'

'You won't believe my invoice. This is the last time, Bax. You're the original disaster magnet. I can't work with you any more.'

We don't talk again until we say 'goodbye' at Heathrow. Even five years ago my rage would have been enough to incinerate the average soaking hippo, but as you get older you understand that unless there's some benefit to having a tantrum, why bother? You look ridiculous purple and it seldom changes anything. Semtex has buggered up the entire shoot, the entire oodh.

But I hired him. Semtex has the eye. You don't need to direct him, and in fact, you can't. When he shoots a riot or anything unplanned, it looks like a four-camera shoot. There are a few who can match Semtex, but they have to have every-thing explained, well in advance; they have to sweat, they take all day. They have to pull out their intestines and have a long holiday afterwards.

The footage he shot in Iraq is the best I've ever seen. You can see tracer rounds coming right at the camera, and the gunfire is so loud you can't hear me behind him making the strange hiccuppy sounds you make when you think you're about to die. He does it without effort. And he has a strange morality unusual in the Vizz.

When we were covering the Battle in Seattle, Semtex put down the camera. He put it down with reverence, the way all true cameramen do. He put it down tenderly, to kick the crap out of a policeman who was kicking the crap out of a woman on the ground, before other policemen kicked the crap out of him. The next time I saw Semtex I didn't recognise him. If you've ever seen someone severely beaten up – they don't look real.

They look as if they've been subjected to special effects. I wouldn't have known the purple pumpkin in front of me was Semtex. I often wonder whether that particular hiding didn't serious affect his judgement. He is the best in the business, but unfortunately there's hardly anyone left in the Vizz capable of appreciating his talent. Or willing to work with him.

So why did I hire him? If you hire a dangerous headcase, can you complain about him acting like a dangerous headcase? Mr

Hugh Briss. Let me introduce you to Mr Hugh Briss, as Herbie would have said. For years I believed there had been a Mr Briss, a legendary arrogant arsehole, or it was some convoluted rhyming slang, before I discovered the word hubris. I thought I could do a better job than other directors. I was savvy enough to solve the Semtex problem. I could rule him.

♏

London is a grey city, and coming back from most countries makes it greyer. If it had a sunny climate it would be the best city in the world, but it doesn't. It has more clouds than anywhere I've ever been. The sky is a great grey lid.

It's one in the morning when I reach my front door. Correction: it's actually not *my* door. I don't own it, but it's where I live. I look at the door and consider that there are two beings behind that door who are interested in seeing me. Many go home to a door with no one behind it. It's not much, but perhaps that's all you can really hope for. That there is a door behind which someone is waiting for you. Not necessarily with much enthusiasm. Ellen is a light sleeper and will take my returning at this hour as a calculated affront.

And Herbie is dead. He's been dead for five years.

I always looked up to Herbie. I looked up to him because he got me my first job, but I remember in particular looking up to him outside the Ritz casino. I was looking up to him then because I was on my hands and knees on the pavement. It had been quite an evening. An evening of two days' boozing, which resulted in me exiting the casino on all fours.

At the roulette table, Herbie had stuck 200 quid, the last of a budget, on the zero. 'Whoops,' he said when the ball dropped right, 'that might be the last of my luck.' We spent the next

24

two days in the casino, careless of time and the world, blowing our winnings and more, inventing new cocktails and bonding with an American basketballer-of-fortune, a sundial designer from Uruguay, Britain's most successful armed robber and a former colleague of Vladimir Putin who said Putin was thick and had bad breath, and was merely a puppet of various mining interests.

Outside the Ritz, I looked up to Herbie, because he had started in Fleet Street and so was barely affected by alcohol, and was managing to use his legs in the conventional manner and stand. 'It's our task to turn time into history,' he announced. I have no idea why he said that.

It was dawn and Herbie looked heroic and important as he said that. Although I was mostly preoccupied with how friendly and comfortable the pavement outside the Ritz was, I replied, thinking of my planned doc about The Ray. 'No, it's our task to turn history into time.' I then crawled into the road to stop a taxi and get home.

I contemplated that Ritz moment at Herbie's funeral. Funerals are designed to manipulate you. The hymns, the music, the readings. Professionals are pouring melancholy and contemplation on you, just in case you weren't depressed enough already.

As the eulogies were read, the profundities and the Bach rolled out, I was a little watery but I was holding out. When they played a recording of Herbie's nine-year-old son playing 'Greensleeves' on a flute, really, really badly, it broke me. Because it made it plain he was a nine-year-old with no dad. The unfairness of everything went into me like a knife, and how no man-made endeavour can budge things.

And naturally, there's the self-interest. I grieved because Herbie had lost his life, but I had lost Herbie. He was my backer. My pathfinder. 'Don't moan too much about losing something,' Herbie used to say, 'because it means at least you had it once.' His advice didn't work that day.

I saw his son quite a bit as I helped to sort out Herbie's affairs. I cleared out Herbie's bedsit, not that there was much there anyway, and it had been burgled the day of the funeral. His safe had been taken, which clearly demonstrated, if you needed a demonstration, that nothing is safe. I doubt he had anything really valuable in it, but I had been curious to get a backstage look at Herbie; it might have been like peeling open his head, and there might have been some worthwhile heirloom for his son, some natty cufflinks or an antique pen.

Of course, I did stuff like take Herbie's son out for ice cream and football a couple of times. But so what?

I think about Herbie, and sometimes I feel I've had more luck than I deserve. I've been shot once, had toes broken, genitals scorched, food poisoning, malaria, amoebic dysentery. I have no money. But I have a family. Perhaps I should stop asking for anything? But that seems too easy. Anything easy is suspicious.

THE MEETING
NOVEMBER

I don't want to be in this room.

Not only is this a party I don't want to be at, but it's in the same room, with the same people, and I'm standing in the same corner, for the seventh year in a row. Not only is this shit, but it's the worst sort of shit: the same old shit.

Even the crisps and peanuts in the same bowls could possibly be the same. Don't whinge, Semtex would say. If you don't like something, do something about it. Or shut up. It's an attitude I applaud. Loudly. I've tried to do something about it. Every day. For years. I've made a lot of effort to get nowhere. Or here, as it's otherwise known.

The one bonus in being in a room with a group you want nothing to do with is that you can dispense with witty conversation. I stand wordlessly next to the peanuts and crisps and fill up, thinking of how once the bento boxes flowed freely and now there are only peanuts and crisps, not caring if my filling up or wordlessness are noticed.

'Merry Christmas,' says Johxn as he walks in.

It's pronounced John, but spelt Johxn. There are reasons why the x was implanted. The reasons are very clever, important, political, ecological and spiritual. Johxn explains why he modified his name at length on his blog, citing various rappers, punk groups and graffiti artists. Johxn's entire cultural universe consists of about ten hours of music and a dozen films (and not even films chosen to make him look connoisseurish). Oh, and two coffee-table books on tagging, ones with big pictures and almost no text. If he reads anything these days, it'll be a tattoo on the back of a young lady he's doing.

If anyone misspells his name, Johxn gets absurdly bent out of shape, despite being the only John on the planet who uses an x. I've never read his blog because I'm genuinely afraid that if I did, his arseholery would make me so angry I'd just snap and kill him.

Johxn's entrance is met by a chorus of greetings, ranging from the warm to the calculated cool of those who don't want to be obvious about their grovelling.

If the Allower appeared to me and said, 'Baxter, you've had a raw deal over the years, I owe you. You have a choice: a mountain of gold or a licence to kill Johxn with absolute impunity,' I know what I'd do. I have a family. But I'd think about it for a while.

'Welcome to our Christmas do,' Johxn continues. It's only November but you can't expect television execs to do anything in December, even host a party. 'You're my favourite producers.'

If this is to win favour, it's pure futility. Nothing he can say will alter the reality that his guests would relish seeing him dead. Zyklon Annie and Edison would off him in a second, although Annie would obviously like the opportunity of torturing him first. Even Jack the List, who's so insatiably self-satisfied that he does help little old ladies across the road and donates to animal charities, would, with immunity, douse Johxn with petrol and ignite him.

'And I've got good news for you,' Johxn announces. The room braces. Johxn's news is either not news or bad news. 'I have money. Big money.'

Is this a Johxn joke? Is he lying? Is he kidding himself? If there is some truth in this, what insane ordeal is he going to put us through before we can be admitted into the presence of ... money? Am I concealing my desperation? It doesn't matter so much if you're broken and cowering, as long as you don't look it.

'I'll send out a proper notice in due course, but I wanted to let you know. Big money is in town.'

Money. We thought we'd seen the last of that.

'You can write me the cheque now,' says Edison. You'd expect him to go first. That's fine; let his noise give me time to plot. One thing's for sure, Johxn's not giving a commission now. Apart from being the most decision-averse individual I know, he wouldn't want to miss out on causing widespread suffering for months and months.

The problem is the custard. There isn't enough to go round, because we are too many. Because technology has betrayed us. Because history has shafted us. Because the universities pour out grads who don't know shit, but who do know how to switch on a camera. Because now any twelve-year-old with a phone can do what we do. Because everything's up for free on the web.

When I started in the Vizz, very few got rich. But it was, as they say in Addis Ababa, *jiben* comfortable, there were freebies, comps, goodies, ligging, blagging, skanking. There was a safety net, if your triple somersault didn't come off.

The nineties. Most of the noughties. You wanted for little. You were cool. You travelled the world. You had guaranteed-to-get-you-laid, guaranteed-to-stop-the-dinner-party anecdotes about Death Row or a sleb's bathroom or what you saw in a politician's desk drawer, or about drinking champagne with a mass-murdering dictator (only the one glass, they're really tight, dictators). You were *jiben* guest-listed.

31

Last week, Zyklon Annie was spotted stacking the shelves in a supermarket in Willesden. It wasn't research or undercover work, she was doing part-time work for tiny amounts of money, putting toothpaste on a shelf. The only part of that report that amazed me was that she was able to get the job.

Years ago, she believed her programmes could make or break governments. While the progs didn't match her delusions, she did advise the nation. She made serious progs that the educated paid attention to. Now she stacks shelves, and I've lost my home.

Johxn comes over to hog some peanuts. He glares down into the bowl. 'Jess, could you come in here?'

Jess, his new PA, rushes in with a notice-my-smile smile. She's by a long margin the cheeriest soul in the room, despite being Johxn's PA. She's twentyish and from some small town in an uninteresting part of the Midlands or the North.

Who's happy to be in London? Anyone not from London. Those who've just disembarked from the boat, hopped off the plane, alighted from the train. Anyone who grew up in a gooseberry patch in Flanders, a one-grocery drive-through in the Algarve, a Gdansk housing estate, a quaint Shropshire village. I was born and raised in London, and like everyone I know who grew up in London, I want out.

'Jess, look.' Johxn holds out the bowl. Jess peers in (100 per cent enthusiasm, because that's what you're supposed to do when you want to do well in your career, be enthusiastic). She's perplexed about what she should be looking for. Is there a hilariously deformed peanut on top? Has Johxn left a message in the peanuts? Is there a tiny end-of-year thank-you present lurking there?

She looks up at Johxn (40 per cent quizzical, 60 per cent enthusiasm).

'This is wrong.' Johxn says. Jess has another dive into the bowl, then gives Johxn a look (50 per cent quizzical, 50 per cent pleading). I inspect the bowl again. I can't see any insurgent peanuts or dead insects or anything you wouldn't reasonably expect to see in a bowl of peanuts. But why should he have a reason to reprimand? He's a Commissioning Editor; he has no reason to have a reason about anything. He needs no why.

'Jess, please take this away. These aren't arranged properly. I'm very disappointed in you.'

This would be embarrassing anywhere, but such pettiness in front of us is embarrassing in another way. It's like a kid entering a cell full of serial killers and seeking to astound them by treading on a very small spider. Part of me wants to quiz Johxn about the art of arranging peanuts in a small bowl. Had Jess poured them from the bottom of the packet rather than the top? But it would end badly. There would be arisings.

Studying Zyklon Annie's face, she'd exterminate Johxn entirely on account of this feeble bullying. She might look like a dumpy, sixty-year-old housewife in a sack, unhappy about her cleaner's mopping, but she's killed. That woman has taken human life.

She might as well have those jailhouse tats that tally up your murder rate, rather than that ridiculous fake pearl necklace. Much tougher characters than Jess have been driven to suicide or death by her. I didn't give her her nickname. Programme-making is her job, destroying humans is her vocation. And as for Edison . . . the stories from Siberia. You kick a single Palestinian kid, the UN wants answers; you kill a dozen extras in Irkutsk, no one blinks.

Johxn is oblivious to the industrial amounts of contempt that swirl around him. It's also annoying that I envy him for that.

The public won't have heard of Johxn. His name hardly figures in the meedja. But as a Commissioning Editor he has his niche. It's a small niche. He's unlikely to get a hundred-foot yacht, but he lives in a different universe. If you're the chairman of a company, even if you run a corner shop, you have some accountability.

As long as he's Commissioning Editor (and how we long for a runaway bus or drug-resistant virus) he can do what he wants. He commissions what he wants from who he wants. And it doesn't matter if you make the greatest, the most successful doc, if he takes against your face, you're shut down. You're not even history. You never existed. I know a once-distinguished producer who is now the day watchman at a nightclub in Bulgaria.

Equally, it doesn't matter if you hand in the pap that Jack the List specialises in. If your face fits, no crime goes unre-warded.

You explain this to civilians outside the Vizz, and they won't believe you. There's this strange myth that things should work. That there are standards. That everything should be proper. But almost nothing is. The fitting job for Johxn in the Vizz would be working at a cinema box office, in a small provincial cinema, something that doesn't even require the social skills of being a waiter or a sales assistant, and which wouldn't have the physical demands of stacking shelves.

You can have regulations and regulators and still having nothing regulated. Nothing is as expected. The worst row I ever had with my wife? Was it over me lunching a Ukrainian stripper? No.

My wife caught us sitting in the Bricklayers Arms. No one goes to the Bricklayers Arms in Gresse Street, which is why I go there. No one *knows* it's there. It's the most central pub in

Central London, and most Londoners don't know it because it's tucked around the corner of a dead-end-looking street. Workers a block away don't know it. You need to be born and bred to know this stuff. A total Londoner.

What are the odds you sit down for a quick lunch with a Ukrainian stripper in the Bricklayers Arms, and in a city of over ten million, who should walk in but your wife, who should be fifteen miles away, at her office? The stripper, even though off duty, is half-naked, and introduces herself as a stripper. It looks like a gargantuan out-of-control fast-as-a-speeding-asteroid marriage-slayer.

Was there a row? A sulk? A raised eyebrow? No. I could have been sitting there playing shove ha'penny with my dad. Ellen instructs me to pick up some limescale remover on the way home. Not an iota of jealousy, not a minim. And it wasn't an act.

I was the one outraged. Outraged that it never occurred to Ellen that I might be making whoopee with the stripper. I almost shouted after her, *I'm here with a twenty-year-old-stripper made up like the Whore of Babylon and you're not even giving me one dirty look?*

Of course, every man is a figure of fun in his own household.

m

We, the so-called independent producers, have to sit here like poodles and listen. We are about as independent as galley-slaves who have a choice between rowing or being thrown overboard. They should call us the dependent producers because that's what we are: dependent on Johxn throwing us work.

There are several stories about how Johxn got his job, none favourable. He is the least able person in this room, and

35

indeed, in many, many other rooms. He lucked out. That's that.

My favourite rumour is the Big Boss who hired Johxn, just before he left to be a Bigger Boss elsewhere, hired Johxn, who had come into the building to interview for a receptionist's job, but walked into the wrong room, precisely because he knew Johxn would silt up everything. Choke the works. He left him behind as a comic time bomb.

There's a hatred that can be beneficial. That can gee you up. Get you over the finish line. Then there's a level of hatred that's simply bad for you. I have a chainsaw in the back of my car. It's a small chainsaw, but it'd do the job. I'm confident I could get at least two of Johxn's limbs off before they carted me away. Knowing the chainsaw's there soothes me. As long as the emergency exit's there, it's all manageable.

'Is this going to be a formal tender?' Zyklon Annie snaps.

'We're here to party, Annie,' Johxn responds.

Annie's face looks as if it had been dropped from a twentieth floor. All the exceptionally ugly women I've known have gone to extremes – they become either wholly jolly or wholly evil. Annie's great claim is that she makes radical political docs – this from a woman who, like most yapping lefties, has the warmth of a granite tombstone. A woman whose social conscience is so hard to detect that, unlike other embittered elderly women, Annie doesn't even have a cat, because owning a cat would oblige her to do something for another living being by opening a tin of cat food. Long ago, in prehistory, when I was starting out, she interviewed me. I've been waiting to settle up ever since.

Interviewing is her kick. She holds interviews constantly, usually when there's no job she can offer. An interview is the one time when you can insult someone to their face or humiliate with little fear of comeback. Dozens of meedja graduates come to her whirring blades every year.

Impossible questions will be asked. If you claim an interest in foreign affairs, she will quiz you about an obscure African country. What do you mean you don't know who the Education Minister of Niger is? Didn't you say you were keen on foreign affairs? Are you only interested in white countries? Are you a racist? An elitist? Or an ignoramus?

'Tell us about the money, Johxn. Have you actually got the money?' Edison asks. Edison's in a carefully relaxed pose, so relaxed he might as well be in bed. His wide-legged sprawl means that his bulging crotch is extended to meet the world, though there must be hardly anyone left in London who hasn't encountered this organ.

'Yes, there's money.'

'Whose money?' asks Edison, with a languid and thoughtful sweep of his long blond hair. Edison does this every five minutes or so to show how, well, languid and thoughtful he is and how he is a hairdresser's dream.

It isn't enough . . .

'Doesn't matter.' Johxn's right. It doesn't matter to me or anyone else here. We don't care if it reeks of frankincense or murder. Johxn could tell us, but he won't. London's charm is that money, like a bus, will turn up eventually. You may have to wait, the wait might be long and uncomfortable, but money will turn up, because we're stable, sort of, in comparison to the many joke states and kleptocracies on this planet. We have laws, sort of, and we have better nightclubs and prostitutes than Zurich or Frankfurt.

'Are you sure you have the money this time, Johxn?' Edison probes. This is cheeky. This is Edison playing the I-don't-need-your-commission-so-I can-be-cheeky card to get the commission and also a reflection that the exalted Edison sees docs as rather beneath his dignity now.

'Yes, I have the money,' says Johxn. I'm not the only one thinking back to the many times months of research went down the drain because Johxn pretended to have money he didn't.

It might be the Qataris, they're pissing money around like a man who's drunk a brewery. Every few years a posse of big spenders comes to town, depending on geopolitical tumbling. Saudis, Kuwaitis, Russians, Azeris, Chinese, as well as the lone wolves of larceny. The world's most successful thieves will gambol on the Thames sooner or later. We're stash city. The Big Bag. The Vault Almighty.

I went to school with the guy who runs the Qataris' money in Europe. I cheered him up when the whole class jumped up and down on his new satchel until it disintegrated. Has it done me any good? Has it got me an inch closer to those petrodollars? No. This is why you should never help anyone. Ever. We're all going to be shat on. Nearly every day. It's much harder to take when the shitter is someone you helped.

'Sorry if it sounds selfish, but I'll take it all,' says Edison.

Possibly my greatest crime was getting Edison into the Vizz. Fifteen years ago I gave him a job as a researcher. Operator, bandit, pet-napper, carpet-bagger, horndog, sponger, con man, gigolo, spiv, bamboozler, mock-human, oxygen thief, back-stabber, back-scratcher, backdoor man . . . these are the words that come to mind when I see Edison. If you can do something for Edison, Edison can do something for you, and Edison will do anything for you or to you. Don't be shy.

One lunchtime, returning to the office with a much-anticipated coronation turkey sandwich on toasted granary with extra mango chutney, I discovered Edison sitting with his towering Amazonian cock out of his trousers.

I didn't know what to say and I never ate that coronation turkey sandwich, or a coronation turkey sandwich ever again. In case I hadn't got the hint, Edison explained: 'I'm always happy to be the wife.' Other pearls from Edison in the two weeks before I fired him were: 'Why don't we just rob a bank?', 'Are you absolutely sure you don't want to buy me a car?', 'It would be great if there were time-travel because then I could go back to give myself a proper blow-job' and 'I am the greatest Brazilian director in the world' (this without so much as having filmed a clapperboard).

When I took him on he hadn't had a hot meal for three days and he was sleeping at Heathrow airport, where he had flown in from Manaus. He soon acquired not just the string of menopausal women and propertied gays (whose muscle tone was no longer what it was) favoured by hustlers to keep him in the style his imagination demanded, but many young handers-over of cash and hot meals.

You can't say Edison isn't willing to work, languidly. Edison's flaw? Too much Machiavelli, seeing far too many angles. If he has a door open in front of him, he'll still go, languidly, round the back to pick a lock. We're all trapped in ourselves.

But he's one up on all of us. He has directed a feature film. When I found out I almost blacked out from envy. Whatever anyone says about wanting to work in silver daguerreotypes or on a real-time chronicle of life on an Albanian collective farm, anyone who has ever looked through a lens wants to play in the big league.

I've never been obsessed with features because I've worked enough with actors to know I can't stand them. Being an actor is the very definition of not having character. You do as you're told. And they will do anything. There's a difference between being willing to work hard and make sacrifices and being willing to do *anything*.

Plus, the incessant demands from actresses to get their clothes off. It's a constant battle to keep them dressed. All they want to do is flash their bits. And the whinging. The concern about poverty, human trafficking, refugees and climate change. Gaze on my mighty conscience and weep. No, you can't bang on about spirituality when you'd let an entire nation perish for your close-up.

Most films are nonsense, but they are the big boy's toy. You are, as a helmer of a feature, a multiverse boss.

I dread to think what the casualties must have been on Edison's film. Crew and extras froze to death or were crushed by equipment; it was the sort of publicity money can't buy. But it was a proper, no-dispute film. Shot in Siberia with murder-money from ollies with unpronounceable names. Hollywood stars. Hordes of extras. Helicopters. Focus-pullers. Top catering. Some story about Avar hardmen breaking out of the gulag.

My joy when the film didn't even get shown at some crappy festival in Montenegro was almost indescribable. It's not nice enjoying someone else's failure, but you have to take what you can get.

Something must have gone badly wrong. Something, because you can always get a film screened somewhere. It might be one screen in a small, provincial town to three members of your family, but you can always have that. That Edison's film never saw a screen meant something calamitous, some hideous beef between its Avar, Chechen and Dargin backers.

And if there's one business where risk is abhorred, where failure is a deep, deep brand on your forehead, where a mere molecule of trouble will have investors beetling for the bunkers, it's features. So Edison's film sits on a shelf in Dagestan and he will never be allowed to make another. So Edison's film sits on a shelf in Dagestan, but Edison made a big-time, top-catering, helicopter-filled movie. Not everybody gets that. Better to have directed and tumbled into obscurity than to have never directed.

♏

'I want something special,' says Johxn. Of course he does. Now we're back to the old routine.

What a gobsmackingly wide word 'special' is, how useful for the stupid. It's the usual deal: Johxn doesn't know what he wants and we have to waste our time and money helping him find out.

'I want something extraordinary, whether it's politics, the arts or some inspirational individual. You all have your speci-alities. I'm talking about a mini-series or a whopping three-hour fucktastic doc that will be talked about not just for decades, for centuries.'

I'm tired of standing by the peanuts, there's an empty chair so I take the weight off my feet. I'm seated for about five seconds before the chair collapses under me with a firm snap-ping sound. I end up on the floor. In circumstances like this you have to accept that you're the destination for everyone's laughter. You just have to take it.

Everyone looks, of course, but they say nothing. I'm waiting for some quip, perhaps for Johxn to comment, 'I should add I'm not interested in slapstick, Bax,' or, 'Always ready with a heavyweight contribution, eh?' But nothing. I can't figure whether the silence reflects well or badly on the gathering.

41

'Great news, Johxn,' says Millicent. Silly Milly means it. If anyone else had said that it would be 100 per cent insincerity, or insincerity with a dollop of arse-licking. But she means it. Her optimism is so strong, you feel more cheerful by being in the room with her.

Silly Milly's speciality is art. When you go into some dingy warehouse (and in the art world there is only the dingy warehouse or Mayfair) and you have the familiar dilemma of whether a pile of rubbish in the corner is a pile of rubbish or a searing indictment of Western materialism, that's Milly's thing.

You won't find anyone who has a bad word to say about her, but you won't find anyone who has a good word to say about her work. She does the best roast chicken with stuffing I've ever eaten and she encourages art and artists by getting it on with them, their friends, neighbours and guests. If it's down to a popularity contest, Milly will win, and I suppose I could live with that.

'I'm looking for something radical,' muses Johxn, staring into the distance as if the fate of humanity depends on him. *Radical* is another word that is largely meaningless apart from the speaker expressing the view: 'I am better than you.' A word much used by fantasists, those who see themselves as Super Spartacus, Jesus Guevara Christ, a wagonload of Levellers. 'Something . . . post post. Really meta. Meta meta,' Johxn continues.

'Meta meta,' Milly chimes in. It'll be all over London in an hour. What do the others here see when they look at me? The also-ran. Baxter Stone. The Prince of Darkness. Semtex's handler. No one likes me, but in the Vizz, that's a compliment. They fear me. A lot of them really do. You have no control over your reputation, you really don't. I don't know where the rumours come from. They grow, and change, like kids.

On my left Jack the List throws me a conspiratorial glance. Why are we suddenly on the same team? That's what's amusing about people, they ignore you for a decade or even reduce you and your family to penury, and then they're gagging to go on holiday with you.

Next to Jack is Fletcher, old-school Central Office of Information and nudist. Once, before I could stop him, he showed me some snaps of his textileless holidays. Was it part of his mission to convince everyone that he is devoted to the birthday suit and that's why he drags his family down to the Cap d'Agde, and nothing to do, at all, in any way whatsoever, with watching young boys romp around naked? He ran an agency representing child actors for years, but eventually it was noticed he wasn't getting the kids any work.

It's not enough . . .

What a bunch. 'What's the deadline for this?' I say, simply to say something.

'Bax, don't worry. You're a worrier. You worry too much about stuff like that,' says Johxn. 'Stuff and things. Things and stuff.'

Of course there is no deadline, because if you don't know what you want, why would you know when you want it by?

It's not enough to be a four-faced, venomous, betrayal-loving brazen whore . . .

What a bunch. Since I've been in the Vizz, there has been a conspiracy to erase intelligence, to cull anyone with a backbone or imagination, anyone you'd actually want to invite into your home. The few admirable figures I came across when I started out are dead, mad or banished.

43

Even if this room represented the best of London, we'd still be in trouble because not everyone can succeed. It's one of the greatest lies, that everyone can get custard if things were arranged a little differently. Better education. Better government. Better this. Better that.

There isn't enough custard. Someone has to clean the toilets. Someone has to be last. There has to be failure, and indeed failure is booming.

On the other hand, there has to be success. Someone has to succeed. And it's so unfair, it's fair.

Anyone, no matter how dim, ignorant, lazy or useless can succeed. The feckless, the incompetent, the braindead, the truly out-to-lunch, the nail-chewers, the badly dressed, the bad-parkers, the hideous, they're not discriminated against. They're all in with a chance. Many industries, not just the Vizz, testify to that.

But there is no money. It's the end of money. This cash Johxn has is like the last of its species in a cage we're all marvelling at. When I started, the Vizz was powerful. Now it's just one more poor relative tugging at the public's sleeve for attention. It's exciting to see an empire fall, but it's not comfortable. The tumbling pillars can hurt.

Mindless pap gets a bad press. There's always been mindless pap, and there's nothing wrong with mindless pap. Who hasn't indulged in a bit? The problem is when there is *only* mindless pap. And pap served by a small group of pap-providers.

We're in a disaster movie. Who will get to the final reel, because it's certain most of us won't? We're already bitter and twisted, but most of us will end up extremely bitter and twisted, and poor. That's a word I never thought would be associated with me. Maybe not rich. Maybe not famous. Maybe not as happy as I dreamt, but poor?

44

It's not enough to be a four-faced, venomous, betrayal-loving brazen whore. To make it you've got to be a lucky, four-faced, venomous, betrayal-loving brazen whore. That was what Herbie used to say. *Braindead brazen whore* was another favourite phrase. Towards the end, Herbie was very despondent about our post-brain society. I suppose that's one of the few benefits of being dead: you don't have to attend ghastly meetings like this.

'Really looking forward to seeing what you come up with,' concludes Johxn. That might be true, since our existence provides him with so much fun, but I doubt he ever reads our submissions properly.

Last year I sent off a proposal at two in the morning when I was legless, having decided to emigrate to Argentina to teach English. In the middle of a proposal about the smuggling of weapons-grade plutonium, was the sentence: 'You are too thick to understand this, my old china John, because you are a very stupid prick and too illiterate and lazy to read this far, you over-promoted simpleton, you phenomenally fortunate pond creature.'

I was convinced that Johxn didn't read anything but the title of any proposal and the first paragraph, and glance at any illustrations (we all figured out long ago proposals with big, colourful pictures fared well in Johxn's office; after all, it's no more use sending an intelligent letter to someone stupid than sending a stupid letter to someone intelligent). I was proved right, but I was in agony for a month and lost a stone.

Johxn strides out as if he has something important to do. I fear I'm sentenced to a session of bogus camaraderie in this salon of evil before I can escape.

'He does do good self-importance,' comments Jack the List. 'He could be mistaken for someone who – what's the expression? – works for a living.'

This is interesting. Jack prides himself on maintaining a level of bolshiness, but such raw disrespect in a room of intergalactic snitches and manipulators can't get you anywhere; there is no obvious upside.

'I really enjoyed your doc last week,' I say to Jack. This is true. I loved watching it. I had a hoot. But what I don't add is that I loved watching it because it was so dire. *Jiben* shitty. Praise will, at the very least, confuse and wrong-foot Jack, might even do me some good. There are certain words that go deep, that brush past the filters of scepticism. I had a girlfriend who called me her 'lord and master' – naturally her irony couldn't have been greater, but the reptilian strand in my brain didn't pick it up.

Jack the List does mostly the list. It's hard to tell his docs apart. *Britain's Richest, The World's Richest, Meet the Rich, Meet the Super-Rich, The New Super-Rich, The Real Super-Rich, So You Think You're Super-Rich?, The Lives of the Rich, How the Rich Live, The Truth About the Rich.*

And of course once you've made a couple of docs like that, you're an expert on infiltrating the Royal Enclosure at Ascot, you're a master of treading the gangplanks on Cannes yachts and you know how much armour-plating a Rolls-Royce can bear. So every time some dozy Commissioner wants an easy, cheap slot-filler on the 'New New Rich' or 'Rich vs. Super-Rich', they phone Jack, who has the contacts and knows where to position the tripod at Henley.

Being super-rich isn't enough. What's the good of being super-rich if the world doesn't know about it? They're all delighted to take part in Jack's docs. They all feature Jack. They feature Jack heavily, sipping champers, wolfing down truffles, stuffing his face in chocolatiers, adjusting top hats, bounding off private jets. But Jack always uses the Jack *scowl*.

In real life, you couldn't be sure what this odd pursing of the lips means (25 per cent smirk, 25 per cent smile, 25 per cent grimace, 25 per cent puzzlement).

If they were standing next to him, the super-rich might think some champagne bubbles had got up his nose, or he'd hit on a tough gold-sprinkled praline. The scowl is innocuous up close, but when you get to the editing suite and add *voice-over* you learn that Jack is sneering.

Because, of course, when Jack asks, 'Is that toilet made of platinum?' or, 'Why did you build a replica of Las Vegas in the middle of the Mongolian tundra?', he's slamming the unjust wealth and sniggering at the bad taste of the ollies. Jack hasn't forgotten his Marxist roots as he marvels at some twat buying a diamond-encrusted dog bowl.

Was I the only one who could see Jack was living the high life (and let's not forget the unrestricted cocaine and complimentary ballerinas off-camera) by sticking moneybags in front of a camera to explain why they'd been delighted to pay the price of a London house for a bottle of cognac?

You'd imagine that the super-rich might get upset when they realised that Jack was laughing at their platinum loo and call in a discreet professional killer (they're willing to travel and much cheaper than you'd think). But no. Whether you control a quarter of the world's aluminium or you're lying in a doorway sporting a body odour that has been a week in the making, almost everyone wants to be in the Vizz.

Eventually, however, the murmurings that Jack wasn't a hard-hitting journalist but a virtuoso gatecrasher and forager got to him. He announced it was important that under-reported aspects of conflict zones were brought to the world's attention, so he produced a number of docs on shamefully neglected beauty pageants, such as *Miss Sarajevo* and *Miss*

Baghdad. Again, you saw a lot of Jack doing odd things with his lips in a masterclass of ambivalence. Whether you, the viewer, see this as embarrassing or empowering, I, Jack, agree with you.

♏

Zyklon Annie already has her phone stuck to her ear, presumably so she doesn't have to talk to us, and to give her an excuse not to get in the lift with me, but she has turned her gaze to Jack. His badmouthing Johxn has caught her attention. Is Jack losing it? Is a competitor about to splatter? Or is he *acting* as if he's losing it? Is this a trap? You can see her war-gaming it.

'What are we all doing here? This is such bollocks,' Jack says. I never thought I'd agree with the man who came up with such an insightful one-hour doc on Miss Syria and is a leading authority on how to choose a butler, but he's taken the words out of my mouth.

Jack's only misfortune is that he strayed out of Eden. He had it good in his patch, boogalooing with the super-rich, helping out distressed beauty pageants, testing polo mallets. He was a laughing stock, but he should have considered that most of those laughing at him, like me, were only a few quid away from rummaging for some cardboard so we could kip down in a doorway.

He had a great time in Damascus with Miss Syria and her friends. He'd gone native and after twenty years in the Vizz, he vowed he would make a proper doc this time. A thorough-bred doc. A doc that would get shown at the real festivals. A real doc. Real current affairs. About a real person. Without Jack gurning in every other shot.

Here's a tip for any prospective journalists. If you go to a strange country and you see the picture of one man

48

everywhere, in every office, in every school, in every hospital, in every garage, in every fucking building and public space, it doesn't matter how joyful people look. It doesn't matter how tidy the streets are. It doesn't matter what you're told. Something is very wrong.

Jack made a doc about Assad. How he was elevating Syria. How well educated he was. How far-sighted. How charming his wife was. How he was loved. How schoolkids wanted to be like him. How great the zoo was in Damascus. Everyone was so happy.

The doc aired a couple of months before Assad started gassing and starving his own citizens and barrel-bombing the survivors in the hospitals. The lion at the zoo was eaten.

You'd guess that making a doc like that – a doc that is so shameful, unremittingly embarrassing, nightmarishly mistaken, that idolises a mass-murderer – would *disqualify* you from making another doc. That you'd have your licence ripped up in front of you. That you'd be barred. Of course not. It's the Vizz. But Jack still has the laughing-stock problem.

I have better things to do than to ferret out Jack's intentions. I rush for the lift and as I was congratulating myself on shaking off the gang, Edison slides in. Why?

'Bax, Bax . . .' Edison pauses, because he's languid and thoughtful. 'Baxter,' he says, to show that he does remember my full name, which is nice after he's proposed bank robbery and intimacy, and in the hope, like many mountebanks and car salesmen, that the repeated use of my name will win me over. 'Baxter, how are you?'

Why are there embassies? For instance, the Russians know that the Americans are spying on them, and the Americans know the Russians are spying on them. It's a form of arrogance, another appearance for Mr Hugh Briss: we permit it, because *we* can do it *better*. Edison knows we're in a life-and-death struggle, that I'm blagging to the max, but he still thinks he can put one over on me.

'Fine. How are you, Edison?' I give him back his name. This is the blessing of etiquette; it allows you to say nothing and eats up time when you're stuck in a lift with Edison. I'm surprised he's bothering to talk to me, because technically, irrefutably, he's a couple of grades above me on the basis of a movie, however unreleased or unreleasable. He's a big-budget brave. Is it unravelling for him too?

'Fine? Are you really fine?' Edison gives me a languid look. What a rudimentary trick. You repeat the question to emphasise this isn't mere chit-chat, but a heartfelt enquiry about your well-being, because you truly care. Most of us, of course, are bursting with grievance and welcome the opportunity to spill.

'Really.' With someone like Edison, it's name, rank and serial number. Maybe something about the rain. You never give out any information, of any sort, because it may be used against you. I consider making a dig about unreleased films, but I'd lose in that exchange. 'I hear you were in Syria.'

'Yeah.' Languidness. 'It's a nice war; promising, if you can find the time. Plenty of sex.' More languidness. 'Did you ever find Herbie's safe?' he asks. He can't resist the dig. Fair enough. You should kick a man when he's down because then he might not get up again.

'No,' I say in the most not-caring voice I can muster without sounding as if I'm not caring too much. The lift seems stuck on the first floor. Will I be here with Edison all afternoon? My 'no' seems to work.

'Heard about Jim?' Edison offers after a minute of silence.

I nod. I have heard about Jim. Found hanging from a tie in a hotel room in Nairobi with Japanese octopus porn playing on a large plasma screen. What is it about my gender? They can't give their knobs five minutes' peace. The only surprise was that Jim had a tie.

Mind you, you can never know if it was an accident. My experience is that those who commit suicide aren't the self-harmers, the mopers and overdosers. Those who do it are serious, you never see it coming, and they get it right.

I'd had lunch with Jim six months earlier. Obviously, I hadn't wanted to have lunch. It was embassies. He might let slip some info useful to me, without me giving away any info that would be useful to him, or he might make the mistake of doing me a favour in the expectation that I'd do something for him.

Jim had turned up an hour late looking manic and then, shortly after we had ordered, whimpered, 'I'm so afraid of the dark,' before curling up in a ball on the floor and wailing uncontrollably. He'd been doing coke non-stop for days.

An ambulance was called. Although I repeatedly explained he wasn't my friend and I'd like to sit down and eat the guinea fowl with plum sauce and samphire that had just been delivered to the table, the ambulance crew urged me to accompany them. I worry about the level of my ruthlessness because I couldn't sit down and eat that guinea fowl.

Yet it's an indication of how far gone I am that I didn't feel any sorrow for Jim's demise. My reaction: one less competitor. No one starts out in life wanting to be the person who gets satisfaction from someone over-asphyxiating while a hapless cephalopod comes to an undignified end in Jap minge. You get formed.

'At least Jim died doing what he loved,' I remark as the doors open. Edison likes this, and while he's chuckling, languidly, I duck into the downstairs toilet with a swift goodbye. This should shake Edison, and if he follows me in, I'm locking myself into a cubicle.

When I walk out of Wacky Towers, I'm pleased the street is free of anyone involved in the Vizz. A photo of a smug black cat has been fixed to a lamp-post. 'Is this your cat?' is written above it in the manner of so many missing pet notices. Below it: 'I ate it. With a white wine mushroom sauce. Yum Yum.'

As I walk towards the tube, there's a guy with a blanket, the cardboard mat and the traditional dog on a string. I've seen him many times before asking for small change. He doesn't look at all awkward when it's blazing sunshine, sweltering, everyone's stripped to the waist, and he's still under the blanket. It's an integral part of the show. It occurs to me that the only difference between the two of us is that it's not quite so obvious that I'm fucked.

Correction: he's certainly pulling in more dosh per hour than I am.

How many of us are going home to cry? I wonder. It's easy to front it up for a few hours at a meeting or an office, but what happens when the doors are closed and you're alone? Isn't your real life when you're alone? Isn't that why most of us don't like to be alone?

STATUES
FEBRUARY

This morning we have a light coating of snow. Winter's fare-well. With a glance of particular bitterness towards me, Ellen leaves for work. It is, of course, my fault she has an early meeting, my fault there is snow, my fault she has to work at all, my fault she is my wife, my fault I am looking relaxed at the kitchen table with a coffee as she departs.

'One of us has to work, after all.' She really loads that sentence with rage. I consider protesting, but it would be useless as she's locked into martyrdom, and as I'm relaxed at the kitchen table with a coffee, in an old T-shirt, the protest that I actually am working wouldn't be very convincing. It's also true that my working hasn't produced any results or, more importantly, any money. I don't have a Big Idea for Johxn's Big Money, after months of racking my brains. Lots of good Small Ideas, but no traffic-stopping, get-down-on-your-knees mega-doc.

Yui gawks out of the window.

'The snow is helpless,' says Yui. 'The snow is helpless.'

'It is.' I haven't a clue what's she's talking about, and I can't be bothered to interrogate her for half an hour to figure it out. I tell her to take Luke to school.

Yui would happily do nothing, but when you ask her to do her job, she is gracious. I tell her twice, to make sure.

Apparently, in the French Foreign Legion they issue all orders twice to avoid any misunderstanding. Yui looks displeased when I do this, but having had a number of crises by trusting her English I'm sticking to the system.

She stayed with us after we lost the house, less out of au pair loyalty and more out of having nowhere else to go. Yui is a model au pair in that she likes Luke and, as she has the curves of a credit card and, indeed, the appearance of an Auschwitz survivor, she is no threat to domestic harmony. She doesn't speak any language, however, which is a drawback.

Her parents were Japanese but she spent her early years in Brazil, before moving to Spain, Jordan, Korea then Germany, before arriving in London. A reliable source assured me that Yui's Japanese is barely that of a two-year-old, and that's probably her strongest language.

Yui does paintings of her vagina a lot. I was stuck with her in a traffic jam for an hour once and she almost managed to explain to me why. Obviously I'm not the man to judge these works, but it seems to me she has absolutely no talent. I considered putting her in touch with Milly, but Milly finds painting unspeakably eighteenth century, and there's something unlucky about Yui, she's embedded in misfortune.

I've had bad luck, but I can't deny I've had good luck too. Ellen. I'd be lost without my wife. I was about to go up the stairs from the tube at Victoria Station one Saturday when I saw a beautiful blonde lumbered with a massive suitcase. I was younger and buff and I flew up the stairs with the suitcase. I almost twirled the suitcase round over my head and yodelled, although halfway it occurred to me maybe I should slow down so I could come up with something witty to say. I couldn't. I couldn't believe how beautiful she was.

'Thank you. Perhaps you should ask me for my phone number,' was what Ellen said. It terrifies me to think if I had been a minute earlier or a minute later, I would have missed her. I've never met anyone like her, before or since. Someone who really knows me and still likes me. I'd be dead without her.

The best thing that ever happened to me in my life, I had nothing to do with, I had no say in. It just happened. Like bird shit dropping on your jacket. Correction: like a butterfly landing on your lapel.

The second time Ellen and I went out, I thought to myself, 'I'm going to marry this woman.' Then I noticed an attractive brunette in a corner of the club, and I thought to myself, 'You know, I could do that brunette, doggy-style on the table, and still marry this woman.' How much are you entitled to?

I should add the third time we went out Ellen ended up talking to some guy she knew vaguely, quite warmly. I wanted to kill him. I don't mean that in a figurative way. I mean I wanted the balm of extreme violence. I wanted to sink a machete several inches into his neck and chest. If you don't want to kill, it's not really love.

♏

I head off for the doctor. The curious thing about doctors' surgeries these days is that the receptionists, who barely speak English, who have zero qualifications, who are on burger wages, treat you like dirt, while the doctors who, if nothing else, are educated and well paid, feign courtesy, or are, at least, more courteous than the receptionists.

At the desk, the receptionist, having ignored me for a few minutes, gives me a yes? glance. He's some Latin, wearing a blue suit. He'd get marks for sartorial effort (the receptionists

57

typically have a promotional T-shirt or a charity-shop cardigan) but the suit must have been cut for his much younger brother, and he's been wearing it night and day for the last five years.

'I have an appointment.' Wordlessly, the receptionist points at the computer screen on the wall where you are supposed to check in. I have some sympathy for receptionists, as they do have to deal with the magnificently thick and the aggressive.

'The screen isn't working,' I say. It sums up medical care, that screen on the wall. A computer check-in that doesn't work. Not to mention the touch-screen. I don't have a medical degree, but I would guess that a touch-screen in a surgery is not a good idea: one thinks of the flued-up, the lepers, the Aids-dribbling, the bearers of H. pylori and E. coli, of strep, of resistant tuberculosis all leaving their mark, not to mention that the elderly or ill might have trouble with the microscopic instructions.

I don't want to be in this room. I'm sure it's a waste of time. GPs want to get rid of you as speedily and as cheaply as possible; if you're under thirty it's a mystery virus, if you're over thirty, it's your body falling apart. I've always had to attend three or four times to convince them I'm ill, which is a waste of their time as much as mine. Despite having waited three weeks for this appointment, I have to stew for another forty minutes with a throng of Sudanese and Iraqis before I'm summoned in.

It's another doctor I've never seen before. In prehistory, you had a GP who saw you regularly, someone who would have a vague idea of you and your ailments. In this practice, I've never seen the same doctor twice. London.

The doctor is spraying the patient's chair with some disinfectant aerosol. He's just out of med school. He doesn't look as if he wants to be here either – welcome to life, hotshot.

58

'How are you?' he asks. Every time I'm asked this by a doctor I'm tempted to reply: 'Fucking ill, or I wouldn't be here, would I?'

'Fine, thank you.'

'What can I do for you?'

I haven't told my wife about this because she'd think I was making it up, and would end up angry. I've heard from my friends that this is what wives do, they give support by not offering any. If Ellen found me lying in a pool of blood her response would be: 'Stop feeling sorry for yourself.' Correction, it would be: 'I'll tell you when you're ill.'

Her lack of sympathy is compounded by her ridiculous good health. In the last ten years she's had one brief cold that didn't even exhaust a single box of tissues. She doesn't believe in illness. I've seen prime ministers and Afghan warlords run and hide from their wives, truly sprint, because whatever it is you do all day – save economies, sell walking canes, eulogise platinum, beautify fruit, rule wisely – eventually, ultimately, finally, you have to go home and wives know how to hurt you.

Though in a way, we like the nagging, up to a point. Where's the joy in snoozing in bed if your wife doesn't come in to condemn you as a lazy pig? 'You're not going out dressed like that.' Isn't that the voice of your mother (well, those of us who had mothers)? Nagging is the sound of home. Nagging offers some comfort. Up to a point. Like everything.

'I'm seeing things,' I announce.

The Doc's annoyed now.

'Seeing things?'

'Very briefly, for a second or two, when I wake up. I see things.'

'You mean things in the shadows.'

No, you stupid fucker, not in the shadows. I see things in glorious electromagnetic splendour right in front of me.

'No, I see things, clearly.' I add, 'Objects.' To make it clear it's not some insane vision of celestial cities or seven-headed whales.

The Doc now checks my records carefully for any note of me being a timewaster. He's worried that he might have to, you know, do something. I wish I could have a certificate to confirm that I am not a hypochondriac, someone who is desperate to have a conversation or is in need of a chit that will get me off work. No, I'm here because there's some oddness going on.

'Objects?'

'Yes, a wastepaper basket. Or a chair. They're there in the room for a second, then they're gone.'

I'm lying about the chair. All I ever see is a wastepaper basket. But just seeing wastepaper baskets is even weirder. I reach out to see if it's there, or blink, and then it's gone. As hallucinations go, it's dreary. If you're seeing things why not a starship engine or a parachuting giraffe?

With ill grace, he does the prop thing. Like a good shaman shaking his bag of bones, he goes for the lightstick to pry into my eye. It's either the stethoscope or the lightstick, to show that he's a real doctor, with real equipment, really doing something.

'You seem fine.' He sits back down to deliver the verdict. 'What you've experienced is hypnagogic sleep – you think you're awake but you're not.' Ah, the old fob-off. Why do doctors refuse to listen? I am awake, it's one of the things you can be sure of. Sometimes when you dream, it feels real, you're stuck in the bathroom straining to remove an impossible stain from the tub, but then you wake up. That's how you know it's a dream.

He writes hypnagogic sleep down on a piece of paper for me. So I'm not going to get two aspirin. 'You can look it up on the web.' I gather doctors used to be annoyed about the web – patients looking up all sorts of symptoms, drugs and side effects and then having the temerity to ask questions.

'Thank you,' I say. There's no point saying what I think. If it carries on, I'll come back. I haven't got the money to go privately.

At home I do look up hypnagogic sleep and vaulting from one medical link to another, I come across something that fits the bill.

Charles Bonnet Syndrome, where you do see things, typically ordinary things or individuals, although interestingly never anyone you know. Some speculate it's the explanation for ghosts. Or since the figures you see are often miniatures, step forward leprechauns, elves, fairies, imps and other mythical short-arses.

The syndrome is typical in those with failing eyesight (where it seems the brain improvises to fill in the gaps). But not always. And, of course, many sufferers don't report it because they don't want to be logged as mad or to discover they have some tumour growing in the ideacave. I ignored the baskets the first couple of times.

Most of the day has now gone. Before the web no one had access to so much information, knowledge and rubbish. It's certainly made my job easier, but the irony is I can't make money from it.

When I was growing up I had fantasies of going into the big record shop in Oxford Street and just helping myself, filling up a trolley and not paying, and now, in effect, I can do that. I can grab a dozen recordings of Beethoven in less time than it takes to walk to the shops; I can watch my favourite film in Arabic. But so can everyone else. For free. It's that old 'be careful what you ask for'. If you're a creative it's all there for free, but you struggle to make that stuff they call money.

Can I make a doc about Bonnet? Would it appeal to Johxn? Tricky without special effects – very interesting but lots of dodderers explaining how they saw a tribe of headhunters toasting cheese sandwiches in their front room? One for the files, but not for immediate action, unless we get a season about the elderly and their problems.

♏

It's sunny and mild, so I go for a run along the river. London: robbing and killing people since 50 BC.

There aren't too many people on this Vauxhall stretch, the tourists only start swarming at the Houses of Parliament. To my surprise, I feel good; no, correction: I feel great, I feel like a fucking nuclear weapon.

When I was a kid, I was convinced that when I was older and ludicrously successful, I'd be running along the Thames because I'd have some mansion slap bang in the centre of town. Though I imagined I'd be running along the North Bank, because, although I hate to admit it as a South Londoner, the money and goodies were pretty much on that side of the river. We're harder and we have the more interesting criminals, and the ones that didn't get caught, but the real swag was across the water. Always steal it legally.

It's changing. Twenty years ago Vauxhall had all the charm of a derelict car park, one terrible tandoori restaurant and a tranny pub. Now it has M16, a dozen gay saunas and bondage clubs and several chintzy eateries. The Americans are building their new fortress embassy here. Vauxhall's always going to be a shithole, a strange mating of a motorway and a railway station, but it's becoming a very affluent shithole.

Occasionally, you get what you want but it's never in the way you thought you'd get it, because you weren't careful enough about specifying the details, or because the Allower just won't allow it.

I'm running along the Thames now because we happen to be living in someone else's house, which is only a five-minute trot away, not because I'm a big deal. I am a director, but I'm a director at a time when being a director is about as lucrative as stacking shelves in a supermarket. 'When you're young, you plan to beat the world. And that's good, that's how it should be,' Herbie used to say. 'But you can't beat the world, you can't rule it. And even if you rule the world, even if you do get to rule the world, so what?'

I'm coming to understand what he meant, but not ruling the world doesn't mean you have to end your days divorced and broken in a bedsit. It bothers me that Herbie was cleverer than me, friendlier than me, more educated, more experienced, and it did him no good. He was just crushed. Roadkill.

And I'm angry that his safe was stolen before I could get my hands on it. I suppose, selfishly, I was hoping there might have been some parting gift, some last advice. He was the last of my soothsayers.

I run easy. That's one of the benefits of getting older, you hardly care what others think, though not caring is also the slippery slope to being the cackling self-abuser on the train. Two black guys jog past me, smooth. Jamaicans? They're eighteen, nineteen, their gear is boxfresh, their hair looks as if it had been styled five minutes ago. They are so ripped and confident they must be . . . something. Models? Athletes? Dancers?

When I was younger I wouldn't tolerate any overtaking. Every challenge was met and fought furiously, if not defeated.

Now I don't care if some spherical housewife clutching a colossal water bottle staggers past me. I certainly can't match these two.

However, when they are about twenty feet ahead of me, I have a spurt. Hitch onto their energy. Clear the system. I know I can't catch them, but I can be towed by their energy for a while. I up my pace. To pursuit pace. A last hooray.

To my delight, I'm closing the gap. I'm warmed up, I'm totally nuclear. I up it to attack pace, something I haven't bothered with for a decade. I keep on closing the gap. The two haven't responded to my challenge, but they haven't slowed down either. I'm zipping past them, and then putting yards between us. I thought they would give me a cardio boost for fifty metres or so, but I've left them standing still. I've burned them off. Big time.

It's embarrassing. I almost turn to remonstrate with them: it's shameful that fit lads like that have eaten the dust of a pudgy, over-pizza'd director about to hit fifty. I didn't look that ripped when I was nineteen, or ever.

Have I been sent a message? A lesson from the Allower? Is this instruction in how the impossible can be caught napping? If so, it's too late for me, my heart is pickled in pessimism. You simply get these surprises now and then. If I'd wanted to catch up with them, I wouldn't have. If you really don't want it, you can get it. It's a miracle, no less, but it's done me no good.

I ease off and yield to the wheezing as I near the Houses of Parliament. You ponder on history as you get here and see the buildings and bridges, see the brown sludge that is celebrated as the Thames.

Julius Caesar. Queen Boudicca. Henry VIII. Shakespeare. Francis Drake. Thomas à Becket. Newton. Mozart. Dozens of Rothschilds. Cromwell. Charles Darwin. Lenin. Stalin.

Churchill. Sherlock Holmes. Florence Nightingale. Freud. Einstein. Picasso. The Duke of Wellington. Jack the Ripper. Haydn. Maria Callas. Jimi Hendrix. Ho Chi fucking Minh. Namey names. They all gave water to London.

Names. Dates. Names. Dates. But there is no history. There's no trace of them. History doesn't exist. There is no Thames. The Thames is just a name. The brown sludge you're looking at now will be out in the Channel in a few hours. Water doesn't care whether it's water here or in Ulan Bator.

As I reach Westminster Bridge I turn back. The crowds are so massive, there's no point trying to weave through. I believe I can speak on behalf of most Londoners when I say to tourists: fuck off.

Fuck off, and don't ever come back. There's nothing to see. That's why they're always looking around, gaping, craning their necks and consulting maps. They're wondering why they're actually here and what they should be looking at. But there's nothing to see. Maybe a few buildings. You don't have them back home? You live in a yurt? Fuck off. And don't come back.

♏

From a certain distance I have everything: a home, a wife, a son, an au pair.

Of course, I hardly ever see my wife or my son (this seems to be standard these days), my au pair doesn't speak any language, and the house doesn't belong to me. It's hard to see anything. You're too far away you can hardly see anything. You're too close you can hardly see anything.

To avoid doing any work, I surf the bitching pages to see if there's any amusing gossip or even unamusing gossip. Or something about me. I must cut down on this, but there's something reassuring about being insulted. You still exist.

From Lovable Psycho: *Seen grovelling yet again the other day, at Wacky Towers, the Immense Immenso, formerly known as the Prince of Darkness. We know who ate all the pies.*

How do they have time for this? And I haven't eaten a pie in years. Lovable Psycho must be one of the scuttlers in reception. It's a law that the bigger the online mouth, the weedier the person. I once tracked down one of my baiters. He was so small – like a stooped, tired rabbit, with a basin haircut – that I couldn't hit him, and so pathetic he had already been thoroughly punished.

Immense Immenso? I've put on a few pounds, but really. I still have a six-pack, even if it's hard to see under the fat. I go to the kitchen for some toast and poached eggs but discover some smoked chicken and potato salad at the back of the fridge, so I feel it's my duty to polish them off before they expire.

'What do you call this?' Ellen asks. My wife has returned home unexpectedly to pick up a ticket she forgot for a terrible concert I refused to go to. It's unfortunate because being caught with food, however humble, it's a scenario that plays into her 'my husband is a ne'er-do-well, layabout blubberama'. A scenario that doesn't preclude another one of her pet scenarios: me being a cold-hearted, callous, never-at-home workaholic careerist.

'A late breakfast? An early lunch? A snack?' Ellen's on a roll. 'Brunch? A nibble? A long-lost supper? An *amusebouche*? The Baxter diet?'

My wife has terrible taste in music. You can't have everything. I'm paying a heavy price for having refused to attend a middle-of-the-road concert. Ellen, like most women, could survive on an apple and a yogurt a day, fortunately. The food bill is ridiculous enough already. If I could stop eating I'd be rich.

'I call it eating some smoked chicken with potato salad.' There's no sense in giving ground.

'I showed some pictures to my friends the other day. They didn't recognise you. "Where's Bax?" they said. "And who's the roly-poly you're hanging out with now?"'

This is the great benefit of marriage: you're constantly under attack. It keeps you ninja-sharp. But I'm bang to rights, eating at 11.20, in a pair of tatty underpants that my wife attempted to throw out last month. All I can do is act nonchalant. Ellen sees Herbie's viewfinder on the table, bordered by a few morsels of potato salad.

'Herbie again? How long's it been?'

'I don't know.' Of course I know. Five years, four months.

'If you need advice, you can always ask me, you know.' No, I can't. Ellen is always wrong. I stopped betting with her on election results, football matches, the weather, how late trains would be, which direction to drive in, because it was no challenge and because she never paid up. But her being always wrong doesn't mean that doing the opposite is always right (unless it's which direction to drive in).

When someone close dies, a part of you feels snubbed. Let down. I suppose I miss Herbie mostly for selfish reasons, because I could always go to him for a good conversation. Good conversation is almost the best thing of all.

A good meal, a good car, a good penthouse, a good blowjob, these can easily be found, especially if you have money, but good conversation? That's rare. And I could always go to Herbie for solid advice. For illumination. To be able to see into the corners, around the corners, though you didn't always like what you saw. Every time I talked to that man, I learned something.

It was an awful moment when Herbie gave me his view-finder. I knew then it was a surrender on his part, an unwelcome ageing, I just didn't realise how complete the surrender was. He was dead weeks later. I've hung on to the viewfinder because although it's positively Stone Age technology now, it's a keepsake. But it's also a grim memento mori (another term I learned from Herbie).

'Are you still arsing around looking for that safe?'

'No,' I reply. That's true. I have given up on that one. I spent months chasing down crims, buying policemen drinks, posting notices, a reward (I didn't even get a response from cranks or con men). I can't see what more I can do. I have given up. More or less. Ellen does her 'I don't believe a word' expression, one of her best.

'I'm off. One of us has to work,' she announces. It's the point where many women would say, 'My mother warned me about you.' But she didn't. I get on better with my mother-in-law than Ellen. I've never once had an ill-tempered word with her, whereas there have been several occasions where I was hoping Ellen might just fall under a bus, freeing me up to play the tragic widower and to pull a Russian ballerina, going cheap these days. No, my mother-in-law is always baking me cakes and special treats, telling me that I look thin.

♏

Johxn phones. 'I have some work for you.' This doesn't happen. He doesn't phone you, and he doesn't just offer work. I can't quite believe I've heard that, but I manage to do so, because we all believe deep down that one day we will be rewarded, that one day we will win the lottery.

'I don't know if you've heard, but Fletcher's dead,' he says.

I hadn't heard. Should I pretend to be mournful? But really, an elderly paedo?

'He was going to do a series of short films for me.'

I'm outraged that Johxn's giving work to someone else, and I'm surprised. Fletcher was there when they created television. He was so *old* and middle class and, the kiddy-fiddling aside, extremely courteous, traditional, elegant, cufflinked: all the qualities Johxn hates. The man had starched shirts, something not seen in the Vizz since the late 1960s. What did he have to offer Johxn? Did he have something on Johxn?

'It's a series on the statues of London. Five minutes on little-known figures of British history. It's got a presenter, Professor Headley, who's an expert on that stuff. All you have to do is point the camera.'

'Thanks for thinking of me.'

'Actually, I wanted Edison, because this is right up his street, he's got such a unique vision, a meta-vision, but he had to pull out at the last minute. You can't always get the talent you really want. It was very disappointing.'

'Sounds great,' I say, because that's what you have to say, and it's work, even if it's served up on a huge insult, but I fear there's more punishment to come because Johxn doesn't do great.

'The prof's a bit busy, so it occurred to me you could pick out half-a-dozen statues for him.'

'Okay.'

'And, you know, you could do a treatment. A treatment. But you know, like a short script. Hmm? The basic information about the figure, some interesting facts. You know, five fucktastic facts. Quips a bonus.'

'Right.' So you want me to research, write, produce and direct this.

'But there's something I need you to do for me first.' Is Johxn going to ask me to pay a deposit?

℩

I go out on foot to see if I can locate a little-known statue that is photogenic, fascinating, weighed down with anecdotes and a profound insight into humanity. You know, fucktastic.

At Horse Guards Parade, I chance upon an equestrian statue. It's Frederick Roberts on his charger, obviously some military bigwig. Is he little known? I've never come across him. Johxn certainly won't know about him. Indeed, that part of the brief is easy, since everything – science, geography, culture, history, you name it – is little known to Johxn.

How does Roberts, rate in fucktasticness? I look him up. First Earl Roberts, 1832–1914. Who did he kill? Nearly everybody. He was the Empire's enforcer, a long career outside of Britain, rubbing out resistance from the Indian Mutiny to the Boer War (the one with the embarrassing concentration camps) and died frothing at the mouth in 1914 because no one had listened to his warnings about the Germans.

I now understand why his name isn't bandied about more these days, despite being the British Army's best and most-decorated commander after Wellington. I was joining the Army when I met Herbie on the train. I come from a military family, but I discovered that was not me. On the other hand, I've never understood why, if you've got the obligation of being a serial killer, you'd waste your time dismembering prostitutes when you can join the Army and kill to your heart's content and get medals and a tidy pension for it. There's always aggro you can volunteer for.

Roberts also took part in the Abyssinian campaign of 1867, which must have been the high point of gunboat diplomacy. Mad Abyssinian despot takes two British missionaries hostage and we send an entire army, an *entire* army, to get them back and trash the country. Wahey. The Foreign Office wouldn't even send a letter of condolence now. And of course Roberts did his time in the Second Afghan War. Your army ain't nothing until it's been to Kabul.

When I jumped from assistant cameraman to researcher I had to cover the Soviet War in Afghanistan that was just folding up. I found two mujahideen in a house in Neasden. They were cross-legged on the floor because there was no furniture in the house.

'We are soldiers,' they told me. They had been sent to London for some reason, but they never got further orders. They sat there for a couple of years, then one went off to work at a cats' shelter and the other for a company that puts 'the fun in funerals': rock 'n' rock burials, witchy wakes, pirate-based send-offs, etc. I bumped into them every now and then and they were always thankful to me because I had brought them some teabags and chocolate digestives when they were on the floor, waiting. The smaller the gift, the greater the gratitude.

In 2001 I got a call from Ahmad. 'You know that Arab turdchewer, bin Laden? He says he has something important to say. He wants to do an interview. I can put you in touch with that chicken-snatching pimp.' I wasn't keen. I'd been to Kandahar and nearly died from a variety of causes. Afghanistan was right at the top of my list of countries I never wanted to see again, but I went to sound out Johxn who was in charge of current affairs.

I told him about Osama bin Laden's offer. For a while he thought bin Laden was a Pakistani cricketer, but when I gave

71

him the background, he said no. I tried again a week later, allowing for Johxn's extreme thickness and knowing that his mind was as fickle as the weather, but he said no again. 'No one's ever come to me with such a lame, unfucktastic proposal, Bax. Don't ever waste my time like this again. I have to say, you're not cut out for this work, you're really not. It's not too late to retrain, you know.' A month later the planes crashed into the Twin Towers in New York.

Roberts might be a good choice, as a model war criminal. But even if we slag him off as a war criminal there will still be complaints that we're whitewashing him. On the other hand, we could big him up as an unappreciated administrator who knew how to get the trains to run on time and raised respect for law and order. That would be fun, but career-ending. I probably need a safer figure than Roberts. I carry on the search for fucktasticness.

I don't have any luck, and I give the crowds outside Buckingham Palace, or as we used to call it Fuckingham Palace, a wide berth.

Down on your luck, young man? Go to the Queen's gaff because without having to suffer the expense of an entry fee to a club, without buying overpriced drinks or putting on your best clothes, you will meet some young lady from a far-off country who wants to practise her English, be taken to places tourists don't know about (and even your shitty local will count as delightfully authentic), and have a story to tell her friends back home. If you can't pick up here, you should really give up. I decide to check out Piccadilly, and I'm halfway across Green Park when I sight a familiar figure having a run.

It's the Prime Minister, flanked by two goons. He's not enjoying his run, struggling along. The goons don't seem to be armed, but I suppose it's an impromptu dash for a few minutes out the back of Number Ten, so it's unlikely that any terrorists would be hanging around Green Park on the off-chance the Prime Minister might pant through once a year. Maybe the old lady on a bench has an Uzi in her bag ready to hose down disgruntled voters.

Of course, the Prime Minister has a good excuse to be out of shape. Plenty of problems. The country. The world to lick into shape. Some twenty feet from me, he spots me, looks away, re-spots me and I can see him think: 'Now what?' Our gazes lock.

He can't stop, because when you're running, you don't stop, and you don't stop even more when you're a running Prime Minister.

'All right?' he gasps with what is meant to be a matey nod of the head. The gasping is to underline he's out on a run, in case I haven't fully grasped that, and can't stop however much he wants to, the nod to show how chummy we are nevertheless.

Senior politicians never want to stop anywhere because the public only want to complain about something, ask for something or lecture you about how to do your job. Seeing me, he's afraid I'll ask for a handout or pester him about refuse collection in my neighbourhood.

I nod and smile. I may be on the ropes, but I know the Prime Minister well enough to receive a nod from him in public. I also have enough on him for one very entertaining magazine article.

'Good to see you. Ellen well?' he asks backwards.

'Yes, thanks,' I shout. Name-recall: the trademark of the consummate politician, as well as the round-the-clock willingness to take the time to lie. It's impressive. I watch him run off, like the last of my hope.

Two tourists (they must be from abroad they're so tanned) watch. 'Was that . . .?' they ask. 'Yes.'

At Hyde Park Corner I consider the statue dedicated to the Machine Gun Corps of the First World War. It's certainly a little-known statue and probably deserves to stay that way.

First of all, why a naked David? Why? Why is he standing with his hand on his hip and a big chopper? Was he celebrated in the Bible for getting his kit off? Was putting his goods on display to put Goliath off his game? It couldn't be more gay if there was another naked figure pumping away from behind. Did the sculptor just have this superbly buttocked David handy when the war ended so he could quickly offload it in the memorial boom?

And it's a copy. (I only know this because Luke did a sketch of Donatello's *David* from the big book.) Depending on your mood, it's a homage or a rip-off of Donatello's *David*, which might be David. Or not. Which might have been Donatello slobbering over a Florentine rent boy. Or a rich allegory of political wisdom. Or both. Which was a copy of a piece by the Emperor Hadrian's favourite sculptor. Does anyone ever make anything up?

Machine Gun Dave doesn't have the helmet and the boots of Donatello's statue. A good pornmaker knows that a naked body is more naked if it isn't naked.

There's something slightly creepy about celebrating the machine gun. Most combatants in most wars don't want to be there and simply want to survive and hardly ever kill anyone (apart from my Uncle Joe), and can live with the knowledge that the enemy they did kill was the price for survival. But when you're mowing down hundreds of soldiers every afternoon, you, single-handedly, only stopping for a cuppa, how do you live with that? Or maybe that's why they had to put up the memorial.

I carry on over to St John's Wood. I badly need the exercise. And it's strange how London's not that big if you don't mind walking, and if you know the back streets it can be relatively quiet. Pleasant. It's only an hour to cover the really worthwhile bits.

It's difficult to know what time to call. I really want to get it over with. Just before I go in, I phone Johxn to make sure he hasn't changed his mind. I wouldn't be doing this unless I were desperate. I tried no a few times, but Johxn stated baldly, without any of the savoir-faire of the classy blackmailer, that I wouldn't get the statues unless I carried out this errand for him. If I didn't have a family I wouldn't do it. If I were on my own, I'd sooner starve, I really would. Most crimes, I suspect, are committed on behalf of children.

Luck. There are bizarre patterns. For instance, I have bad luck with restaurants. When I could afford to eat out, every time I wanted to go to the new hip place shooting up the top ten, it would be closed. It would be closed because of a fire alarm or because of a fire. Or because someone had just been murdered there, because of bankruptcy, because it didn't open on a Tuesday evening, because it didn't open on a Wednesday lunchtime. It would be closed because someone was filming in it. There was a message. I'm not sure what it was.

I've also had bad luck with employment. Correction: apart from once, when I was nineteen and I was travelling through Ecuador and I ended up as the curator of textiles in a museum outside Quito. I was on a train and started chatting with Rafa, who was the director of the museum. He invited me back to show me around. He then offered me a job. I was running short of money so I was delighted. I assumed he wanted me to sweep up or sit in front of a valuable exhibit.

'I would like you to be the Head of Textiles,' Rafa said. I laughed. But he was serious. I explained I barely knew what a textile was, that I had no interest in textiles, and that my employment history was working a cash register at a supermarket and setting up tripods. 'That's fine. What you need to know is the difference between seventy and thirty. I keep seventy per cent of your salary, and you keep thirty.' He explained that he could give the job to a friend or relative, but Quito was so small it would eventually emerge that it was a friend or relative whose knowledge of textiles extended to putting on a shirt. It couldn't work. On the other hand, no one knew anything about this dapper young Englishman who had gone to a world-famous university.

'I haven't been to university.'

'You don't understand this game,' said Rafa. 'In this game, you can go to any university you want. You can go to any university without leaving this office. And you don't need to read a single book.'

'I don't speak more than a hundred words of Spanish.'

'You're not here to speak Spanish, you are here to . . . textile.'

'But they must find out eventually.'

'Eventually,' Rafa said. 'Then I say you're an international con man who fooled me, a simple, trusting museum director, and I tear at my hair in rage. Tear, tear, tear.'

It was probably the best year of my life, since not only was I the Head of Textiles, I was the only person in the department. There was no budget for textiles so I decided everything was curated fine as it was. I turned up a couple of times a week to have a drink with Rafa, and I made extra money teaching a bit of English.

I don't know why I left. Many mornings I wish I'd just stayed as Head of Textiles. Before I left, Rafa got me to steal some of the mid-range exhibits and sell them. Tribal shit. I sometimes wondered whether I just used up all my employment luck in one go; or maybe I sold something I shouldn't have sold.

♏

I ring Chloe's bell.

'It's me, Baxter? We met a couple of times at Johxn's. Sorry to bother you.' I consider simply blurting it out and running.

Chloe hesitates for a moment. 'Oh. Come in, Baxter.' Then she lets me in. I follow her in, instead of blurting and running. Her flat is everything my home is not: tidy, fresh, expensive, tasteful, though maybe not as tasteful as she thinks.

'This is a surprise,' she says.

'Yes. Sorry about that. This is a bit bizarre . . . Johxn's a bit like that, isn't he? Johxn's sent me with a message. He's asked me to say, to tell you, that your relationship is, well, over.'

She doesn't seem too surprised, or too upset. Maybe I can get out of here without too much shame. I don't know much about Chloe. She has some pointless semi-job cushion-arranging or antique-hunting for the rich. Getting invited to some plutocratic tables was doubtless one of the attractions for Johxn.

'What a shit,' she observes. I make no sign of agreement. If I start down that road there'll be no stopping, and should it come up, I wouldn't be able to deny it convincingly. I asked Johxn if there was any mitigating factor he could offer, their inability to agree on the early films of Truffaut, for example. 'No, I've got a better deal, that's all,' was his comment.

His new girlfriend is a much younger Chinese girl. We always had the Hong Kong crew here in London, and I found them viciously tough, but the Mainland lot, fucking hell. My son will definitely be taking Mandarin lessons. 'But it's much kinder if you handle this, Baxter,' Johxn had insisted. 'You're a true diplomat. A people person.'

'I suppose there's someone else,' Chloe reflects. Should I mention that the new girlfriend is younger, a porn star? I feel a little sorry for Chloe, but she did make the mistake of going out with Johxn in the first place. We all make mistakes, though. That's one other area I've had luck with, I've never had the shag of shame. I've never woken up next to someone I've wanted to slink away from.

'Don't you feel awkward being his messenger boy?'

'Yes.'

'Do you do this sort of thing for him regularly?'

I nod.

'Has he got you to do worse things than this?'

That's a tough one. How exactly do you rate these labours?

'I don't know. Probably.'

'I'm sorry you've been dragged into this, Baxter. I suppose Johxn blackmailed you. Can I offer you a drink? This makes a change from getting dumped by e-mail.' That's one of the reasons Johxn sent me, I guess. No trace. No paperwork. No evidence that could be used against him. He's fantastically stupid. But quite sly.

'Thanks, but I have to go.'

'Yes, there must be other things for you to do apart from Johxn's dirty work. I suppose I should send a message. He still owes me for our holiday.'

I refrain from comment, but boost my air of sympathy.

'He's so awful, he's so rude about everyone. You know that he calls you the Immense Immenso?'

No, I didn't. Now I do. I thought I couldn't hate him any more, but it's happened.

'You were a friend of Herbie's, weren't you?'

This surprises me. Chloe knew Herbie? Of course, Herbie was well connected and sophisticated. He was educational to know. In addition to hubris and many other things, he was the one who explained to me that the Renaissance happened in Italy not France. I don't know why I thought that, but for a long time I did. The word sounded French. And that it had something to do with wine.

But I don't mind admitting I'm wrong, something I notice most people do. No one knows everything, no one can be right all the time, so why not say: 'I was wrong. The Renaissance didn't happen in France.' But it's rare to find that. The words are so easy to say, but nearly everyone finds that admission as hard as sucking their toes.

Herbie as a friend of Chloe? That's a surprise. Herbie was a slob. A haircut: maybe twice a year. Once he was having a cig outside the office, a sweet old lady slipped him a fiver. And he didn't have much time for the upper crust. It's hard to imagine him with Chloe, who probably dusts her pot-pourri and whose underwear must cost more than Herbie's entire wardrobe, and them having a conversation about what colour a pelmet should be.

But Herbie was in essence the last of Fleet Street, rather than pure Vizz nobility. Those chain-smoking lushes who could find out anything about anyone by going down the pub. The sodding researchers and young producers now, they couldn't find their way to the loo without the web.

Herbie started out in papers, so he had the foot in the door. The foot in the door isn't always about aggression and front, it's also about winning trust and getting strangers to open up to you. He was friendly with thousands of characters all over London. That's why he was so good; if you needed to interview a blacksmith or an expert on bell-ringing, he'd have a number.

'I was very fond of Herbie. His divorce finished him, poor thing.' Chloe has poured me a shot of Buffalo Trace, one of Herbie's favourites.

'Thanks. Yes.' That's true. The divorce really gutted him. Some men step out of a marriage like they step out of a bathtub. Jack the List, for instance, started off with a radical Maoist Peruvian, but then went off with a charming, younger Vizz exec whose father owned two yachts (one for each hemisphere) and a real castle. I admired the way he simply dropped, without any guilt, the first wife, who, despite being a Maoist, had supported Jack for a couple of years by working in an off-licence.

Most of us would have been plotting to come up with a justification or two, a look-good scheme for abandoning the warty revolutionary, for forsaking the stockpiling of ammonium-nitrate fertiliser and moving into a riverside penthouse, but not Jack. He dropped her like a red-hot anvil. Correction: you'd notice dropping a red-hot anvil, it's the sort of thing you'd remember. No, Jack's wife just never existed.

Herbie was like one of those birds that mate for life, the divorce ripped out his guts. That he was married at all was surprising. Herbie was someone who needed a carer more than a wife; love is quantum physics strange.

'The divorce, and other things,' I agree. 'He was pretty much a receptacle for tribulation, at the end.' You listen to roots reggae, you'll find yourself using the word tribulation more than the average Londoner.

'Herbie liked you a lot. He said you had the eye.' I wish Chloe hadn't said that. I feel I've let Herbie down. 'He showed

me your film about the bouncy castles. I thought it was great.'
She laughs to ratify that statement.

Booze. Praise. Correction: *not really deserved* praise. I am
being played here. Johxn had offered me that bouncy castles
doc in the hope that I'd turn it down. It's an old trick when
you want to fire someone or get rid of them, you ask them to
do an impossible job or a job you know they won't do, so
they storm out in a huff, firing themselves.

I flatter myself that I turned it round. There was a lot in
that doc to suggest how insubstantial the Vizz is, how full of
hot air. It was mostly about John Scurlock, the Louisiana
engineer who invented the inflatable. I felt I was being very
mature, very meta, but no one noticed. Although it wasn't the
worst thing I've ever done. Never work with kids, though,
unless you're willing to hurt them.

Johxn refused to broadcast it at first. 'Bax, this is no good,
I can't show it. You've really let me down.'

'What's the problem?'

'Everyone's happy.'

'Everyone's happy?'

'Yes, everyone here is happy and laughing and jolly.
Bouncing up and down. That's not what docs are about.'

He got into a jam at the end of the year with his budget, so
he was forced to put it out. It had the highest ratings of the
series.

♏

Chloe sits down and has a shot of bourbon too. 'I suppose it
was his son that was the start of it.' Herbie's eldest son died in
a bike crash. That *was* the start. It was one thing after another.
Herbie was very resilient, probably more than me, but when
you're targeted, singled out like that, who can take it?

'I'd reckon that's what sank the marriage. Too much grief and recrimination,' I say. 'Then he had a series of disasters professionally. Johxn—'

'Don't tell me. He left him in the shit.'

Yes. Johxn just turned off the tap. Herbie was really good-natured, even when Johxn practically destroyed him by not giving him any work. Herbie did have saint-like tendencies. Naturally he didn't like Johxn, but he was the only one of us who didn't hate him.

One evening in a dark leafy street in Hampstead, after Edison and I had left a party, we discovered Johxn staggering in the driveway, off his tits. Edison picked up a rock from some pretentious twat's Zen garden and said: 'Why don't we kill him?' With Edison you knew it was a legit proposal. It was a while ago, so my feelings weren't as hardened as they are now, but I did consider coming in from behind and kicking the year out of him. It was only the knowledge that we had been seen leaving the party at the same time as Johxn that stopped me. I knew I wouldn't be able to lie competently about that in court. My pleasure would seep through.

'Johxn does have a habit of leaving people in the shit.'

'He was telling me you're obsessed with Herbie's safe?'

Here we go. Herbie's safe. 'You know Herbie was from the West Country? The West Country is different. The Geordies, the Scots, the Brummies, the Scousers, the Ulstermen, the bluff Yorkshiremen, the ten people who live in Cumbria, they all say they don't care about London, that London is full of shit, that they have their own thing, that they don't care about London. They're lying.

'The West Country? They really don't care. They just don't. There's a story that, long before the Vikings, long before

Christopher Columbus, the fishermen in Bristol discovered America. They refused to tell anyone.'

'Herbie had such tall stories. He told me he knew where King Arthur was buried.' Chloe laughs in a way that suggests she's already forgotten about Johxn.

Not sure about that King Arthur story.

'He told me he knew who really shot JFK.'

Maybe.

'Oh, and he had a great one about how the Nazis cracked anti-gravity two days before the end of the war, but they destroyed all the research because they were such sore losers.'

I can believe that one.

'And you think he kept some of these amazing secrets in his safe?' Chloe asks.

'I don't know. You'd assume that, as he was so desperate by the end, if he had some great card to play, he'd have played it. But Herbie was a man of his word. If someone had given him some file or footage but said you can't use it for thirty years or until I'm dead, he would have respected that. Or he just didn't play the card because he was from Taunton. Logic evaporates out that way. Or. . .'

'Or?'

'Or there's nothing, because he was also a practical joker. He sent me round to Buckingham Palace once; he told me the Queen was waiting for me to do an interview. I talked my way inside I was so convinced it was genuine. Herbie laughed so much he had to buy a new pair of trousers.'

'And you've been looking for this safe for years?'

'It disappeared after he died. It was stolen.'

'By secret agents?'

'Or by the local junkie. It was one of those mini safes, too heavy to carry any distance, but you could lug it to a car.

Herbie would tease me about it. "Herbie's safe has got more than Pandora's box." I had to look that up. I thought Pandora's box was some restaurant. I badly wanted to find it because there might have been some great ideas in it. Herbie was a genius in some ways.'

'How do you mean?'

'He saw things others didn't. It was what? Nearly thirty years ago he said to me Islamic terrorism would be a problem. I laughed. It was Herbie winding me up again. It was like saying Norwegian wine would take over the world.' Herbie knew the small stuff too, he knew things six months in advance of most newshounds: which politician was going to be caught diddling a deadly actress or which grandee was about to go bankrupt.

Chloe gazes at me. Is something embarrassing en route? 'Baxter, you must keep looking for the safe.'

'Why?'

'Because Johxn's looking for it too.'

Now that's interesting. Did Herbie have something on Johxn? Had he caught him out on something? Was Johxn dipping into the till? Shaving some budgets? Inventing budgets? Fraud sounds too much like hard work for Johxn, but who knows? Well, well.

'You're a big hunk, aren't you, Baxter?' Chloe says. 'A bit flabby, but you've got some serious muscle, haven't you? Can I hire you for a job? How much for donning a balaclava and breaking a couple of Johxn's bones? Nothing life-threatening, just pain, lashings of pain. What sort of money are we talking?'

♏

When I get back home after checking out some more statues and a couple of centuries I knew nothing about, Johxn phones me.

'Did you take care of that topic?'

'Yes.'

'How did the topic go? Was anything said?' I reflect. It would be good to have some fun, inventing a rant about micro-cocked shits, but I can't take any risks. At all.

'She wasn't happy.'

'We all move on. She needs someone a little more . . . Hmm . . .' Johxn can't find the word. It must be difficult operating with a brain that has no thoughts and a tiny vocabulary. He is perfectly suited to the post-brain world. Again I restrain myself.

'Listen, Baxter, Edison is back on the statues job. He was free this morning so he was able to get cracking on it straight away, while you were . . . hmm . . . busy.'

I'm unable to react.

'But I've got something else for you. Is it true you were a bouncer?'

'Yes.' It is true. A friend started a club in Southend. I was on the door for five evenings because he couldn't find proper heavies. It was probably my boxing past that made him think I was suitable. It didn't matter that I'd only boxed for a few months and that I was useless at it. I was a boxer, so I could bounce. And if you're the man on the door, everyone assumes you're well hard, because you're the man on the door. You must be some hardcore kick-boxing head-butting mental pugilist or you wouldn't be there, would you?

'Did you have to thump troublemakers?' How popular violence is, particularly with those who've never had any experience of it.

'I never had any trouble.'

That sounds so . . . lethal. So masterful. It's nice to tell the truth once in a while. I'd have been in big trouble probably if there had been any trouble. But there wasn't any on the five nights I worked. It was another great job. My last great job. The only disturbance I had was a pensioner who lived nearby who had locked himself out of his flat and believed I could do something about it.

'You are a big lad, aren't you? All those pies, the liquid lunches. I need you to meet me tomorrow. I need some back-up.'

'What is it?'

'I'll tell you tomorrow.'

'Seriously?'

'Just be there, Bax.' Is he into some drug deal? Has he spunked finance from dodgy foreigners who want to slice him to death? Does he expect me to beat someone up? I go to bed thinking he can go to hell, but the next morning I wake up and it occurs to me that I might as well go along because I have nothing else to do, and if it does get dangerous I can run off and leave the xenos to kick him to death.

I only had one proper fight, as an amateur of course. When I was seventeen, I took boxing seriously for several months. I liked the sound of Boxing Baxter. My Dad and Uncle Joe, the men of the family, smiled approvingly. I joined a club in Peckham, which at the time was rated as the hardest in London. Not the most successful, not the most trophied, just the hardest. I did roadwork, I went swimming, I skipped around manically, I hit bags. I tried strange oriental techniques for hardening knuckles. I was battered by huge black men and by small black men. I was already well aware that I wasn't a gifted boxer, as was everyone else at the club, but I was going to work. I believed in work.

The club went up to Birmingham. The atmosphere on the coach was jolly and homicidal. We sang dirty songs and

86

scared people on the motorway. I hadn't had sex for weeks. I can't remember the name of the kid I fought. All I remember he was from Salford. My trainer whispered, 'Kill him,' as I got in the ring.

I learned an important lesson that night. For me boxing was an activity, a sport. Something I did. For the guy from Salford it was everything. It was his only hope, his life. This guy was so hungry, it was like fighting a black hole. He'd lose an eye, teeth, motor skills to win. He'd die to win. He wasn't a much better boxer than me, because I never heard about him afterwards, but he did knock me out in the first round.

The coach trip back wasn't enjoyable.

When we meet on the corner of New Cavendish Street and Wimpole Street, Johxn looks awful, as if he's having a bout of malaria (could it be something that serious?), and hands me a card with an address on it. 'You'll have to walk me in.'

'What?'

'You have to drag me in,' he says. 'Imagine you're throwing me in, Bax, rather than out.'

He is pitifully skinny and small. I grab him by the arm and try to march him into the premises of Kemal Khan, dentist. Even small individuals can use their body weight effectively when they don't want to move. He whimpers slightly. The advantage of having had a younger brother is you learn to grab by the ear and then everything's fine, and it's even more humiliating for Johxn.

'You'd better stay in case I make a run for it,' he croaks.

I wait in the waiting room, possibly the last and only place on earth where anyone reads *Country Life* magazine. I listen for screams of pain, but none materialise. Too late I wonder if dentists can be bought off to let the drill stray into a nerve.

Cash in hand. Who'd know? You always get the solution too late.

I am aware that my activity as a thrower-in, hanger-on, side-kick, toady, however you want to paint it, doesn't guarantee me anything. I'm not naive enough to believe in gratitude, or the certainty of trickle-down. The only advantage I get from sticking to Johxn is that by sticking to him, I'm preventing some meedja grad from We-Smoked-Bare-Dope-Bruv University getting to Johxn and jumping the queue. It's pure blocking.

When he comes out, Johxn says: 'I'll sort something out for you, Bax.' He hails a taxi, without offering me a lift, which is fine by me.

I've waited patiently, now he's worn, now his guard is down. It's one of the basics of conducting a tricky interview. As he opens the taxi door I say: 'I hear you want to find Herbie's safe?'

Johxn jumps like a baboon with a red-hot poker up its arse. So it's true. Very interesting.

That evening, on the web: *Seen bodyguarding the X-Man, pie-eater extraordinaire, the Immense Immenso looking, inevitably, immense.*

I put 'lose weight' on the must-do list.

♏

I wake up screaming.

'Nightmare?' Ellen asks, with that total lack of sympathy only a wife can muster.

'Nightmare,' I agree, not wanting to say there was no nightmare. A nightmare would be fine. You can wake up from a nightmare. You can't wake up from your life. My wife goes off to make a coffee with an I-know-exactly-where-my-life-went-wrong look on her face. Victoria Station.

She'd do a decent job of burying me and telling a few affectionate stories about me to our son when he's older. That's all you can ask for.

I'm cracking up. Knowing you're cracking up doesn't much help you in the business of avoiding cracking up. The morning light creeps in and helps. Light always helps. As I let my wife take full advantage of the bathroom, because giving women unlimited bathroom time is always a winner, I consider my options and gather some aggression.

Herbie used to say you need four girlfriends: two you're auditioning, the one you're with and the one you're leaving. It was ironic because he was monogamous, unflirty and not attractive to women. But he was making an important point: spread it around. Insurance. Insurance: you can never have too much.

I had to go from one shitty island in Micronesia to another. It was four hours in a boat about the size of a soup tin. I really had no choice. The other option involved flying back around the other side of the world and paying a fortune. I was unhappy about the soup tin, the vastness of the Pacific and the gormless guy in charge of the soup tin. 'You have a radio, right?' I asked. 'Sure.' He pointed at a box. Two hours out, the engine cuts. The guy fiddles with it, then announces: 'It's dead.' We're in the middle of the Pacific with one bottle of water and a bag of dried apricots I carry when working in strange shitholes. 'So?' I indicated the box. 'I didn't say the radio worked.' I've never been back to Micronesia.

I don't like phoning around, begging, but that's what I have to do. Albert Einstein allegedly said doing the same thing and hoping for a different result is the definition of insanity. Maybe so. But that's what we do. You ask the beautiful girl to dance forty-nine times and she says no, but the fiftieth time she says yes. Maybe she feels sorry for you, maybe she's tired of you asking, maybe you have a better shirt.

How much luck have I had? I've had some opportunities. I've collected an Oscar for Best Director. I was in LA the day before the ceremony. A friend was directing the show and I went to see him as they were having a run-through. He asked me to go up and collect. So I walked up to some applause (there were six production people sitting around) and I gave a short speech.

'There's actually no one I'd like to thank, because I did it all on my own. And I'd just like to say to the industry: eat shit and die.' It got a laugh, but like most jokes it had some truth. I was getting bitter. It does you no good. It gives you no advantage but there's nothing much you can do about it.

So I know what it's like to pick up an Oscar, the Oscar that anyone who's looked through a lens wants. I have enough imagination to colour in the rest. In a way, I've had that experience. And I have won awards. It's impossible to make a doc without winning a bronze medal at some festival in a city you've never heard of, very often in a country you've never heard of. And of course, the awful thing about success, apart from the money, which is agreeable, is that, well, as Herbie put it: 'Success? At best, it's idiots liking your work. Otherwise it's idiots pretending to like your work.'

♏

As ordered by Ellen, I pop into the crowded local supermarket to get some haddock for supper. It's the worst situation: having to soldier your way through a supermarket for one item.

At the check-out, there's a woman between me and the dumpy woman at the front, who's wearing an oversized combat jacket. Mrs Combat watches her shopping being scanned by the assistant. She makes no attempt to pack the items as they clear the conveyor belt, and she has a lot of items. Mrs Combat watches her shopping with the sort of detachment you'd watch someone else's shopping. She's not waiting for something bulky to go to the bottom of her bag. Her arms remain lifeless by her side. She has the nonchalance of a conqueror. The woman in front of me notices Mrs Combat's not packing items away. The cashier notices Mrs Combat's not packing items away.

The women are aching to say something, but after all, there is no rule that says you have to pack your shopping away immediately. We're not in a race. Not formally. I strain to beat back my annoyance because I'll be playing into Mrs Combat's hands. I say nothing.

Mrs Combat lets thirty odd items pass through the check-out and then, as if she's suddenly noticed them, slowly, *very* slowly, unfolds some plastic bags. She then packs her shopping, gazing at each item with deep contemplation, as if she's never seen a piece of cheddar or a rasher of bacon before.

There are three shoppers behind me. It's too late for me now, all the other lanes are packed. I'm firmly in neutral, because I know what's coming. Payment will be another leisurely saga.

It will be a virtuoso performance of looking for her purse in various bags and pockets. Deep, deep contemplation of her purse. Deep, deep contemplation of the several compartments of her purse. Hesitation between cash or credit card, then slowly choosing a card that won't work. Repeatedly. Before initiating another lengthy search mission for a voucher she's remembered. A voucher for a piddling amount. A voucher that won't be valid, but will allow Mrs Combat to enter into a lengthy discussion about the validity of vouchers and how that validity is made known to the public.

Finally she will count out the money, very slowly, in small change, with deep contemplation. We are hostages, us shoppers, held against our will. Mrs Combat has conquered and fully subjugated this check-out.

You get the lost-in-space quite often in this supermarket. The elderly, the ill, the stoned, who are barely aware of their surroundings, but this is different. This is no accident.

Mrs Combat is in her early forties and done. She was never a looker. She's unemployed. No person who is regularly employed could move that slowly, like a tired sloth, for so long, except, okay, perhaps someone from Lambeth Council. She's done. It's game over, and all she can do is be an obstacle. Like those who buy a dog or a gecko so they can lord it over something, she's enjoying the hold. The power of making us wait. I don't know what her story is, but it's a story that ends with her done, which makes me feel better.

I have my bag and money ready when I get to the front, and I clear the counter with my haddock in under a minute. This doesn't help me at all.

♍

I go round to see The Other Commissioning Editor, Wurly. Wurly, also known as the Lesser Commissioning Editor. I know it's pointless because he has a tiny budget, and for reasons best known to himself he won't give me any work. But I don't have anything else to do and having a meeting will give me some sense of self.

On my way to Wurly, I pop into the Club. I'm not a member, but because I've been drifting in for twenty years, everyone accepts I am. Precisely because it's known as the place where the magnificoes of the Vizz go, they're rarely there. The odd party or screening. No, the regulars who clog the bar are estate agents from Belfast, bored and boring lawyers from contract factories, novice whores with a degree in meedja studies. Nearly every time I've gone there some chancer fresh from Scotland has latched on to me who wants to get plugged in. You do? So do I.

But this is desperation. I have a coffee, hoping maybe my luck's changed. It hasn't.

Edison is holding court. He addresses those gathered in the bar: 'I'm much more intelligent than any of you, and if I can't really make it, you lot have no chance.' He is listened to respectfully. Why isn't he doing the statues? Should I ask? I can't face a conversation with him.

Outside, some tramp who has arranged a number of empty plastic water bottles into a crude replica of a camera with a telephoto lens expresses delight at my appearance. 'Oh, I can't believe it . . . no one's going to believe this . . . it's . . . it's . . . wow!' He pretends to take my picture with his pretend camera like an excited paparazzi. It works. A bit. Like my collecting the Oscar. I do get a tiny hit of wow. I'm tempted to give him something for the counterfeit fame, but don't.

Wurly will never be a Big Boss because he has a flaw. He's not a complete bastard. There's a vein of decency or softness in him. Take your pick. If you can't hammer the puppies, you won't make it. I gave him his first job as a researcher when he was so timid he couldn't even make a phone call on his own. I practically had to stand there and hold the phone to his ear and dictate. You'd think this support would work in my favour; it doesn't.

But, unlike Edison, he hasn't forgotten that I showed him the portal into the Vizz. So I enjoy going round to plague him, because I have nothing else to do, and he does feel awkward. Not very much, but a little. Tormenting others is free and can require no physical effort. In a way, there's little point having massive success now, because at forty-nine I can't fuck all night.

Aside from the matter of being married, I always saw success as having a place in Ibiza with a dozen talented ballerinas. You need those ballerinas in your twenties when you really could get through two or three in one go. I would have really flexed their flexibility.

Similarly, I don't need a flash place in Ibiza, because you need a tan in your twenties, because you want to attract even more women to your bed. When I jog around Vauxhall on those two or three sunny days that allow you to take off your top, although I consider my spare tyre to be very minor – correction: my spare belt – quite becoming for my age, I notice how everyone under the age of thirty averts their eyes and small children comment: 'Mummy, why is that man so fat?'

What I need is stability, peace and quiet and not ballerinas whining about how they need a trip to the foot doctor or they've run out of that essential nail varnish. So I can work on the *Magnum*.

'Hey, Bax.' Wurly gives me a big smile. The big smile will be my pay-off for visiting. I'm getting warmth but no work. I think back to how Wurly was when I hired him. I haven't really suffered, in the starving way, but Wurly has had the easiest of rides from my opening the door to his sitting at this desk. He was just out of the University of Not-Trying-Very Hard-Up-North, a pale creature who'd ventured out from under a rock and regretted not being back there. I'm glad I didn't go to university. No one good did.

I could have destroyed him, as Zyklon Annie does with the newcomers. I could have crushed him like a bug. People are like balloons, they genuinely do inflate and deflate with success. When I met Wurly, he was a tiny, flat balloon, just fallen out of the packet. Now he's zeppelin-sized, because he has a regular salary, a high-back chair and he has power over a few dozen like me. How we can expand.

Precisely because it's the last thing he wants to discuss, I ask, 'So, any work?'

He winces. He doesn't do poker face. 'If only you'd been around two weeks ago,' he says. I know very well what he'd have said to me if I'd been around two weeks ago. If you phone up every week, you're a nuisance. If you phone up every two weeks, you're too late. And one of the worst things about being a freelancer is that you have nothing for six months and then three offers on the same day, so you have to peer into the future to guess which job is the one that will lead you to glory.

We talk about Jim. Wurly insists he has it on good authority that it was a compilation of executions playing, not octo porn. We talk about Fletcher. Wurly insists that it wasn't a pine-apple, but a small durian fruit – the king of fruit, as it's known. I can imagine a foodie snob like Fletcher calling at New Covent Garden to score durian instead of getting a pineapple from round the corner. One day some layabouts in an office somewhere will recount my death too.

Wurly's office has a stunning view of the city and the river, gleaming in golden sunshine. Even as someone with little feeling for beauty, I feel the beauty. You feel major, just sitting in Wurly's office. The office is how it should be. I never imagined, however, growing up, that one day I'd have a conversation in a fancy riverside office on the finer points of the death of an unconvicted paedo.

We talk about Semtex. He's been in, touting his Roger Crab idea. 'I can't give him work,' says Wurly. 'You know how mental he is, but I wanted to treat him to lunch.' I can see what's coming.

'He started scribbling on the menu "Twice-murdered monkfish in a despond reduction", or some drivel like that. We were asked to leave. Even lunch is too dangerous.'

'That surprises me, Wurly,' I say. 'I've never had any trouble with him, anywhere, let alone in restaurants. He's so unfussy. He had a terrible childhood. Really unfortunate. He's to be admired for the way he's overcome all that abuse and poverty. Not many could do that. That's why we all like to help him out. And that Roger Crab profile is a sure-fire winner. Did you upset him?'

I see a little darkness traverse Wurly's face at the possibility that he might have been insufficiently supportive of someone from a lower income bracket and who has been the victim of a fashionable crime. I'm happy to talk. I've got nothing else to do and I know I must be irritating Wurly. I reminisce about how I got him his break. He's squirming when his secretary comes in and says there's a problem. Silly Milly can't do a job.

'I can,' I say, having no idea what the job is.

'No, you don't want this job,' says Wurly. This annoys me. This is the voice of a man who's never eaten shit, who's never known desperation. This is why I don't like Wurly. There are very few who have any character who haven't eaten shit.

'Bax, this job is beneath you, it's beneath your dignity.'

Beneath me? The only thing beneath my dignity is the mantle of the earth's core. It occurs to me I could just sit in his office until he gives me a job. For hours. For hours. Wurly's too wet to call security. Finally, he gets up. 'I've got to go to a meeting, Bax.' And leaves. I consider sitting there, but I know

Wurly's not going to risk coming back to his office today, just in case I'm still here.

♏︎

It's only when you've completely given up that you succeed. I'm in bed, so depressed that when Johxn phones up to offer me work, I'm actually angry about being disturbed.

'Statues is back on. Don't say I don't look after you, Bax. Half-Semtex is waiting for you at his place.'

I walk round to Half-Semtex's place. He's a good cameraman, but as his name suggests he's not as good as Semtex. Someone once remarked, 'You're good, but only half as good as Semtex.' Suddenly everyone forgot his real name and called him Half-Semtex, even those who didn't know Semtex, even his mum.

As I suspected, there is a supermodel doing the dishes in his dingy kitchen. She's really going at it in an I'm-doing-the-dishes manner. The first time I went to Half-Semtex's place there was a ridiculously beautiful blonde, with an apron, dusting away with a big feather duster. Half-Semtex is a strapping lad, but it was odd that someone so beautiful was doing his housework, with so much vim. Was it one of those strange hire-a-model-to-do-your-housework perversions?

He doesn't introduce me to the dishwasher. Perhaps he can't remember her name. I haven't been to Half's place that often, but every time there has been a staggeringly beautiful woman labouring away, painting, baking, giving it the full domestic throttle.

Was Half-Semtex a notable London degenerate who hired supermodels to do his grouting? If not, what's his secret? It took me a while to twig. He's well-built in the understated way women like, rolls a machine-quality joint, gets into all the top clubs free, he's got spending money, but that's not the clincher. His doomsday weapon, his death ray is that . . . he doesn't care.

No supermodel is badly treated. There's nothing unpleasant in his behaviour, but he doesn't care, and it drives the women wild. If the tall blonde doing the dishes walked out, he'd register it, but he'd know sooner or later another leggy blonde will carry on the work. Doubtless all these beauties go in for tornado-style blow-jobs in bed, but when that doesn't get more than a half-grin from Half-Semtex, they need to find something to attract his attention, to show how serious they are. But they can't have him.

If you don't want it, you can have it. If you're merely saying you don't want a supermodel to clean your windows, but deep in your heart you're hoping it might happen, it won't. The upshot is, however, that Half-Semtex only has a super-model doing his dishes because he doesn't care about having a supermodel doing his dishes, so in effect, he doesn't have a supermodel doing his dishes, and is like the rest of us, except maybe with cleaner dishes.

We get into Half-Semtex's car when his phone goes. His mother has just been hospitalised. Half-Semtex, of course, wants to attend. I can't help being jealous of his laid-back nature. He goes off calm. The downside is you'll never get anywhere with that attitude. Of course, you can always question the whole desirability of getting anywhere.

Nothing is ever easy in the Vizz, but this statues project is looking cursed. I only live around the corner from Half-Semtex, so I go back home while Half-Semtex's agency tries to rustle up a new cameraman.

Luke shows me a drawing he's done. Like most fathers I'm prejudiced, but it is brilliant. I don't know where he gets it from. My wife claims she had a great-aunt who was a painter but she hasn't produced any proof. I can't draw a convincing cock on a wall. Luke's drawing is like something by Rembrandt and he's ten. The problem is there's already been a Rembrandt.

His drawings are truly prodigious. When we pass the drawings around the reaction is that it's a prank. I could probably get him some Vizz action, but I have no intention of exposing any family member to the meedja. We have a suitcase-sized book on the history of art that has somehow survived all our misfortunes and Luke copies out master-pieces, almost exclusively ones that feature executions and torture, but that's European culture for you. The martyrdom of St Valentine and crucifixions figure big, although Luke complains the crucifixions aren't lifelike. 'The nails wouldn't hold,' he observes.

I should take him somewhere. I started going to the British Museum when I was eleven. I'd ask my father for money to go there on Saturdays and naturally the word museum worked its magic. I spent most of my time in arcades in Old Compton Street playing the machines, but I actually did go to the museum a couple of times. When I needed a dump. It's not like now. It wasn't mad. Tidal waves of tourists. Tourist tsunamis wiping everything out. It was a weird playground.

The drawback to being a father is that if you get it right, no one notices, and if you don't, you're the figure of fun.

The agency tells me they have a cameraman on site. I've never heard of him, but there's no time to be picky. Fortu-nately our presenter hadn't left home so he's not hopping around in a rage waiting for us. We've lost most of the day, though.

I try to make a call to the new cameraman, but my

reception is bad. It's those fuckers at MI6 and their big rooftop dishes making endless enquiries about the bondage scene in Istanbul.

♏

As I get to Camden and exit the tube, I'm accosted by a man in front of The World's End pub. You can tell the non-Londoners immediately. They're cheerful.

'Excuse me, sir,' he says. Swarthy, tubby. Suit. Unpractised English.

Being addressed as sir is bad. Courtesy on the streets of London now exists almost solely for the purpose of manipulation, for the extraction of cash. The savvy response in London to anyone talking to you is to walk on, and indeed, if the sir-caller is small and unmenacing, to fire off a 'fuck off' just to be safe.

But you do occasionally get tourists or the bewildered asking for directions, and it makes such a pleasant change from the relentless demands for cash, cigarettes or blow-jobs that you feel like thanking them. I stop.

'I am Masood,' he continues. This is bad. Very bad. No one introduces themselves if they want to know where Buckingham Palace is. Masood is quite chubby. I wonder if he's about to ask for money for food. I'm astonished by the number of beggars who are better dressed than me and who are so lardy their knees are giving way. What does it say about a society when the beggars can't be bothered to make an effort?

My feet want to move on, but my heart isn't dead enough. Perhaps Masood comes from some remote corner of the Middle East where you have to introduce yourself and discuss the weather before you can ask a question.

'I am a teacher,' Masood adds. Right. This is a stick-up.

Masood hails from some strange shithole where teachers have respect. He believes his rank will endear him to me; he hasn't been here long enough to digest that our schools are full of losers, criminals and never-beens.

My feet are revving hard, but a part of me is curious as to what's the pay-off? Living in London turns you into a connoisseur of begging. Will Masood push the frontier of importuning? Will he dazzle? Will he innovate?

'I want to talk to you about human rights in Iran—'

I'm already three paces down the street before he hits the second syllable of the country. Human rights? It's a near universal how everyone expects someone else to sort out their problems.

We have no rights. If you want to do something about human rights in Iran, off you go, don't loiter on my pavement. Iranians annoy me because they'll always bang on about how astonishing their culture is. Or was. They were masterful with the aubergine in antiquity. So what?

Done anything in the last thousand years? The skateboard? Hip-hop? The slinky? The vibrator? The computer? Powered flight? Antibiotics? The mobile phone? Reality television? The Frisbee? Opera? Electric Guitar? GPS? The satellite? Velcro? All Iranians do is sell oil and fish eggs. The only Iranians I've ever liked were Otanes, and Youssef. Otanes didn't want to rule or be ruled, which is how you end up, wanting to be left alone, but when you start out it's You versus The World. You wanna break it. You want to rule it.

Youssef ran a great café in Primrose Hill, with great aubergines, and he hated Iranians. 'I'd lie about being Iranian,' he said, 'except the thing I hate most about Iranians is their lying.'

The funny thing about the beggars, chuggers and other pests who stop you is that they often get angry if you tell them to fuck off, as I have on a number of occasions. They get in your way, you say no in a civil manner, but they carry on and then are wounded by you making your position abundantly clear.

At the statue of Cobden, I'm surprised to see Semtex setting up, but he's equally surprised to see me. 'I thought I was working with a David Smith,' I say.

'That's me, star,' he says. 'I've changed my name. Legit. By deed poll, so no one can accuse me of any skulduggery. I was told I was working with Edison.'

'You were until about five hours ago, but he's had a better offer. Couldn't you come up with a more original name than David Smith?'

'Totally off the grid. How do you run a background check on a David Smith? I'm fucking invisible,' Semtex retorts. 'I said to you before, I'm not going to have a go at you about, you know, the matter, the fire. That would be unfair.

'So I'm not going to go on about, you know, the big fire. But I'm fully taking the piss in every other regard because you fully deserve it, and because there's so much material to work with.' Semtex pauses to choose another line of abuse. 'Why didn't they get you to shoot this? It's not exactly the chariot race from Ben-Hur. I'm mildly insulted.'

'Why don't you thump Johxn for demeaning you by giving you work?' I've been trying for years to get Semtex to lose it with Johxn, but, like anything you want, it hasn't happened.

I ignore Semtex mostly and he carries on with the cheer of a pall-bearer. I don't care. That's the thing about sulking, it's rather pointless, because no one cares.

Our presenter arrives. When I meet someone for the first time now I can't help wondering exactly how or when they will disappoint or betray me. I instantly realise Professor

Headley won't disappoint me because I'm not extending him the benefit of any doubt. I don't know what's going on in the universities – I've met more impressive apprentice heating engineers. He has the features of an identikit paedo and that shifty manner of someone who knows they're somewhere they shouldn't be.

Why has Johxn chosen him as a presenter? What hold does he have? What bollocks did he spout at a dinner party to bewitch Johxn's puny intellect? Did he just slip Johxn some money so he could be in the Vizz? I don't care. As you get older you understand why so many atrocities happen, why orders must simply be obeyed.

There's a hitch: I have no script. Edison obviously has done nothing, or if he has, is not making the mistake of sharing the information and thus making my job easier, and I haven't had time to do any proper research. Some mystery figure at Wacky Towers, probably a teenage intern, has sent us a list of statues to be done, probably chosen at random.

'Where's my script?' the Professor asks. A not unreasonable question. There are a number of reasons I can't give him a script, chief of which is there isn't one. I'm tempted to respond that as he's the expert and the presenter, perhaps he should have something to say, but I don't.

'I was thinking about that,' I say in my most directorial manner. 'It's too constraining using a script. I want to try it . . . off the top of your head, an intellectual . . . bouquet, if you like. It's just a bit obvious to talk about the statue directly. Let the unconscious loose.'

Semtex reacts by not reacting. You can't fool a cameraman. He studies his camera as if there's some reason to study it. I'm surprised in a way we have a budget for a cameraman and a director. When I started, in prehistory, in the Vizz there would have been four, five, possibly six of us doing this shoot. An assistant cameraman. Sound. A producer or two. A PA.

The Prof obviously doesn't want to do this off-the-cuff stuff, because he clearly knows bugger-all about the subject, but he likes the idea about the intellectual bouquet and since he hasn't done any television before he doesn't have the stones to call my bluff.

He assumes I know what I'm doing, or at least he hasn't figured out that I'm busking. This may not last long. In the days of film you had to watch your time, but the best thing about digital is that you can let presenters or interviewees talk as much rubbish as they want, and it costs you almost nothing. I'm just old enough to remember how the film veterans laughed at video. Disaster always starts with laughter. I don't care if this is a flop because it's not my baby and no one is going to make history in the Vizz with five-minute bombasts about statues, even if they were fronted by someone with something to say.

'These statues are the droppings of an imperialistic society. They are not public faces, but public faeces, immortalised turds,' the Prof gabbles. That must be a line he prepared earlier. 'What we are visually seeing is the hardened excrement of a brutal society.'

Semtex straightens up from the camera eyepiece and a flapping pigeon above him dumps a massive load into his hair. It should be funny, but the Prof doesn't know Semtex well enough to laugh at him, and I don't want to say anything that will set Semtex off.

I pretend nothing has happened and get the Prof to wave his arms about like an irate Italian waiter. That seems to convey truth. That's all they do now – presenters, politicians – they bound around like fucking rappers and wave their arms. Put your hands in the air and wave them around like you really, really care.

We're opposite Koko, which used to be the Camden Palace, which used to be something else. There is no London. Or rather there is an infinity of Londons, which is why there can't be one. Like some weird physics. The London I grew up in has long since disappeared.

'The epicentre of my epiphenomena is my cock,' the Prof continues. How did we get here? I'm past caring. I get the Prof to wave his hands a bit more. He looks even worse doing this, but I'm obeying orders. At the end of the shoot, he hands me a thin pamphlet, which has 'My Cock: A poem' on the front. 'It's a poem about my cock,' he explains. On the back is a photo of a penis. It's grainy. Like a photocopy of a bad picture of a deformed radish. If that were my cock I wouldn't be imposing it on the world. Since I have to work a little longer with the Prof, I resolve to wait till he's got round the corner before I chuck it in a bin.

'Baxter, one of my colleagues was telling me,' the Prof hesitates, 'that you were working on . . .'

'The Ray,' chips in Semtex, still cleaning his hair.

'Yes, I was,' I confirm.

'Did it ever . . .?'

'No. It didn't get finished,' I confirm. Semtex keeps his word and is silent on the subject of the fire and my losing every penny.

News gets around, doesn't it? Everyone loves a good misfortune. Why did I want to make a doc about The Ray? I don't know really, perhaps that's why I wanted to make it, to find out what drew me to him. And it cost me every penny I had because recreating scenes from fifteenth-century France was an expensive business, with all the costume nonsense, although the actress who played The Ray's wife volunteered to do everything naked to save on wardrobe.

'Statues are all wrong,' the Prof says. 'Who knows who the genuinely important are? The most important person in the world might be a bus driver in Stockport.' I wouldn't trust the Prof to flip a burger properly, but now that the camera's packed away, he has said something meaty and understandable. It's tragic and wrong that even a moron can be right. It shouldn't be allowed.

The Prof shuffles off and once he's out of sight, I dump his oeuvre in a bin in front of Koko, which had been the Camden Palace, which had been something else before.

I spent an evening in the Camden Palace when it was the hot club in London. Did that really do me any more good than being in, say, the twentieth-most fashionable? At the time, not really. If I tell anyone now, do they care? Not really. That's history.

I had been there with a friend who was going out with the man who handled the distribution for the Cali Cartel in Barcelona. Did he sample the merchandise ? You fucking bet. He had a bag of coke the size of a dictionary, which he'd brought with him, through customs, in his hand, which gives you an idea of his mental state. He over-died about three months later with practically no internal organs.

I spent the night dancing with three tall Swedish girls, certain that, away from home, in a glamorous club, after an evening of drinking and snorting courtesy of Bax, one of them, at least, would end up in bed with me. No. Three of them. It was so unfair. At least a hand-job on the fire-escape.

That was, what, twenty years ago? And the injustice still rankles. I danced with them for *hours*. To some ropey music. How small things rankle. Now, that's history. I had an offer of a free meal in a New York hotel fifteen years ago, but my fellow diner turned up late, all the tables were taken, so we had to go out, and I never claimed my free meal. It was only one meal. A few bucks. But it still rankles, as if that would make any difference to the quality of my life. It's the small stuff you can't shed.

I let Semtex get on with some cutaways. Cameramen don't risk their lives exclusively for truth and justice, but also for a reputation. You have to feel some respect for someone who camped out on a volcano for days, as Semtex did in Iceland, *praying* it would erupt. He is as excited as me by the prospect of shooting an inanimate, immobile and unattractive object, but he will come up with the goods. I won't admit it, but he's precisely the cameraman I need.

I couldn't care less about Cobden. I know nothing about Cobden, apart from his involvement with the Corn Laws. I don't care about the Corn Laws, whatever they were. Does anyone? They didn't care much about him during his life. That his statue was financed by a Frenchman says a lot. That it's in Camden says more. They had cows and ducks here in the nineteenth century. It was as much a part of London as Edinburgh.

The item will be poor, but Johxn can't complain. I've had no prep time. I can always get the Prof to voice-over some bonus nonsense during editing. And if it's completely inaccurate, someone will write in to Johxn to complain about it, and will get precisely no response. Accuracy, facts, truth, replying to members of the public, responsibility are all so unmeta.

Behind the Cobden statue, there is a small memorial to the Burma Railway. It's a tack-on. You can see that no one hugely cared. It upsets me because my Uncle Joe was there. Because he's dead. He was one of the three people on the planet to have been kind to me other than my parents and there's nothing I can do to alter the fact that he's dead and that he possibly had the worst war of anyone in the Second World War.

I can't go in the Blind Beggar pub now, because that's where Joe bought me my first pint (an obvious fiction) on my eighteenth birthday. I was outside it once in August, gasping for a drink, but when I went in I was just coshed by sadness and had to turn round.

Uncle Joe was short, five-four, and unbelievably skinny. He wore black-framed glasses. He spoke quietly. I never saw him get aggressive, or even excited. But most people who met him for the first time were terrified of him. Everyone just straightened up around him and got respectful. The British Army in the Far East did all sorts of shit they didn't want anyone to know about, and Uncle Joe did most of it. Even civilians can sense a killer passing through. He had that super-heavy gravity.

Who had the worst war? Not the soldiers who fought. The soldiers who were captured. Uncle Joe had four years with the Japanese.

'The big lads were the first to die,' he told me. 'Being small saved me.' He never went to the cinema because he didn't like romances; he didn't mind comedies but felt they were a waste of time; he didn't want to see war films because most of them were silly and unrealistic; the ones that weren't so silly and unrealistic he didn't want to see either, and he didn't want to see gangster films because he did the books for the Krays ('Small boys,' as he once described them to me).

I always wanted to make a doc about Uncle Joe, but he died before I had enough status in the Vizz. And he wasn't a talker. I asked him what it was like being a soldier. 'You want to shoot first.' That's how he summed up twenty-plus years in the Army. I'm not sure anyone would have believed his story. Almost everyone who was captured with him died horrendously of illness or starvation. He had two mock executions. He escaped once. The jungle was worse than the camp. 'In the jungle, all you are is food.' He almost died, but was saved by a dog carrying a durian fruit. He was unable to move from exhaustion, illness, sores, hunger, in the middle of the jungle. It was over, when this dog trots up with a durian, leaves it for him and trots off. That kept him alive until he was recaptured.

He was forced to dig his own grave, but at the very last second the firing squad got other orders. Then, towards the close of the war, he was shipped to Japan. The ship was sunk by the Americans. Almost everyone drowned or was eaten by sharks. A shark attacked Uncle Joe. He punched it on the nose. He got to Japan, where he was outside of Nagasaki when the atomic bomb was dropped. It was only when he was in his seventies that doctors discovered he only had one kidney, one missing from birth, which meant he could have dodged conscription.

'That's the only real question,' Uncle Joe said to me. 'When they ask you to dig your own grave. Do you?'

I sit down and eat my sandwich. In some parts of the world having anything to eat is a luxury, but in London, the division comes over sandwiches. Do you buy your sandwich or do you have to make it yourself? Once I used to think nothing of having a three-course meal, with booze. Then I used to think nothing of buying a sandwich and a coffee. Now I do.

'Have you heard of Göbekli Tepe?' I ask Semtex.

'No.'

Semtex's now setting up a crude trap for pigeons, using a camera case. It's not fitting for a vegan, but he grew up in the hippy wastelands of Wales where there was doubtless nothing else to do but torment wildlife and learn the didgeridoo. He reaches over and rips off a bit of my sandwich and places it as bait. I pretend nothing's happened.

'Who's Göbekli Tepe?'

'It's an archaeological site in Turkey that's reckoned to be the Garden of Eden, because it was the first garden. Eggheads in white coats with many test tubes have discovered that's where wheat was first cultivated.'

I wonder whether it was worth asking Semtex about Göbekli Tepe. Is it worth asking anyone about anything? What does it tell me?

'How's Ellen?' Semtex asks.

'She's fine, thank you.'

'That's the great thing about being a failure, Bax.'

'What?' I note that his hair is still shitty, and that I won't tell him.

'You can be sure that someone's with you because of you. It won't be because of your incredible wealth and power. It won't be because you're going places, star.'

Is Semtex narked because of the pigeon or the sandwich? Does he treat my eating the sandwich as a provocation? That I reached for the sandwich viciously? That I'm beating him around the face with this sandwich, whereas I'm just having a bit of lunch? It took me years to figure this out, but he has a real aversion to sandwiches, to the point where he'll cross the road to avoid a sandwich bar. How do you develop a horror of sandwiches? I have to admit in the past I have taunted him and made him shudder with an overloaded egg mayonnaise.

'At least I use my own name.'

'You haven't found Herbie's safe, have you?' he says, in another round of retaliation.

'No.'

To my amazement, a pigeon waddles into Semtex's trap and he slams the case on it.

'What?'

'I'm not harming it at all,' he says. 'We'll go home and when the mood's right, I'll shit on it and then send it on its way. To settle the score.'

I should probably keep my mouth shut, but I can't hold back. 'But that's almost certainly not the pigeon that bombed you.'

'It's about sending a message.' I can't argue with that. We are all battling for justice in our different ways.

We part and I carry on down Camden High Street. On a lamp post is a picture of a cat lolling on a sofa. 'Tabby found' is the headline above it. Below: 'Jiffy (according to his collar) has a good home now, comfy in my lower intestine. Never vindaloo a cat. It's just wrong – it swamps the delicate feline flavour.' If you eat, can you complain about being eaten?

A charity shop across the road draws me in to look at the books, to see if there's something that might give me an idea to win over Johxn for his Big Money Gig.

I like Göbekli Tepe, or Potbelly Hill as the Turks have it, but I need something more. It's not very Johxn. The ideal project for Johxn would be a one-legged ex-slave black tranny whose pioneering calculations on gravity were stolen by Isaac Newton, illustrated by woodcuts from a Luddite lesbian in Bedlam. The trouble with the net is that while it's great for research (I can remember when you had to phone fellow humans and winkle info out of them, word by word, or even walk to a library, in the rain), it's great for everyone.

Everyone can go click. What I want is a story in a book, sealed away in a few hundred copies. Some vintage shit. Some shining criminal. Intrepid explorer. First-rate eccentric.

The books are disappointing, schmaltz and erotica. On my way out I notice a small stack of tatty 45s. I don't know why I look. A moment of nostalgia? They used to mean so much. An era when you bought music song by song, not by the terabyte. I flick through and I'm astonished by what I find. Pressed off-centre. Faded lettering that was faded at manufacture. A real rarity.

You used to come up to Camden for the bootleggers. Whatever else, the web has wiped out those greasy shits. Now we can all summon up one hundred Bob Dylan bootlegs for free while we brush our teeth. I wasn't expecting to find some musical treasure these days.

Before I turn the corner in to my street, I slip the record halfway down the back of my trousers and cover it up with my jacket.

I didn't want to buy it as much as I did want to buy it. There are a number of reasons why I shouldn't have bought it. For a start, I no longer own a turntable. I had to sell it and learned again that painful lesson: you buy expensive but you always sell cheap, so cheap that you wouldn't go through with the sale if you weren't desperate. I also don't have room in our new place for a turntable. I can barely get in because of all the boxes, although I suppose if I had the money for a new turntable I might well have the money to get a place that would have room for a turntable.

There is also the fact I haven't a clue whether the single I've purchased is any good. I haven't heard it. It's a single so rare I can't believe I've found it, so listening to it or enjoying it, in a way, is irrelevant.

Bongo Herman's 'Bongo Riot' is lodged next to my buttocks because I don't want my wife to find it. How much trouble I'd be in is hard to say. 'Bongo Riot' itself doesn't matter. It's a few quid. This purchase doesn't in itself make any material difference to our situation.

But marriages aren't about reality or truth. They're about warfare and the ammunition needed. So Bongo Herman, while insignificant in himself, could become a deadly weapon. A back-breaking straw. The danger lies in what Bongo Herman could symbolise: we are in debt up to our necks and I am throwing money out the window. Like an Olympic javelineer.

That we are only slightly in debt for the moment and that I'm not throwing money out the window wouldn't prevent that statement.

Secondly, even more fiendishly, my wife could exclaim that not only was I starving my family, but, far worse, I had the inclination and the time, the sheer nonchalance, the naked, steaming braggadocio, to mull over the concept of buying a record, to go hunting for a record, to chat carefreely, sultan-like, like a spliffed-up cavalier, with the employees of a record shop, to flick though vast piles of records, when I should be devoting myself to extricating us from the mess.

If I'm caught with Bongo Herman, for the rest of my life, and it will be until the day I die, I'll be hearing how I squandered the grocery money and starved my son because of an obscure Jamaican that even Jamaicans don't care about.

I should say I'd do the same. You can't give an inch in a marriage. It's a relentless, bare-knuckle punch-up. I have a list of slip-ups I constantly refer to. Ellen burned a steak and kidney pie, slightly, once, fifteen years ago, but that's an incident I segue into the conversation every now and then as suppressing fire.

I bought the single because if I hadn't it would have been an admission of defeat. It would be admitting that I'd never have the space for a turntable or the money for a turntable or access to my vinyl collection, currently stored in a friend's garage in Hammersmith. It would be an admission that there's no hope. Storage and parking. Storage 'n' parking, that's what London's about.

And Bongo Herman is one of my heroes. You'll need to find a really thick book on reggae to find his name, but he was there at the start, he was there at the height, he was there during the downfall, and he's still there. He played with everyone, although you might not notice that, because he's often unacknowledged and there's a problem with bongos. You can't hear them when you have a powerful reggae bass and a studio full of powerful amplified instruments blasting away.

I admire him because he can't win. He's fighting an unwinnable war, a one-man guerilla struggle against vastly superior sonic forces. But he still fights. He always fights. Although he knows he can't win. There's another insurmountable problem for Herman. That the best bongo player in the world is almost indistinguishable from someone who's been playing the bongos for ten minutes. Skill counts for almost nothing in the bongo world.

♏

Mind you, you can never be sure how your wife will react. I remember sitting down to tell Ellen that we were wiped out, ruined. Strictly speaking, it wasn't my fault. Fires can start anywhere. It was my fault, however, I'd put so much money into that one doc about The Ray, which was going to be my *Magnum*. If it had been an uplifting story about digging a well in an impoverished region of Africa and how the water changed everyone's life, it wouldn't have felt as bad as a doc about The Ray, a man whom the prosecution alleged used to juggle with the body parts of the young children he'd murdered and sodomised.

I'd put it off and put it off, but finally I couldn't carry on with the weight. I was absolutely convinced it would be the worst day of my life. I was adamant she'd just leave and that I'd be seeing my son on odd weekends. Dreading the screaming and the weeping and the blame.

Ellen sat there so quietly I wondered if she hadn't heard or if she was in shock, so I explained again that we would have to sell the house. That everything was gone. She nodded and said: 'You'll think of something. You always do.' And then she went off to watch her soap opera. I was the one in tears.

It's also true that Ellen wants nothing to do with anything financial. You say 'bank' or 'interest' and she sinks into a coma. Instantly. I handle all the money not because I'm considered competent, but because she wants nothing to do with it. Using the cash machine is as far as she's willing to go.

Contrast this with the time I unpacked her boxes. We had just moved into our first home and because I was stuck waiting for something to happen, I thought I'd unpack a couple of her boxes, dust off her knick-knacks, put them out on a shelf so she could see what was there. I thought it was a minor favour, a bit of time-saving house husbandry. To earn some merits. She went crazy. She was sobbing. If I'd ripped up all her clothes or tea-bagged her best friend in front of her she wouldn't have been more upset. It was not normal. I offered to repack everything in the boxes. But no, that was no good. It wouldn't be the same. She'd been looking forward to unpacking those boxes herself. I had a miserable week.

A yellow Lamborghini is still blocking our driveway. Parking is such a problem. We've all committed parking crimes. It's odd that there's a yellow Lambo in Vauxhall, on this side of the river. You get the Arab playboys in Kensington or Knightsbridge in their Ferraris and Lambos, circling Harrods, occasionally getting up to a heady thirty miles an hour in the chocka traffic.

It could be that the owner of this Lambo worked for years cleaning windows and skipping meals to get the money, but it's unlikely. That it's a convertible makes it worse.

It's not blocking in my car, because my car is parked elsewhere. It's in such a good parking spot in Soho that I haven't moved it for four months, because I don't want to lose the space. If the Lambo were there for half an hour, so what? But it's been there since the morning.

This is London. You don't leave your top down. That's not asking for it. It's begging for it. This is London. It's just the right height for me to take a lengthy piss into it. I don't want to be pissing into a yellow Lamborghini, but I'm obliged to. The driver is right down on his knees begging for it. I can't, in good conscience, just walk on.

Back home, Luke is lying on the floor, playing with some tiny plastic soldiers piled up in a mess. I don't recognise the uniforms, they're probably designed that way: generic, eternal soldiering.

'Which war is this?'

'It's not a war. It's an orgy.'

It's a different world. Last December some nutter with a megaphone turned up outside Luke's school and started shouting, 'There is no Santa Claus' to the kids in the playground. One of the kids, eight, responded, 'We know that, you saddo.' And scored a direct hit in the nutter's face with a hard-boiled egg.

Ellen is fiddling in the kitchen. Like a man who hasn't got a rare Jamaican 45 down his trousers, I saunter over to one of my boxes and pop Bongo Herman inside. Now he's just more junk, old junk, and not a gold-embossed certificate of my wickedness. Mission accomplished. To wind down, I go online to the spleen pages.

Lovable Psycho writes: *It's an insufficiently known fact that the Immense Immenso has a looong history of violence!!! When he worked on a natural history quiz he was owed money and hit upon the tactic of going into the ower's office and blowing holes in it with a sawn-off acquired from his geezer mates down Sarf until the reddies were produced.*

Well. I did work on a natural history quiz. I was owed money by the well-known bastardo Harvey. I never went to his office with a shotgun. I never got my money. My fellow director, a minor aristocrat, who was also owed money, did walk in with a shotgun. That's one of the advantages of belonging to the upper classes, the posh get a firearms licence with no questions, or by suggesting there's a mole on their estate they need to take out. Soames didn't shoot anything. The gun wasn't loaded or even pointed. It didn't need to be.

The other item that catches my eye is from Secret Dictator: *Much-loved broadcaster and boy-botherer Kevin Fletcher is deaded. Unlock your sons. Family statement states Fletcher died of septic shock after an infection from working his allot- ment vegetables. The horticultural factor is true, but our sources insist that it was a pineapple, although, naturally, an ethically sourced and organic one and one that had journeyed deep into his rectum.* Underneath there is a heated discussion on whether Fletcher fiddled girls as well as boys, Secret Dictator insisting that Fletcher was an equal-opportunities paedo, doing all genders, ethnicities and social backgrounds. *He was a heroic anti-fascist who fought discrimination all his life.* I see another entry: *Interesting that the late Fletcher was*

117

seen dining with His Immenseness the day before his admission to hospital. Coincidence? Another completely false murder charge for my collection.

One of the benefits of employment that's often overlooked is that it suppresses thought. Unemployment allows you too much thought. Too much thought, like too much anything, is bad for you.

I'm tired after the Cobden shoot, but not tired enough. Deep inside, in a way, again I reflect, I am a worthless person. Even the things that seem to offer redemption – my love for my wife, my love for my son – merely shelter want. I love my wife because, partly at least, I want to be loved; my son is, after all, my son, my continuation, there's plenty of selfishness there if you care to delve, plenty of me, a trail of me. I'm worthless and I'm almost the best person I know.

♏

The next day when I wake up I glimpse the wastepaper basket. I'm not bothered any more.

It's a pleasantly late start. I meet Semtex by the Temperance monument in Clapham. There is no sign of the Prof. There is, however, a sign of Edison.

'I'm back on this one, Bax. Sorry no one told you,' Edison says.

'Johxn okayed this?'

'Yes.'

He says yes far too quickly. Naturally, I refuse to believe him. If he told me my name was Baxter, I'd check my passport. I phone Johxn.

'I'm here with Edison. In Clapham. He claims he's back on the job.'

'Hmm,' says Johxn.

118

'Where did he get that idea?'

'Hmm,' says Johxn. Edison meanwhile has phoned through as well so we're all on conference.

'We had an agreement, Johxn,' insists Edison.

'You said you had a gig in France.'

'But now I don't, and I've done all the work on this project.' No one's done any work on this project.

'Hmm,' says Johxn.

'You should tell Bax he'll just have to pass,' Edison insists.

'Hmm,' says Johxn. There is a pause. I'm getting so angry I'm weighing up going into town and satisfying my urge with the chainsaw.

'You'll have to fight it out,' Johxn announces.

'Sorry?' I say.

'We're all getting too artsy and meta-artsy these days. We're all so unmanly,' he elaborates. Speak for yourself, chair-warmer. 'You and Edison should have a good, old-fashioned straightener. May the best man win.'

'You're saying we should have a fight?' chimes in Edison.

Semtex's face is all grin. 'I'll hold your jacket for you.'

I'm now so angry I no longer care that Edison's bigger or at least taller than me and fifteen years younger. I'm departing the realm of reason. Why not? Why pretend there's any civilisation? Let's get to the grunting.

'I can't believe you're saying this, Johxn,' continues Edison. 'I can't believe you could say something so uncivilised. I want nothing more to do with this project.' Edison shakes his head and walks off. I'm a bit surprised but still so angry I have to go over to a park bench and kick it. I come off worse.

In my first week at kindergarten some kid took my chair. I wanted it back and the teacher noticed our tugging it back and forth, but instead of giving us a homily on sharing and the immorality of brute force, she said: 'Go on, fight it out then.' I won, but I didn't like it.

'I didn't think Edison'd bottle out,' I remark.

'He's probably heard that story about, you know, what's-his-name,' Semtex replies.

'He fell down the stairs.'

'That's what I always say in court.'

'He was blind drunk.'

'And he heard that story about you killing those stuntmen you owed money to.'

'I didn't kill anybody.'

'You've got extraordinary form for violence.'

'Coming from you?'

'What exactly happened to those stuntmen?'

'I'm not taking this from the man who's so quick to take offence, he doesn't even wait for the offence.'

'Why wait ? I'm a prophet, star.'

'What about Bangkok?'

'Here we go with that Thai shit. Being quick to take offence, Bax, is a sign of intelligence. Why wait for someone to piss on you? I go as they reach for their zipper.'

The Prof fails to show for another hour and a half. This supposed intellectual Godzilla can't find a street clearly marked on a map in Central London.

Eventually he hoves into view, looking rattled, which is his way of apologising. He should be cleaning out the cages in a pet shop, a small provincial pet shop, not shaping anyone's youth. I let him rabbit on without interruption, so he can deceive himself that his analysis of the Temperance movement is real razzmatazz, a real crowd-pleaser.

It amazes me how people can't do the simplest things. I'm almost unable to fly now, I'm so infuriated by the non-sitters, the throng of passengers who can't just get on, put their luggage overhead and sit down. The digressions, hesitations, U-turns, unpacking, repacking, unpacking and diversions those simple tasks produce. You know before you get on the plane what you have to do, you have *hours* to prepare for the two simple actions of stowing your luggage and sitting down. What do you get? The gormless who stand in the aisle as if they've never been asked to sit down before.

Before he leaves, the Prof asks me what I thought of his poem. It was brilliant, I tell him. Lying just powers the world. He hands me another tissuey pamphlet entitled 'My Brother's Cock'. There is no illustration this time. I rub the paper in the hope that I can actually have the satisfaction of wiping my arse with it, but it's too shiny, so I dump it in a bin.

♏︎

In the evening I do some scrolling. Quirky Pliers writes: *Unemployed? Try the Immenso method: take someone else's job. The Lord of Lard turned up to a shoot by our favourite Brazilian, and chainsawed a bench to make it clear what would happened if he didn't hand over the helm. The Clapham Chainsaw Massacre will live in our memories for ever.*

Cruelty Club comments: *He was lucky. Look what happened to those stuntmen.* Tired+Emotional agrees. So does HotbabeAgainstInjustice.

♏︎

I phone my brother. He sounds okay. He sold up years ago and moved to Arizona with his American girlfriend. He bought a hundred acres in the middle of nowhere. The nowhere that other nowheres look down on. I guessed it was an eco-thing. His girlfriend works as a moderator on websites

121

turfing out the too-obvious Nazis and paedos. Part of me was slightly concerned he'd do something mad like grow marijuana, as he's the one who always got caught.

He only ever stepped over the line three times, and he only did it because of the charge of being boring, but he got caught every time.

The day before his birthday, the day before his licence started, he took delivery of his Kawasaki bike. He'd saved up for it for several years doing shit jobs. The bike gleamed in the garage, like something from the future, from a much more advanced and cooler civilisation. The evening before his birthday, five hours before his birthday, he cracked and took it for a ride, a one-minute circuit round the block. We lived in an ultra-dreary suburb where nothing happened, ever. The biggest drama for years was a stray dog, a friendly one.

Vince was wearing full biking regalia. He was stone-cold sober. He is the most cautious driver I know. He didn't speed or rev up the engine or go for a wheelie. He was stopped by the police. The policeman had absolutely no reason to stop him. It was the first and only time I ever saw a policeman in our street. It was as if he was there by appointment.

No licence, no insurance. The court was unbelievably unsympathetic. They threw the book at him. You know when that happens, it's not an accident. It's a message.

I love my brother, but he is, or always was, a little boring (the reason he bought a bike was for outlaw cred). You knew if you left him alone in the house he wouldn't burn it down or have an unsuitable party. It's better than having a brother who will burn the house down. But it's not as good as having a brother who might burn the house down. He always did as he was told, followed the rules with a good grace. It was this incident, amongst others, that convinced me that, whoever runs this place, the Allower, goodie-two-shoes aren't appreciated. You should laugh at a cripple, or steal something, if only once a year, as insurance.

I asked Vince: 'What have you got there on your hundred acres?'

'Nothing really.'

'Is it beautiful?'

'Not really.'

'Are you doing anything with your land?'

'No.'

'So why did you buy so much?'

'It's for . . . you know.'

'For who?'

'You know. I'm waiting for . . . you know.'

He'd always been a keen sci-fi fan. That's mental illness, it can be very slight, and like cancer very unobvious until it's too late. Vince had arranged a landing pad for aliens in Arizona. Can I do anything? No. He hasn't done anything certifiable. He's bought some land in Arizona, admittedly an hour's drive from the nearest shop, with his own money. That's his business. His Christmas photo showed him shaved clean, even the eyebrows gone, because apparently the Ebes don't like hair.

Vince is waiting for the aliens to land on his welcome pad. To his great annoyance, another alien-fancier bought an adjoining property, with 200 acres and a bigger welcome pad, so now he's worried the aliens will snub him. You're never safe. I considered flying out to talk to him, but you can't even shift the ideabins of sane people. He sounds happy.

It took me quite a while to notice that, while I may not be in Arizona, sweeping a huge landing strip, I'm not so different from my brother. Ancient civilisations, aliens, angels: we all want the cheat-sheet, the answers delivered in an elegant envelope, the helping hand, Herbie's safe, the winning ticket, the *deus ex machina*.

I'm also waiting for aliens to land. We all are in some way.

♏

The next morning I get an e-mail from Johxn. The statues are going on ice. Everything cancelled until further notice.

I don't even start to figure out Johxn's logic because that would be a waste of time. I'm sure further notice means never. I can't say I'm attached to this project, but I was looking forward to some money. I should have known it was too easy. Of course, I'd suffered, but I hadn't suffered enough. There hadn't been the necessary protracted bouts of pure despair.

The thing to do is to forget all this, to walk away from the statues and not look back. Don't look back. To proceed with some new ideas. To think of Bongo Herman and his struggles with Bongo Les. I try that for a few minutes, but then, as I'm alone in the house, I climb back into bed, pull the duvet over my head and making whining noises for longer than I imagine it's possible to make whining noises on one breath.

JERUSALEM
APRIL

We trudge up the road to the Jerusalem sign. It's savagely hot. I wish I hadn't decided to go on foot, but parking's such a pain here. The security's so tight if you so much as stand on a corner for a minute a soldier will jog up to ask you what you're doing, as much out of boredom as professional concern.

Putting Liliane in front of a Jerusalem sign is a bit obvious, but why not? My poorly remunerated contract doesn't have a reinventing-the-wheel clause.

If you want to know about the end of the world, I can tell you all about it. I'm helming three one-hour docs about it, financed by simple Norwegians and Finns, who really should only concern themselves with growing timber, but who for some reason have left Johxn in charge. All you need is an office in London and someone, somewhere will believe you are important.

I wasn't the first choice. Naturally. The hot director of the year gave it all up when he met one of the top fashion supremos on a train in Milan and explained that all he'd ever really wanted to do was design bras; he drew a few outlines on a napkin and was hired to start a new range. No one saw that coming. However, Edison getting machine-gunned in a Bolivian hotel was long-awaited. He took four bullets, but survived, saved no doubt by his huge ego. Unbelievably, it was a case of mistaken identity. The erring hitman did nevertheless receive fan mail and presents in jail.

Four or five other directors turned it down because they had other offers. No one at the height of success wants to work with Johxn. I, at the opposite end to success, don't want to work with Johxn, particularly for what he's paying me, but there we are. I still have failed to come up with a Big Idea for Johxn's Big Doc, but so has everyone else. It's good to have company.

♏

Everyone believes the world will end. Quite detailed etiquette is offered for the end, as if for some social function. We all like an end. Not unfinished business. No one likes the party going on without us. Although quite a few cultures go in for the cycle business. Our world, furnished as we know it, will end, but another one will spring from it and carry on happily without us. So maybe not the end.

Liliane starts her piece to camera. The heat's getting to her. She snaps out her lines. I make her start again. And whirl her hands more. Johxn was very firm on that. 'You need to get the number of handies per minute up; that's what makes a good piece. That's what makes contact.'

'Everyone comes to Jerusalem,' says Liliane. 'It's probably the most fought-over city in the world.'

'No it's not,' says Semtex. 'What about Byzantium? Or Babylon? Every army in the world's conga'ed through them. Oh, and Baghdad.'

You can't fool a cameraman. You can fool an editor, you can fool an expert, a politician, an aye-aye-keeper, an exec, but you can't fool a cameraman. They have seen it all. You can make them suffer, you can stand them in icy radioactive water or in vicious crossfire, but you can't fool them. They might have limited knowledge, they might not be able to recite the dates of kings and queens or clarify a word like epiphenomenon, but you just can't fool them. They know. They see.

'The whole world knows you were in Baghdad,' counters Liliane. 'There's no need to remind us about your stories, again, Semtex. You are a very briny pickle. A briny car-bomb cheater.'

I had been with Semtex then. In Baghdad. In the bad times. We were sitting in a café, in a street we weren't supposed to be in. Some smug American, who didn't know his Dr Alimantado albums properly, had told us it was too dangerous a district to visit, so we had to do it. I suspected he was right, but he was such an arsehole and reggae lightweight I had to disagree and walk big. We were drinking tea and enjoying the sun and the waiter was trying to convince me, in German, a language neither of us spoke, to have the *masgouf*, a supposedly great Iraqi fish dish that tastes like mud.

A Toyota Corolla pulled up and parked opposite us. I noticed because it was the first car I ever drove. The driver got out and looked at me. He had the look, that look of perfect assurance you see in very rich bankers, film executives, Edison, the unshakeable conviction that this universe was made for you.

However, something terrible was going on with my crotch, and I was wondering whether I should cancel the entire shoot. The problem was that cancelling would look like cowardice, an unforgivably major loss of bottle, but it would be almost as bad to admit it was because my scrotum was itching so severely I wanted heroin. I was wondering whether I could tough out the itching for a few more days, when my chair collapsed under me, as its legs were shattered by a chunk of exhaust pipe propelled by I don't know how many kilos of high-explosive.

Some nationalities shout more than others. They love it in Iraq. We were at peak shouting and wailing. I'd say if a car bomb had gone off in Tokyo the Japanese would have been cooler, more shogun and inscrutable about it. I looked down the road at the bodies, realised that there was nothing useful we could do and left. We didn't have the camera, thank God, so we didn't have to make the decision about whether to harvest the misery or not.

Semtex and I would have been splatter if the Corolla hadn't been stolen seconds before the detonation, and was 200 metres down the road when it blew.

I was pretty calm. I surprised myself with my cool. My ears were ringing and I was covered in dust and what must have been particles of passers-by, but I got back to my hotel in a stately manner. Briny. It was only in my room that my legs turned to rags and I threw up. I couldn't stand up for a couple of hours. I actually thought my spine had been hit. As I lay there I considered how you could quip that Semtex had almost been semtexed, but there are some things you can't make a joke about. Many things become funny after a few years, but some never do, not for the participants. It's the next generation of Iraqi stand-ups who'll benefit from that material.

The truth is if people don't know you're weak, you're not. I wonder what goes on in the rooms of others, when the show's over. I'm curious how many hard nuts sob behind closed doors.

I must have used up a lot of my luck that day.

ɱ

I can't believe I'm working with Semtex again here in Jerusalem. If it were up to me I wouldn't be. You do things for your child you would never do for yourself. Even if it had meant my career going down the drain, I would have said forget it. But for your son ...

Not the sort of person you imagine having close friends, Semtex has at least one acquaintance from youth he's in touch with. Who is now the headmaster of the top local school, the one with the absurdly long waiting list. Where my son will be starting next term, to his mother's delight. I make no apology. I don't see why I should be the only utiliser of integrity in Britain. It's no quarter in education in London, like everything else. And anyway, Semtex and I have now been reconciled. Slightly.

You want to sort out the Middle East? I can give you the solution. Easy. Get the Chinese to invade. Soon every jihadi and Hasidim would be arm-in-arm blowing up the rice-eating logogrammers. My enemy's enemy actually is still my enemy if he or she is more of an enemy to me, especially in my backyard. Liliane has welded Semtex and me together, just like old times.

'We haven't had the car-bomb story today, isn't it about time?' Liliane leans forward, very slightly, but in a manner all vertebrates would clock as the aperitif of aggro. Many women are courageous and outspoken simply because they've never been punched very hard in the face.

I also note Liliane's still using her cleavage although she's well into her fifties. She has great tits for her age; French women are really good at that. They invented the cougar. I study her necklace and wonder how much it's worth. That's what's funny, the ones that are worth a million look like the ones worth fifteen quid. You have to examine them, get a jeweller to tell them apart, so what good is that? Ultimately, diamond is merely imitation quartz.

'I'm not the briny pickle, Liliane,' Semtex responds. 'If you want to get your brine-gauge out, Bax was the shiny briny pickle. Bax had some kid's appendix hanging from his ear and all Bax said was, "Isn't it time for lunch?"'

I wish Semtex wouldn't continue with this. Something ghastly happens in my guts when I hear the word Baghdad, and I feel faint. It would be embarrassing to faint if you've just been categorised as a shiny briny pickle, but I can always claim malaria. That's the good thing about having had malaria or being shot, you can always collapse or get legless and say it's malaria or 'I've never been the same since I was shot.'

It's odd that Semtex is quite so cavalier about it. Or maybe not. I had my back to the blast. He actually saw the blast and the crowd ripped apart. It was almost the only time I remember him without a camera. Like most pros he was glued to it, and most of the time in Baghdad he had it rolling, but there comes that moment when you want a break. To have one drink without the fucking camera. That bomb must have been the most pictorial monument he'd ever witness, probably the image of his life. It was as close as you could get to something like that and shuffle away. And he had his hands in his pockets. The Allower has a wicked sense of humour, and a way of reminding you who's boss.

'Isn't it time for everyone to do their jobs?' I love playing that card.

The heat and the intervention from Semtex are wearing Liliane down. It's generally unheard of for a cameraman to be heard, unless it's a question of light. If you're a top French intello who speaks three languages and reads three dead ones (because Pa sorted the top school in Paris), earning beaucoup money at a top Parisian university for doing nothing more than going 'bof' sporadically, you don't take kindly to someone who not only admits to leaving school at fifteen, but prefaces most of his comments with that info, particularly when that individual dresses like a vagrant.

Semtex is wearing a new T-shirt, to be fair, with the Ugaritic cuneiform inscription 'to Ba'al' on it, which he assures me is a fairly obscure cuneiform that Liliane either understands or is not going to ask about. The cuneiform looks sharp. However, I'm sure Semtex has had the same pair of orange combat trousers for the last fifteen years (for undercover or hush-hush work he has black jeans).

My wife for one is just beside herself, furious in the way some are about famine or torture in strange countries, furious at the mere *concept* of someone wearing the same item of clothing for decades. 'He wore the same trousers when he came to supper ten years ago.' Ellen might forget my birthday, but she'll remember that.

Like most autodidacts, Semtex is irritating because, like most autodidacts he knows very little; but Semtex has discovered the most valuable aspect of knowledge of whatever sort is that you can use it to annoy. Get the irking going.

Liliane has twigged that Semtex's comments are infuriation-sprays, so she starts, with added brio, her piece to camera again. I make hand gestures to encourage her hand gestures. Meanwhile, Zyklon Annie is back at the hotel, enjoying the air conditioning and the bar. All in all, I prefer her to be there, but it is galling how unequal the labour market is.

I struggle to not get angry about Liliane and Annie and the heat. Anger rarely does you any good. Occasionally, screaming, especially if the screamed-at are smaller than you (and they

133

mostly are, as my wife would say), can get results. But otherwise anger is the adversary. I think of Bongo Herman and his struggle with Bongo Les and stay cool. You never get it your way; it's not that there is always a fly in your ointment, you have to hope there's some ointment on your fly.

'Jerusalem is a city sacred to three major world religions,' continues Liliane.

'Four, at least,' I correct. 'Rastafarianism?' I know Bongo Herman would want me to speak up.

If you're a sophisticated woman of the world you're meant to have a sense of humour, so Liliane pretends to have one. 'I don't know why Islam is considered different to Judaism; it's just warmed-up Jewishness. All these Semites pretending they're different.'

She won't say that in her piece to camera, since she doesn't want to be stabbed by a failed waiter from a couscous restaurant in Lille. However, she doesn't know that the camera is still running so we can always slip that reflection out for the whole world to enjoy. She starts again.

'Five,' says Semtex.

'What?'

'Five religions. The Canaanites. The Canaanites, who founded Jerusalem, before it was stolen by the Israelites, named it after Shalem, the god of the evening star. *Jeru*-Shalem. Any religion that practises human sacrifice is major in my book. They built this city on barbecued kids.'

'Jerusalem is one of the oldest cities in the world.' Liliane is now ploughing on whatever the casualties.

'I left school at fifteen. I can tell you over there,' Semtex points northwards, 'are much older cities: Damascus, Byblos.'

'They all have visions of how the world would end.' Liliane is sprinting.

'No, they didn't,' interrupts Semtex. 'Armageddon, Ragnarök, they're not the end, they're just the end of a chapter. Armageddon is not really Armageddon, just the end of our waiting-room. While Ragnarök is a messy transition to the same thing after a lot of blood and howling, but they get very depressed up north.'

'Why don't you present this? You squeeze me, squeeze me like a lemon,' snorts Liliane.

She storms off, although storming off doesn't work well in hot conditions and when you have to walk uphill in high heels. She realises quickly that she should have stormed off downhill, although that's away from our hotel, but you can't let a good storm down.

'No one wants a real end. An end end,' Semtex remarks as he pulls focus on the disappearing Liliane.

'The scientists do,' I offer. 'They have energy death. Everything ends not even with a whimper, but silence because we're all too tired.'

'No wonder they don't have any mates.'

Should I soothe the sweating Liliane as she fights to look as if she isn't suffering from the slope? No. We've already had three reasonable pieces to camera today, and that's above the two-a-day, hour's-work average for Liliane.

The French don't have any work ethic. If it weren't for the hordes of tourists going there to buy wine and cheese and visit the topless beaches, they'd be bankrupt. And that Paris, for some reason, is considered romantic by Americans. Although while I've waited ages for some sour Algerian to serve me a stale pizza, I've never found Paris romantic.

The camera is still rolling. Semtex is working on his 'When Lilianes go Wild' tape. Our best tantrum to date was after bribing the check-in to give Liliane a maid's room, unmade.

She levitated – *levitated* – with rage. We have it for posterity. Next best was when we got her arrested as a working girl operating in our hotel in Berlin. That backfired because it took us a day of lobbying to get her out of the police station.

'There's no ha-ha like the old ha-ha,' Semtex observes. It's true, running jokes can run a long time.

I hand Semtex the money. I hate losing a bet to him, I was sure Liliane would go for one of her other catchphrases. She had been squeezed like a lemon only the other day.

All over the world, in memory of Liliane, you get crews putting on cod French accents and stretching the words 'You squeeze me like a lem–on. You squeeze and you squeeze and you squeeeze.' Or, 'I am shatt-airred like glaass.' Or the crowning, 'Zis is slavery, no less.' I might have felt sympathy for Liliane but as I'm in charge of the budget I know what she's getting paid.

'How do you know that stuff?' I ask.

'I read it in the guidebook. This morning.'

'Let's get the cutaways. Why Ba'al?'

'He was the original Prince of Darkness.,' says Semtex 'It's my tribute to you. They'd burn kids to Ba'al. He was a franchise. You bought the Ba'al name and added any extras you wanted. When the Carthaginians were losing their war with the Greeks they burned more of their kids alive because they thought they were losing the war because they weren't burning enough kids.'

'If you're not burning enough kids, you're not burning enough kids.'

I don't know why the Carthaginians are judged harshly for child sacrifice. If you've ever been desperate, you'll feel for them. You have to do something. Something is nearly always better than nothing. I wish Semtex wasn't such a good cameraman, but his instinct, his lens, is always spot on. Once you've had the best, it's hard to deal with the rest.

I hate history. I was there when it started. Herodotus. A series about his book, the one that started history.

It was my first job in the Vizz. The job Herbie got me as an assistant cameraman, after I met him on a train when I was on my way to basic training in the army.

Being an assistant cameraman seemed like heaven at first. It was like being *paid* to go on holiday, in the sunshine in Greece. And working in the Vizz, a glam job. Everyone I knew saved up all year and paid to do that. And all I had to do was carry the tripod, mark things up and try to have as many pleasure events as possible. I've never had any regrets about ditching the army (I couldn't even get the boot polishing right), although my Uncle Joe was always sad about it.

Of course, by day four I was getting bored with the standing around and the glamour of the Vizz was patchy. Particularly at Thermopylae, where the 300 Spartans made their nutcase stand against the million-strong Persian army.

Maybe the most celebrated battle of all time, one that has inspired illiterate teens all over the world to sport Spartan slogans on their clothes, and ironically a battle that was lost. You're meant to win. Consider all the successful generals who must be popping with rage at the Spartans, who got stomped like ants, but who are revered, bigged up as a model. They lost, they were wiped out, chopped up like parsley, barely a squeak under the Persian footwear. Anybody can get killed. I wish I could get as much celebrity for losing. I do it big.

It was Liliane's first job as a presenter, too. Which dinner party got her that gig? Because you only ever get a job by meeting someone on a train or laughing at a dinner party. Has anyone in the whole of world history actually got a job by being qualified and applying for it? Liliane was young and, like any eighteen-year-old, I had a vague hope of sex. Liliane, of course, had no interest whatsoever in the gangly assistant cameraman, which is why I make her walk up and down stairs in Jerusalem knowing full well I'm not going to use the footage. She did it four times yesterday before she stormed off.

Thermopylae is pretty much a motorway now. My lasting memories are of breathing in lead, sweating and getting food poisoning at the one café there. But Liliane's monologue stuck with me. She went on about the 300 Muscle Marys and their preening before the battle. It's one of those recurring themes. What you don't hear about is the non-300. It wasn't just the Spartans. There were others.

I phoned Herbie from the shoot to thank him again for getting me the job. One of my uncle's lessons was: thank people. I've thanked people for a long time. I reckon I've only got one result from thanking people in thirty years. But maybe that's all you can expect from any gambling system, that once in thirty years it pays off.

'The Thespians,' Herbie had said. 'Ask about the Thespians.'

The Thespians. They died unapplauded, at the back. Their PR was lame. They weren't buff and ripped, they didn't have a big rep, they didn't get slammed on the Athenian stage. The Athenians made their name by stealing ideas (and anything else not nailed down – the greatest civilisations are the greatest thieves), the Spartans by spending all their time in the gym. That's when I started to worry there is no justice. It's not what you do that matters, it's the verdict.

m.

The whole Apocalypse project is like a magnificent cathedral built out of various granite grudges and hardwood hatreds. I don't think Johxn is capable of understanding the perfection of what he's put into action.

No one would want to work with Zyklon Annie in the first place. No one. As executive producer all she's going to achieve is to incite even more fury by doing nothing and getting in the way at the same time. Not to mention, outside of British politics she knows nothing and has only left the country twice before.

Then Jack the List is meant to be the producer. He would be on a sunlounger by the pool here in Jerusalem doing nothing, but he had a better sunlounger offer on an oligarch's yacht, plus extra truffles and vintage champagne. However, I know he'll be turning up in the editing suite at some point to disimprove the quality of my life.

I have mixed feelings about his absence. On the one hand, if I had to spend a lot of face-time with him, I'd probably assault him; on the other hand, I'm doing his job for him. Indeed, I'm doing everyone's job for them, but getting peanuts, an amount of peanuts so insultingly small that only a completely desperate man would consider accepting them.

I could do this whole series on my own for the same peanuts, and less debate, so why bother with two more mouths? Johxn doesn't do favours, so why he's giving Annie and Jack a freebie isn't clear. Diversity points could explain Jack getting the gig. He's bi and because one of his grandmothers was Roma, he likes to throw 'gadjo' into conversation and pretend he's especially pally with the horses when he goes to the races.

I know Liliane didn't want to work with me again, but she made the mistake of saying so to Johxn. Johxn told me, with beaming delight: 'She thinks you're a talentless prick, Bax.'

I doubt those were the exact words Liliane used, but they doubtless covered the sentiment and it gave Johxn the chance to call me a talentless prick to my face. Although Johxn, for strange Johxn reasons, venerates Liliane, he's not passing up an opportunity for causing anguish.

Here's the hilarity. It could all work out. Jack could remain yachtbound. Zyklon Annie could exfoliate in the spa, score some expensive toiletries on expenses, make one or two comments for the sake of form, and you know what? Often it's useful to have someone else's tuppence. We all have our blind spots.

Liliane could have something to say that hasn't been said several times by other bof-merchants. Semtex could spend his time producing remarkable images instead of chasing fist-fights. It could all work out fine. The lamb and the lion could team up and open a successful nightclub for unicorns. We could all get served. We could all have our moment, but no.

Annie will be exasperating during editing too, but that doesn't matter so much. The trick is to get your blocks. The juicy chunks. The bits that stick. The confessions. The one-liners. Because you're never in doubt about which are the good bits when you review your footage. It's just the ordering that causes the arguments.

With a feature the advice is if you have a turkey, put the good bits at the end, so that the audience will leave with the good bits in mind, perhaps eclipsing the hour of dross they sat through. Docs are a bit different: you generally haven't got an audience trapped in a cinema, having paid their money hoping they're getting something good.

You have to flash your tits at the top. You have the secret footage of the mass grave or nuclear facility, or your inter-viewee fessing up to some abomination. I can tell in the first minute whether a doc is worth watching because if someone has something, anything, they'll flash it up top, they'll wave their strongest card first – please, please keep watching.

With the blocks it doesn't matter whether you have Frashokereti, Dabiq, Ragnarök, Armageddon in your rough cut, because Annie is going to say no, it should be Armageddon, Ragnarök, Dabiq, Frashokereti. But that doesn't matter because Johxn will turn up to say Dabiq, Ragnarök, Frashokereti, Armageddon, and even that doesn't matter because on the next viewing he will probably go back to your original cut, because that's the best one. You should never get upset by what people say. Until the final cut, until you go to transmission, it don't matter.

It's interesting how all these apocalypses happen round the corner. The final showdown will always be local. There isn't a Semitic religion that suggests the final battle should be in Antarctica or Montevideo, for instance.

♏

Back in the hotel bar I find Zyklon Annie chatting with some young guy she's probably luring to London for an interview, to rip him to shreds and relish his tears.

But we are all part of Johxn's bespoke masterplan to tailor a mini-hell for everyone. I may hate working with Annie, but I have some consolation in that she loathes working with me, as it's apparent to her I can see through her, and what I see I don't rate. That is apart from her achievements as a twisted sadist.

There always comes that point in a shoot, usually at the end, when everyone drops the courtesy, reaches for the blade, and says exactly what they think. But sometimes it comes earlier.

'How was Liliane?' Annie enquires.

'Not so good, you know, women's stuff,' I say. You might as well go nuclear first. Not that Annie would be any less prickly if I said good evening.

'I'm not sure you're cut out to be a producer, Baxter. You don't have ... the people skills. You're not quite ...' She grimaces because she's on the long, hard road to precision, no matter what the cost in the all-important battle for purity. 'You're ... you're suitable for ... fieldwork ... of a certain level. Basic fieldwork.'

She grimaces again as if pained now by having to tell a harsh truth. 'But when it comes to people ... Perhaps you should watch ... more television. Do you watch anything apart from your own programmes?'

Wow, she's good. I realised a long time ago that we're not here to enjoy ourselves. That doesn't mean you have to eat shit all day, every day, but you do have to eat shit most days. I get annoyed with those who are convinced they're being picked on because they are black or gay or trans or come from some strange village or speak with a northern, southern, western, eastern accent, and are missing the big picture: that most of the time we're all munching shit.

I thought about having a fancy calendar printed with pictures of coprophagous creatures, like the animals I'd reffed in my natural history quiz: the gorillas, the rabbits, the giant pandas, the hippos and obviously the dung-beetles (who, in the Allower's sublime sense of humour, are guided in their dung collection by the stars) and us, *Homo* so-called *sapiens*.

That way I could humorously distribute my philosophy as a gift, but then I decided that it was a waste of money and who cares what I think? I m not sure why people want to get others to listen to them; to be view-pushers, opinion-leggers;

like drugs, unleashing your tuppence generally changes nothing. I agree with your critique of the back four in Saturday's match. Or I disagree. And?

Annie likes to pause as if she's curating words, but she has carefully prepared them earlier. Not everyone refers to her as Zyklon Annie, of course; she's also know as the Bag Lady, because of her lack of style and the plastic bags she carries around, stuffed with documents.

She fiddles with some papers in her lap. This is another part of her shtick. Reports, magazines, white papers are always at hand, which she consults and shuffles and piles up but rarely reads, like those people who wear non-prescription glasses because they think it makes them look more intelligent. I don't know why she's doing this; she must know that I know her routine. This pantomime is fine for recent graduates of We-Actually-Read-A-Whole-Book-From-Cover-To-Cover-Phew! University, but it won't get traction on old Bax.

'It's a pity you don't have the finesse . . . or you don't yet have the finesse of someone like . . . Herbie. I was just thinking of Herbie, someone just blogged about him. It's a pity you let him down so badly.'

She's cutlassed up, swinging straight for my jugular in the middle of the shoot, in a bar in Jerusalem. I suppose she thinks it's an entire Pearl Harbor, coming in low while I'm pressing my trousers. Classic terrorism. You let off one bomb, and then as the survivors are pulling themselves together you let off another.

I knew what was coming. I'd made the decision early on simply to ignore anything Annie said, whether I was accused of child murder or inventing slavery, but she's definitely been brooding on this. These are lovingly marinated provocations, and I sense bubbling in my head. This woman who has never removed a lens cap, who couldn't switch on a camera, this woman who couldn't produce a jet of piss into a bucket, a woman whose people skills are limited to driving others to despair, is telling me I should watch some television and that I let down Herbie . . .

I'm lucky I have a Glenfiddich on the rocks, so I can take a long sip. One of the tricks I learned from Herbie is that you let attackers in, you open the door as they take off for their flying kick. Use their momentum against them. Thank them. And when they're confused, when their backs are turned, fuck them up.

'Yes, it's true, I could have done more for him.' Because it is true. On the other hand, there were plenty of others who could have done even more for him, and didn't. The ex-wife. His brother. Johxn, Jack the List and the others, the many others, he advised, trained up, who now have comfy perches in the Vizz. Who are hi-viz in the Vizz.

'You didn't get him any work, did you, Annie?'

Like a briny politician, she acts as if the question never happened.

'It was suicide, wasn't it?' she asks.

'No.' Because it wasn't. Rather a broken heart. Surely talking about dead people so much in our business isn't a good sign? I have another elongated sip.

She cranes her neck. 'Is your chair wobbling?'

'No, Annie, it isn't. Is your eyesight okay?'

I get up. She lets me take a step or two.

'Baxter, I almost forgot . . .'

She hasn't forgotten anything. This is totally total war.

'You've heard that Gavin Herron died?'

No, I hadn't heard. Annie explains that he died from leukaemia, penniless, alone in some hospice run for distressed former television execs (who the fuck would stump up money for that?), although why he was considered an exec is beyond me, since he was possibly even more useless than Johxn.

'He left instructions that there should be no funeral service,' continues Annie. He wasn't entirely stupid, The Heron, he knew no one would bother turning up. That's the consequence of being a small provincial shit, no one cares.

If you're a big fat bastard, you have a gravity. Applause. An uncanny attraction. Always be big. Always go over budget. If Johxn were to go under a bus, they'd be a huge turnout at his funeral, if nothing else so the attendees could laugh it up, or maybe take a sneaky leak on his grave afterwards. Put my name down for that.

'He was a friend of yours, wasn't he?' Ah, Annie wanted the delight of dishing out bitter news. But sloppy research. He wasn't my friend, far from it.

'No.' Annie can tell I'm not lying.

Having endured the barrage, I feel some me-time is in order. So I rush towards my room before Semtex can drag me into some fiasco, but as I approach the lift, I cross Liliane drinking with a German in an alcove bar, I recognise him as the Big Boss of one their channels. Am I going to have to bomp a weighty German before I can get to my room? Your life entails you chatting to an astounding number of arseholes, but I don't see that I should willingly add to that total.

'The eons pick their partners,' Liliane says. What? Quoting profundity-peddlers, or transcendence-touts, especially unfamous ones, is a vice of Liliane's. Don't go too obscure, however, or your dinner-party guests won't get the reference and you can't establish how good the school you went to was.

Then, of course, there are those like me who don't get the ref, and who couldn't care less about some obscurists who croaked not as noticed as they wanted to be, because their phrases didn't catch on 200 or whatever years ago. View-pushers whose views weren't pushed that far. Or did Liliane say 'ions'? I'm so tired. The trouble with living in the dank cave that is London is you get malleted when you reach a sunny clime. A few hours in the sun and I'm done. And quantum physics is the new mysticism for anyone who's got tired of Atlantis.

'The clypeus is black,' I respond. It's important to have some stock phrases that you can draw on when you're too tired or frightened to think. When you're caught doing something you shouldn't be doing in a strange foreign country, for instance.

I learned that after a Shia gunman at a roadblock in Basra had gone mental on me as I tried to parley, screaming and waving his gun. I just stood there with our useless fixer while the rest of the crew sat in the car. For ten minutes. From their perspective in the car it looked as if I was staring him down. 'That was definitely impressive,' Semtex said afterwards. But I hadn't been impressive. I froze. I didn't know what to say or do but after a while the gunman ran out of abuse and let us go because he wanted supper.

Of course, generally, if you're really doing something you shouldn't be in a military installation or president's swimming pool in a strange foreign country, you're 100 per cent fucked, but there is the paramount rule of acting pleased when you're discovered, because you wanted to talk to precisely these thugs with the spotlights and the guns. You should look as if you were looking for the ones who were looking for you.

That's why it's important to have some phrase ready when the guns are pointed at you because you might find it hard to compose under those circumstances. Unless you have some convincing cover story better than, 'I heard a small child calling for help and a camera, so I climbed the twelve-foot wall and brought one.' A simple sentence can be very effective, such as 'My garden is full of daffodils.'

If you repeat your line with confidence and a little chuckle, several times, it could defuse the more minor debacles. The problem with English, though, is that lots of non-Anglos speak some and some speak it well enough to know that you're talking gibberish and they might get angry.

The merit of a sentence like 'the clypeus is black' over a sentence like 'my garden is full of daffodils' is that it *sounds* simple. And anyone who has basic English will understand 'is black', so it sounds as if you're cooperating, you're bending over backwards to explain why it is you cut through the razor wire in the middle of the night, but who knows what a clypeus is? In my experience security heavies have no schooling in insect anatomy.

I smile and press the up button on the lift.

'What exactly is an eon, Bax?' Liliane asks.

'No idea.'

'But you are a native speaker. You should know. I'd like to improve my English. I'm asking for your help.'

'Too late for that, Liliane.' Presumably because I'm trying to get away, she introduces me to the Big Boss. Of course, you're assuming I should be boozing it up with Baron von Freeloader, but no, it's precisely the opposite tactic. Going right past him because I'm so wedded to my art, so strapped to my vision that I don't even notice that a moneybags German gagging to spend is right here in front of me.

The Germans have money to invest, and they adore co-producing because, seventy years after gassing millions and wrecking Europe, they want to be liked and come on holiday with you. There's nothing more effective than ignoring people, as long as you can be certain they notice you're ignoring them.

I have one foot in the lift when he says: 'Ah yes, you made the man with the spoon programme. It was wonderful.'

I like to see myself as in control, but this is too much. Someone who has seen one of my docs, someone important, not obviously mentally ill, someone who likes it, someone who has nothing to gain by telling me so is telling me it was wonderful.

So here it is, the moment I've been waiting for all my life: the life-changing moment. Sweaty, tired, in the lobby of a not-very-expensive hotel in Jerusalem, it's all going to turn around. Baron von Freeloader is going to shower me with money and everything will be pure super-paradise, having finally made contact with me in the lobby of a not-as-expensive-as-I-would-like hotel in Jerusalem.

Lee was the guy with the spoon. He liked to stick a spoon into his ear. He did it all the time, to the exclusion of all the other activities you'd associate with being human. 'It's just better than life,' he'd say. It was hard to argue with that.

A vicious itch in his right ear one day had made him reach for a teaspoon, to use its handle to police it. But as he pulled down and pressed the handle against his meatus he felt more than relief, he felt bliss, non-stop. He limited himself to a few hours spoon time a day, in the evening, after work, but gradually he sat all day with the spoon lodged in his ear, not going out, not working, not bothering with friends, not doing anything really. Lee rated the pleasure as less intense than climax, but more satisfying, and it was constant as long as he had the spoon in place.

'Folk feel sorry for me, but they shouldn't. No one's had it as good as me. If they only knew,' he said.

The medical fraternity debated whether this was some neurological curiosity, a strange mis-wiring, self-hypnosis or raw nuttiness. Yes, Lee was from Yorkshire. Ten years after I made the doc I was passing through Ilkley, and knocked on his door, and I did have to knock because the bell wasn't working, and he was still there, with the spoon, and as we talked it was clear that was that. It's so easy to fall off. The spoon just wiped out the need for anything else. And after all, most of our endeavours are about catching some happiness or manoeuvring into a position where we can catch some happiness by getting money or esteem, so if you can have it all in one cheap sitting, why not?

This ambush praise has me almost in tears and my voice crumbles slightly as I say, 'Thank you.' The Baron von Freeloader is my new best friend.

'You are probably my favourite documentary maker,' the Baron adds. This is probably the high-point of my life. When I least expected it, in the lobby of only a three-star hotel. All the decades of hard work, the ruined weekends, the skipped holidays, the lack of expensive restaurants, now seem worthwhile. My eyes are watering, but not, I hope, enough to be noticed.

'Well,' the Baron continues, 'you and good old Jack the List are my favourites. I adore the way it looks as if he's simply making moronic tributes to the super-rich. He is so subversive.' He laughs to show we're all first-name mates in the club of great talent. Tax. I can't say I'm surprised any more. You can't have praise like that without tax. Supertax to the point where, as far as I'm concerned, the praise is almost gone.

'Bax is a gonfalonier of revisionism,' says Liliane. I can't be bothered to track this down later, so I ask: 'What's a gonfalonier?'

149

'Get a dictionary, Bax.'

'Ach, yes,' says the Baron, 'I heard some rumours you were working on some great opus, some historical piece in France.'

'I was.'

'When can we get to see it?'

'You might have a long wait. We had a bad fire. All the material was lost.'

'An inferno,' says Liliane.

'I'm sorry. You were well insured?' the Baron commiserates.

'I was well insured.'

I want to change the subject. Behind him, on a television screen, Barcelona are playing Real Madrid. Barcelona have just gone a goal up. I decide to do my thing.

'Real will win two–one,' I say.

'It was a pleasure, Baxter. An honour. I wish I could stay, but I have to leave for the airport,' the Baron says, actually getting up and walking off. So much for the bonding. I don't have a card to give him. You'd think if you met one of your favourite doc makers and you were a money-burdened commissioner of documentaries you'd want to propose some deal or suggest staying in touch, but no, it doesn't work like that. The Allower doesn't allow that.

♏

Back in my room, I take it all in. Have I just witnessed the rarest of things, revenge? The much-talked-about thing? Revenge that has powered as many fantasies as any stretch of flesh, the desire that has powered more drama since its invention in Athens on 13 March 666 BC?

Gavin Herron dead. The Heron had messed me around royally. Based up in Leeds, he kept on inviting me for

150

meetings at nine in the morning, so I'd have to start driving at five to get there. Did I want to go? Of course not, but when someone who can pull the trigger calls you, you jump.

He cost me a small fortune in travel and time, making me come up with treatments for docs, with no result. I should have stopped, but it's like waiting for the bus, once you've waited fifteen minutes, you figure there's no point in walking. The bus will have to come soon. So you're still there an hour later, when you wouldn't have been if someone had told you there won't be a bus for an hour and a quarter. I even made one doc myself and sent it to him. This was a man who was *paid* to watch docs, that was his job; he had the half-hour doc for six months and he never looked at a minute of it.

The Heron had left his safe, if provincial, perch and gone freelance and gone caput. He hadn't been fifty. Dying alone, that's grim. I check the trades and read that he wanted to be remembered as having 'done his best'. Maybe he had, considering he was a talentless, feckless clodhopper. I wish I could sit back, have a drink and really enjoy this, but I can't.

I certainly wanted him humiliated, out-of-pocket, broken and suffering. But let the punishment cohabit with the crime. I can't feel sorry for him, my damage was too great, but I didn't want him bumped off. Maybe not an eye for an eye, but let's say an eye and a front tooth for my eye, a bit of interest for my trouble. A poorly paid part-time job lecturing at We-Read-A-Whole-Book-Once-From-Cover-to-Cover-Phew! University, not complete annihilation. It's disappointing I can't really savour this. Why this need for justice? Where does it come from? Another one gone, and we are still too many.

I book a 4 a.m. alarm call for Annie and Liliane, and disconnect my phone to avoid reprisal. In any case, they have the wrong room number for me and I've checked in to the hotel under a misspelt name. These pranks are childish, but you have to take what you can get.

I'm on the second floor. I never like to be any higher in a hotel, because on the second floor you're going to survive if you have to go out the window. You might break a bone or two depending on how the architects envisaged the concept of floor, but you'll survive. I check the fire-escape plan because I can imagine Zyklon Annie setting off the fire alarm to wake me up along with everyone else, or, indeed, starting a fire.

I did actually catch her outside the back of Johxn's offices with a box of matches once, doing what can only be described as trying to burn down the building. 'What are you doing?' I asked. 'Just curious,' she replied, gathering up the used matches. I would have cheerfully grassed her up, but I rather approved of the project and wished her the best of luck. Working in the Vizz does terrible things to you.

♏

The next morning someone from the Jerusalem Film Thing turns up to chat to us about our shoot, to ask friendly questions about us and to discuss tripods. He's not from the Film Thing, of course. Correction: he is on paper, but he's some spook investigating whether we're a dangerous conspiracy. We probably are, but not in a way to concern him. Intelligence people are all the same, I can spot them a mile off.

I almost got a job with MI6. I was doing the daughter of one of the bosses. Here's a tip: if someone never talks about their work ever, not one word about how small their office is, how long the commute is, some gripe about their boss, they're either spooky or an accountant. One afternoon, he looked at me and said. 'You wouldn't be interested in a job, would you?' I said yes. That was the last I heard about it. Maybe I failed some background check as I wasn't into flagellation, or it could be because I tried it on with his other daughter. Youth.

I almost got a job with the CIA. Or I think it was the CIA. I met an old American pilot on a train, who was shot down in the Pacific during the Second World War, then flew U2s when they didn't exist. 'I really miss it,' he said. 'If you've ever flown a U2, you'll always miss it. Always. It was better than anything else. And I do mean anything else.'

We talked about the war as I'd done a doc on Pearl Harbor. I showed him round the East End, told him about my uncle's exploits. We went drinking, he told me he did some courier work, visiting US embassies, carrying codes or encryption keys, I suppose. At the end of the evening he offered me a job. 'We're always on the lookout for talent. It's dangerous, but not that dangerous, and if it weren't dangerous it wouldn't be any fun,' he said. I said yes and I never heard anything more.

I almost got a lot of things.

♏

I go up to my room and phone the wife. I've travelled a lot over the years and I know there are couples who spend every minute of the day together because they run a company. I'd argue there's something to be said for a bit of distance every now and then. Ellen has the sort of stable job, managing a call-centre for a small insurance company, that I couldn't take. The idea of going to the same place, day after day, at the same time, doing the same thing, day after day, terrifies me. I could do that for two or three months, tops. It's the only consolation in my shambles, that this life is the only life I can lead. Vizz life.

'You annoyed me in my dream last night,' Ellen says. There is no winning. 'Luke's too busy to talk to you.'

I check the football. I see, as I foretold, Real Madrid won 2–1. It's not that I know about football. You could ask me to predict the result of two Rwandan teams I'd never heard of and I would get it right. As long as I didn't bet on it. Or get anyone else to do that on my behalf. It's not allowed. I tried hard.

The Allower has given me this one superpower, but I can only use it to impress. I did attempt to get work as a commentator, but of course those jobs go to sleb players and managers. I did get a nice Caribbean postcard from a former Head of Sports to whom I'd been sending my predictions as proof of employability, who retired very early and unexpectedly, saying he was sorry that he 'couldn't fit me in'.

I haven't checked the chatter for a long time, so I have a quick one. It amazes me how the Vizz isn't really about making films and docs, but is all about backbiting, backstabbing or backsliding into addiction with the drug du jour.

Raging Ant reports: *The Prince of Darkness seen darkening the door of Jerusalem with Fifi la Folle. Doesn't this mean that the apocalypse is nigh when the chair-crushing beast reaches the Holy City? On my allotment now, watering my tomatoes hard.*

I don't mind Raging Ant too much. If you can laugh about your insignificance, I have some respect for you. It's nice to have some attention because it's better to be vilified than ignored, but honestly, why bother? And you know the bigger the mouth . . .

I got a lot of flak from I-bought-the-Law for years. I found out it was a low-level, part-time TV critic and failed playwright Harry Grant. It was one of those things you couldn't arrange. I was going for a blood test in Harley Street, and as I gasped my way up the stairs to the fourth floor, Grant came out.

I don't believe in telepathy, but, instantly, we were both thinking the same thing.

We're on the fourth floor. Only the two of us. Alone in a huge stairwell. With a very small banister. It's a long way down, onto a very hard stone floor without so much as a carpet to break your fall. Grant is tiny, with puny arms so spaghetti-like it's surprising he can type. I, as everyone likes to point out, am quite large. There was nothing to stop me heaving Grant over the banister on a non-stop journey to the ground floor. The best outcome Grant could expect would be to be crippled.

I could have made a remark like, 'It's a long way down, isn't it?' or, 'Can you fly?' But there was no need. The situation was so clear. That was what was so beautiful. And what was particularly funny was that, apart from my docs being shit, the bulk of his posts were about what a violent, extraordinary bastard I was, and he had accused me of beating up two waiters in a restaurant I'd never been to. If you accuse someone of being an extraordinarily violent bastard, you can't really complain if they treat you to some of that.

The look on his face was enough. If you bow down before me, that's enough. I let him stew for a few moments, then I walked in to collect my results. He never mentioned me again.

♏

Prince of Darkness? I got that nickname long ago. I was working for Fouad, who got a lot of work on the ethnic ticket, this despite coming from a family in Pakistan so rich that he couldn't tell you to the nearest dozen the number of servants they had. It makes me angry when Pakistan is portrayed as a poor country. It isn't, it's a rich country with the money in the hands of a few particularly greedy smuggees.

Fouad had got into a deal with Zyklon Annie and they had a bust-up over the budget, who got to walk away with the tasty bits. Fouad would have been quite capable of eliminating Annie, if there had been a button you could push to plunge her into a shark tank. He'd have been pounding that button all day, but his shortcoming in the Vizz was that he couldn't do hand-to-hand face-to-face. He couldn't maintain his hardness in the room with Annie.

I'm not sure why he picked me. Probably because I was in the room when he'd just slammed down the phone. He told me he needed me to go and see Zyklon Annie and make her change her mind.

'What do I say?'

'I don't know. You're the shit-hot talent. Make her see reason. And don't come back otherwise.' It was odd, because I was the junior in the office, and Annie was probably then at the height of her influence, but maybe that was why I was chosen. Expendable. Zyklon-fodder. Or maybe he had some crazy notion that as I was young and fit I could operate some groinal magic on the Bag Lady.

I hadn't been in the Vizz long by that point, but I knew that Annie was as notorious for her stubborness as her unpleasantness. Now older and dirtier, I might have come up with some angle to get leverage, but then I simply felt defeated.

There was an Italian restaurant around the corner in Charlotte Street that did a superb lasagne. Lasagne is like poetry, something that is often abused and something that everyone thinks they can do. It's often done on the cheap with a tomato puree that has lost the will to live, but in defiance of blandness and spitting on monetary gain, this place did a better-than–your-mother's lasagne for small change.

I ate with relish as I wondered whether the French Foreign Legion still recruited. I decided that rather than wasting my time being savaged by Zyklon Annie, I'd just go back to the office, collect my contacts book and seek my fortune elsewhere.

It's that important lesson: when you give up, you succeed; but you have to be sincere about giving up, you can't be faking.

I walked up the stairs to the office to see Fouad beaming. 'Congratulations, Bax,' he said. While I had been meandering back from my lasagne, Zyklon Annie had phoned up to make peace. I have no idea what made her soften up, but it wouldn't have been anything less than something very much to her advantage. But it was assumed my absence had worked this miracle.

A week on, Fouad caught me alone in the edit suite. 'Ella, Ella has to go,' he said. Ella was a producer on a big Civil War series that Fouad was executiving. She was, by common consent, utterly useless, but she wasn't alone in that regard in the Vizz, so I didn't see why Fouad was that bothered.

'She's draining the budget, Bax, you have to get rid of her.'

I was still little more respected than the cleaner, so again this request seemed odd.

'How?' I was willing, given instruction, to do anything pretty much. Youth.

'I don't know. Use your fucking imagination. And no come-back to me.'

'But how?'

'If you want your contract renewed, you'll find a way. I don't care what you do. I really don't care, but sort it. We only care about results here.'

By this point I wasn't sure I did want my contract renewed. Fouad and I had been up to the Edinburgh Television Festival and I had watched him eat a lobster, which had given me such an insight into his soul that I never really wanted to be in the same building as him again. I was young, I was optimistic, I was sure I'd find something else. Herbie would help me.

And what could I do to get rid of Ella? How do you persuade someone to resign from a plum job, on a big series, which even if it were shit (which it was), was so big it would get noticed? Talk her into forsaking all worldly pursuits and volunteer in a leper colony? Plant drugs on her? Pretend to offer her a better job in Hollywood? Get a billionaire to elope with her? Infect her with some rare, but seriously debilitating virus?

No, I wasn't doing it. Was it because I came from South London that Hampsteaders thought they could get me to shovel their shit? I got more and more angry and wanted to tell Fouad to get stuffed, but he had left.

I went home and smoked some major dope to an unjustly underrated album by Burning Spear and pondered the legs of my date that Saturday, an incredibly tall publicist who had shown such wild enthusiasm to my invitation to see an avant-garde theatre troupe that I was sure I would be putting undue stress on her bed that night. Youth.

I didn't realise that publicists will react with enthusiasm to any suggestion, because that's what they do. I never went out with another publicist or saw an avant-garde theatre troupe again.

Days later, I remembered I had left some magazines in Fouad's office, so I went back in. I had been hoping to avoid Fouad, so inevitably he was right there. Fouad gave me the strangest look I've ever seen, as if I'd just risen from the dead with tentacles coming out of my neck. It was 80 per cent bug-eyed fear, 15 per cent admiration and 5 per cent avarice.

He wobbled out of the room without a word. But cawing slightly. His secretary handed me an envelope that had a six-month contract and a huge salary hike. I didn't get it. It was a few days before someone mentioned to me that Ella had been found dead in her home, in, as the tabloids put it, questionable circumstances.

Fouad got me a new job at another company a few weeks later. 'I put in a good word for you, it's a fantastic opportunity. I hate to lose you, but it would be wrong to hold you back,' he said.

It was even better paid. It was probably the best gig I ever had, working on a show about strippers and their incisive views on globalisation, international politics and currency rates; it was a new, short-lived attempt to make current affairs 'accessible and relevant'. My favourite item was one large-breasted stripper ripping apart a tiny schoolgirl uniform, telling the Arabs they needed more porn and that would bring peace to the Middle East. She was right.

My new boss was very happy with my work. 'I almost didn't take you on; when a shit like Fouad gives you a recommendation, he's pulling a fast one. He finally admitted he was scared of you, that you were the Prince of Darkness, he babbled on and on. I thought that was funny, but still wasn't going to take you on. When he offered to pay your salary I said yes.'

I never talked with Fouad again, which was fine. I spotted him across rooms once or twice, but he always scuttled off. He now runs a bed and breakfast in the Orkneys, and is often profiled in the papers on the 'getting away from the rat race' theme, an often-used tactic by the formerly important to cover up that they're dead in a ditch. It's like those runners in the park who do a lot of stretching exercises, who act serious, but are only disguising their lack of puff. You're out, you're out, and you're never getting back in again. You're not green, you're not developing your spirituality, or eco-anything. Dead in an undistinguished ditch.

♏

When I was working on my natural history quiz, I came across the bird dung crab spider. First of all, as a spider, it must be frustrating to be compared to something else. You're not known as the death-from-above spider or the wacky weaver or the insanely greedy spider; no, you're compared to a crab (although amusingly some crabs are compared to spiders – why is it so hard to say something about anything?). Secondly, the bird dung crab spider does look like bird droppings, and it's mostly immobile and even smells like shit. It's assumed the foul odour is to attract flies, and also to fend off predators. My argument is if you look like shit and behave like shit, it's no use telling yourself you're a spider; if you're doing such a good job of impersonating shit you might as well be shit, because to passers-by you're indistinguishable.

♏

fffFrank calls from London. I almost killed him, but fffFrank always remembers my birthday, sends a funny card and a silly present, a novelty keyring or a mug with the slogan 'fffFrank doesn't break the bank'. As opposed to those I did big favours for, gave leg-ups, who didn't notice or who forgot very quickly. Or perhaps I'm being unfair to them, perhaps they do remember and that's why they don't help me.

160

'How's Jerusalem?' he asks. He shouldn't be starting with this.

'Great. So?' I ask.

'Bax, it didn't work out.'

'What happened?' I should have known it wouldn't work with fffFrank He's not lucky. He's determined. But he's not lucky. Which matters when you're a stuntman. Which is why I nearly killed him. Or, as everyone insists, I did kill him and two other stuntman, and I would have gone to jail for twenty years, but for my lavishly bribing the chief police officer. I liked that bit. That does sound like me.

'I did everything you said.' Okay, fffFrank's in a defensive posture straight away. Great.

'I waited for him, for hours. Then when he arrived I caught him completely off guard, I levelled the gun at him, I said, "Steve says hello."' And then he punched me.'

'He what?'

'Bax, it was a girly punch. No, it wasn't a punch. Sort of a panic twitch, yeah? But I wasn't expecting that. Caught me off guard and I tripped on something in his cunting garden. He ran into the house, so all I could do was leg it.'

So my plan to carry out a mock-murder on Johxn has come to naught. I thought it was the perfect rebalancing. fffFrank dressed up ninja-style, popping out of a bush at Johxn's weekend retreat, because of course for all his barrow-boy antics, Johxn has family dosh aplenty.

fffFrank would stick the prop gun in Johxn's face and tell him, 'Steve says hello,' so he'd spend the rest of his life wondering which of the 300,000 Steves in Britain stumped up the money for a hit. I'd been really proud of that bit. I was monstrously clever there. Then the gun would jam and the shadowy assailant would disappear into the night, leaving Johxn a pile of quivering jelly.

Except that, as far as he knew, Johxn had decked an armed man; he'd taken out an assassin with a clinical jab. This from the man who'd refused to go to the centre of Liverpool in broad daylight because 'anything could happen out there'. I thought I couldn't dislike Johxn any more, but he's done it, by a sudden act of valour, he's made it harder for me to dislike him, which makes me dislike him even more.

I don't know why they talk about manipulating people. I've never seen it done, and I've been trying hard for decades. People just roll on, do whatever. I can't even get my wife to buy my favourite biscuits.

'Never mind. Thanks for that, fffFrank,' I say. Always say thank you. 'We'll talk when I get back.'

m̤

It was a docudrama about the mafia that featured a yacht being blown up. I didn't kill anyone, and it was an accident. When you work with explosives, there's a lot of protocol, a lot of paperwork. You don't just go down the shops, buy a stick of dynamite, light it and blow stuff up. There are unions and laws and livelihoods involved.

The final checks were being done by a stuntman, fffFrank. fffFrank was originally from Dhaka and was called Siddhartha. He wasn't getting the work he wanted and thought that his long, unEnglish first name was the problem. You'd imagine someone would have told him to shorten it to Sid, but he changed it to Frank.

He still didn't get much work and now reckoned it was because his name wasn't memorable enough. So he came up with the name fffFrank, something easy to say, but a name that would stick in the memory on credits, and one that

162

reflected, he believed, his extraordinary verve in skidding cars. He still didn't get much work.

I knew him through a poker circle I was introduced to by my lying, cheating Pakistani accountant in Brick Lane. I've only played poker properly once, mostly because my wife disapproved of it, and I didn't win. On the other hand, I didn't lose. But it's supposed to be gambling that ruins you, not hard work.

fffFrank was on the yacht doing the final checks. There was confusion over the protocol because the yacht blew up. As I had been promised, the explosion was spectacular. It was a pity the cameras, 20 yards away on a hillside, weren't running, because, if nothing else, as news footage of a stuntman being vaporised, it would have been great.

When you're on a big shoot, it's interesting how many people – actors, electricians, wardrobe mistresses, caterers, hangers-on – have an opinion about what should be done. No one offered me any advice now. I was the man who had vaporised a stuntman.

I was oddly calm. You know that bad things are bound to happen. You know one day you're no longer going to day. People will die. You'll die. You know one day you'll stop working. I didn't expect it to come in my mid-thirties, but there you are.

I took a boat out to the flotsam. I was double buggered. I was thinking, 'That's the budget gone.' The worst I would get would be manslaughter, a couple of years inside. I could retrain as a masseur or a signer. Some quiet job with no responsibility. I'd get to see my son from time to time.

When I saw fffFrank's head bobbing in the water, grinning, with his thumb up. I understood. It would be like my poker. I wouldn't win, but I wouldn't be allowed to lose badly either. fffFrank was temporarily deaf and had most of his clothes

163

blown off, but was completely unflustered, indeed he thought it a lark.

There were a lot of recriminations and lawyers made money, but not fffFrank. He didn't sue. 'Getting blown up, that's what I do.' He somehow saw the whole episode as a favour. He got his notch and was regularly in work. 'I owe you.'

♏

I return to the backbiting pages. How do these idiots find the time for this? I read on with the posts.

Kumquats Happen writes: *True no chair in Jerusalem is safe from the mighty rear of the great Sulky Bulky. Incredible. Word on the street that the well-hung Brazilian (and he should be) has got another beach series from French producers who really should know better. It would be nice to see justice once.*

See justice once? Like it. We'd all like that. Maybe that time with Grant was it. Maybe once is all you're allowed.

Moaning Star writes: *Prince of Darkness? Prince of Lardness more like, the man with a girth like the earth. Lock up your chairs. The Antichrist has to walk in not roll in to fulfil prophecy. The Bible's clear on that. The Antichrist he no wobble like a jelly.*

That's the trouble if you haven't killed anyone for a while. Everyone gets cheeky.

♏

We go to a Thai restaurant, although, as it's Jerusalem, there is no one Thai involved. You can't rely on any nationality any more. I had the best cassoulet I've ever eaten in Miami, the best borscht in Tangiers, and the best tiramisu in Copenhagen.

'It's interesting about Frashokereti,' says Semtex. 'They invented just about everything, didn't they? Those Zoroastrians?'

164

He's in a good mood. It's the new girlfriend. I don't think you can change anyone, but if anyone can it's a woman. Or at least restrain a little.

'And like all pioneers, they don't get the credit. But they probably stole it from someone else,' I say. 'Sticky-fingered Iranians.'

We'd had a good day. When your cameraman is impressed, you know it's impressive. Liliane has done a great piece on how Zoroastrianism came up with the idea of Good vs Evil and the Five Star Afterlife, and how they felt Frashokereti, their vision of the end of the world, would proceed, the good getting the goodies and the wicked burning up in agonising screams. We've become a slick doc-making machine. It took us a while to get into gear, but now we're humming. I allow myself an optimistic thought or two, to see what will happen.

This series could do me some major good. Zyklon Annie has returned to London because of a previous commitment to cause misery, Liliane has opted for a quiet evening in her room, and we're sitting in what looks like a good Thai restaurant. The dishes at the neighbouring tables smell great.

There is a soft 'phut' sound and my chair collapses under me. I find this annoying because I'm not bouncing up and down, and I'm not that heavy. I'm just not. As I extricate myself from the ground, our waiter comes over.

'You're paying for that chair,' he says. I can appreciate the concern for the chair, which was fancy-looking if not robust. Our waiter isn't a waiter. He's obviously someone who's been dragged into the role, maybe one of those out-of-work actors or students temping or a friend of a friend, because he doesn't understand how waitering works. Or he could be the owner. But he's not a waiter. If this were the US I could be suing for the wear to my arse.

165

I say nothing. I have no intention of paying, but I'm not walking out now as I'm very hungry and we've been waiting quite a long time. I'm making a note for the tip. Because there is nothing more important than the tip.

It's the moment of ultimate power. The moment when you can swing the sword, or raise the afflicted. The moment when you stand over the world and you have the power to right wrongs, to rule the world, if only for a moment. You alone decide how much the tip should be: 10 per cent? 15 per cent? 20 per cent? What's it going to be? Here is your chance to give someone what they deserve. To judge like someone with a long white beard. To see clearly. Were they friendly? Were they attentive? Were they too attentive? Did you have to wait for your food and if so, is it the waiter's fault? If the service was bad, if your waiter was surly and slapped down the food with a snarl, is it the waiter's fault? Is he or she being asked to do too much? Are the other waiters bunking off? Having a sickie? Has he been unpaid? Perhaps the waiter is the kindest man in the world who has been broken by an unreasonable kitchen and a loathsome boss? Are you over-rewarding or under-punishing? Have you been taken in by a smile or fooled by a frown? Do you have the hots for your server? Are you giving a big tip because you want to be hailed as a big tipper? Are you buying affection or respect?

'How come you didn't weigh in?' I ask Semtex who has been uncharacteristically quiet, studying the tablecloth and cutlery.

'Julie. She told me to calm down. Not to get conversational again.' He fiddles with his fork. There it is, the wild man of the lens gelded, the mega-nutter manacled, the overlord of over-the-top, under a thumb.

166

The waiter returns with our food. He gives me my red pork curry, and dumps a green chicken curry in front of Semtex.

'I ordered the yellow curry with tofu,' Semtex points out. He did. I remember it, and in any case, as most of the world has already been fully informed, Semtex doesn't order chicken.

'No. You. Didn't,' hisses our waiter. This is unusual. I understand that if you're a waiter you have to deal with stupid, forgetful customers. It's hard. But even if they're completely in the wrong, you're paid to pretend they're right. Take the chicken away. You can heat it up again in half an hour, and if you want, gob in the yellow curry. That's fair.

'He did order the yellow curry,' I intervene in my most let's-all-live-together-in-peace voice.

'Eat the curry!' our waiter screams. 'Eat the curry, you ignorant man.' This is beyond rudeness or a bad day at work. This is straitjacket stuff. I've never seen anything like it. It's as if we've killed some of his family. I look around to see if there's a camera. Is it a set-up? I'd suspect it was Liliane paying for a prank, but why bribe a waiter to have a wobbly if you can't be there to enjoy it?

The waiter carries on screaming at Semtex to eat the chicken. Semtex has met the Semtex of the waitering world. I recall all the waiters and hotel staff who courteously said: 'May I help you?' to Semtex and got decked for their trouble. And now this man is spluttering all over Semtex in his rage.

Semtex lowers his gaze into his lap and fiddles with his napkin.

'Please bring me the tofu, would you?' he asks.

It's an awful, awful sight to witness a once-proud psycho humbled like this. Meekly taking the abuse. It's like seeing some magnificent wild animal, a mountain lion or a golden eagle, in some grimy cage in a gloomy zoo. It's wrong.

167

I wrap my napkin around my knuckles. I get up, and the waiter goes down.

♏

When we finally get back to the hotel, the receptionist hands me a letter. A handwritten letter. I don't think I've seen one in fifteen years.

Mon Cher Baxter,

I am very sorry to do this to you.

I simply cannot abide the shallowness of this meretricious business any more. It's too much like being part of a criminal enterprise, an undignified one to boot. I'm leaving. I should have issued a firm 'non' at the beginning, but ... as you yourself know, we all make mistakes. Please don't waste your time hoping to change my mind.

This must put you in a very difficult position, but I shall make it plain to everyone involved in this project that my decision had nothing to do with you. We've come a long way together. How thin and not bad-looking you were at the beginning! You are fairly professional, by the standards of this inane trade, and you are not the biggest ignoramus lurking in its depths. Don't be down. I absolve you of all responsibility. You have done your best.

Adieu,
Liliane

I like to think I can see things coming, but this one has appeared out of nowhere. I'm fucked. Fucked[10]. It couldn't be worse, career-wise, short of death. It probably is the final nail in my coffin. First the fire, then Bangkok, then the statues, now this. After I've looked up the word 'meretricious', there's a part of me (30 per cent) that admires her for walking away. The Vizz is mostly bullshit, but as Herbie put it, 'Okay, what we do is mostly bullshit, but it's bullshit with some great pictures.' Be principled, Liliane. Be pure. But couldn't you wait another week?

I can imagine how this will reverberate. The chatter. Mass-murdering Bax amusing himself by destroying one of the leading broadcasters of our times. After beating several waiters to a pulp and spending the budget on legal fees.

Annie and Jack are out of it because they're not on site. They can heap the blame entirely on me, in a very big heap. They can defend themselves by saying if they had been there their exec voodoo would have saved the day. I know we're all going to try and charm Liliane back, but I know she won't. I've always had my doubts about jasmine tea-drinkers. We're too far in to get a replacement, but we're not close enough to the end to patch up her disappearance. It's the perfect time to leave, if you want to scupper the project. It's the end of the world for the end of the world.

I fire up my laptop. There's an e-mail from Johxn asking how work is going. Then there's another e-mail from Johxn. It's for Jack. He's done that misaddressing thing and sent it to me instead.

Jacko,
    Cant wait to see u in S Tropez, I'll be bring the clubs. Will Rons yacht be in port. Can he bring more Cristal??? I asked him but hes' v unreliable. And tite! Don't forget 2 remind him. Kraggy?

Dont worry about being away from Israil, El Immenso can handle it. He a strange man, with his obessesion with Herby, and his insistence on using Semmtek, but he can be ok for basics. Only worry is he might upset Lil, but he's so desper8, he'll be a good boy.

Don't forget re Cristal.

Laters.

Jx

It's one of those days you regret they invented writing. Will Johxn notice he's sent the e-mail to the wrong address, and if he does, will he care?

I spend fifteen minutes trying to put out the last small light in my room, so I can get some sleep. I keep flipping the dozen switches on the wall until, eventually, I hit the right combination. The Allower does like his ha-ha.

ZAK
MAY

Now I'm back in London and have unemployed time on my hands, I visit my lying, cheating Pakistani accountant, who has his office off Brick Lane. I attend with a strong foreboding that it's a waste of time. When your lying, cheating accountant just shrugs his shoulders you know you're deep in it. He shrugs his shoulders and I leave. I'm not really hungry but I pop into Zak's for a kebab.

'Haven't seen you for a long time. A long time,' says Zak. 'I thought you might be dead. I've got your doner ready for you, though, just the way you like it.'

Being recognised is a rare pleasure in London. Having lived here most of my forty-nine years, there are at most five places where I might be greeted by name, and that's not guaranteed. Indeed, to have a friendly greeting of any sort you usually need to be a good hundred miles from Charing Cross.

I first went into Zak the Snack's several years ago. I'd never met her, I'd never been into her kebab shop before. As I entered she said: 'It's the Prince of Darkness. Here's your sheesh, bruv, just the way you like it, with extra chilli.' Is Zak a culinary equivalent of a mind-reading act, or as it's the new East London is it some incredibly realistic performance-art installation where the conversations with 10,000 clients will be published in a limited-edition platinum-bound book?

I never asked her how she did it, because somehow that would spoil the fun. It's easy to conjecture. It's easy to conjecture that Lovable Pyscho or Secret Dictator (and I do know who they are) were inside and dashed out the back door seeing me walking down the street, quite rightly fearing for their features.

Does she simply have freakishly good eyesight like those flying aces and she detects me half a mile down the road? I'm sometimes tempted to say, 'I don't want the extra chilli,' or, 'No, I wanted the doner, not the shish,' but that would spoil the fun too, and I quite like getting the grub as soon as I walk in.

'I'm the Curry Mile Exile,' Zak likes to tell her customers. 'I betrayed the curries. I'm a rebel, bruv. Badmash. Not some jat. Went kebab. The turmeric turncoat. The saag subversive, that's me.'

Zak's family are in Manchester, a grand curry-house dynasty from Pakistan, who pretended to be Indian for a while, but then realised it was profitable to pretend that you had a separate identity and cooked spinach in a different way. So Zak defected from the Curry Mile in Rusholme to run a kebab shop in, well, the Curry Mile in London. I've never asked about that either.

'You love rich sauces when you're a kid, because they've got so much going on,' Zak elaborated to me. 'But as you get older the simplicity of the kebab is revealed to you. Chicken tikka masala is nothing but an illusion. A trap. A pit. It's like Bruce Lee said: the best kung fu isn't kung fu.'

I owe the kebab shop, as an institution, my life. There were long periods, in my twenties, when they kept me alive. That was youth, out on the streets in the early hours, on my way to or from some pleasure event. I could film all day and roam all night.

174

Zak's kebab shop does make a change from the Kurdish guy behind the counter telling you about the Swedish couple he bummed while he shovels the onions into your pitta. The clientele, for a start. I've seen the Astronomer Royal, two cyber supremos and a number of Sufi scholars. The shop has this unique atmosphere of prophecy, because Zak is also a thinker.

'I'm the Wilmslow widegirl, I wanted a job that's mechanical. A job that needs no thinking, so I can think all the time. So I can voyage through time and space. I put the skewers on, I take them off. When I'm taking them off, putting them on, I'm not here. I'm not even here. This is tafakkur, big man.'

So you don't just chat about football results at Zak's. Zak is big on the big questions. Scripture. She has a special, Zak's Zaqqum Zootomy, which is essentially a shish kebab with some fiendishly hot peppers, right off the Scoville scale. Zaqqum is the tree that grows in hellfire. The deal is, if you can eat the whole thing, you don't have to pay for it, and you get a lassi on the house. Only one person has managed to pull it off and Zak insists that two wannabe jihadis were so ashamed of having collapsed on the floor, weeping and mewing, while one of their associates uploaded the tableau for world-wide amusement, that they gave up on the martyrdom game.

♏

'Haven't seen you for a long time. A long time,' says Zak. 'I thought you might be dead. I've got your doner ready for you, though, just the way you like it.'

'Shouldn't you know how I am?'

'It's not permissible for anyone to know everything. We're not allowed perfection. Word is you had some real trouble.'

'Which trouble are we talking about?' It's hard for me to keep up. I've only been back from Jerusalem for a fortnight, but Zak is plugged in.

'I heard you had some grand project bankrupt you,' she says. Oh, that trouble. The Ray.

Some like to talk to their hairdresser or to pour out their soul to bar staff. I've never been keen on unloading to strangers, because it doesn't make any difference to your problems. But there's something in Zak's voice that prompts me to blab. Some real sympathy. And maybe Zak's had some lessons in hypnosis. Her voice is always calm and slightly soporific.

One of the golden rules in the Vizz is never use your own money. Use the money of others to finance whatever it is you want to do. I hate history but there was always one thing I wanted to do. The Ray. I put a lot of money into it, because I was fed up with the endless barricades of stupidity. I was going to flank the wank. I mortgaged the house.

'I put the house, the savings, the works into a doc. Tolerated whiny actors and sulky historians, did the whole shoot, sat down in the edit suite to start work, felt great. Felt nuclear. Next day the whole place was a pile of ashes.'

'Insurance?'

You might well ask about insurance. I'm not stupid. Obviously I had insurance. Obviously they didn't pay out. Naturally you don't expect an insurance company to fulfil its obligations, to pay in full, but *something*. Some derisory offer. A humiliating fob-off. No. Sweet fuck all, as they used to say round my way.

I've had colleagues who've put in absurd claims. Jack the List was in town one night, pissed as a newt. Groggy, he sat down in a doorway in Regent Street for a breather. Woke up: it was morning. His wallet gone. His briefcase, with a new, high-end laptop, gone. His handmade shoes, gone. His gold Prince Albert, gone.

He fessed up to the insurance company that he had passed out in a doorway, wrecked. They gave him cash, a brand-new laptop. And brand-new shoes. And a brand-new Prince Albert. For some reason, doubtless hidden in the small print, insurance companies only pay out to idiots or fraudsters.

'They didn't pay out. I shouldn't have used my own money.'

'No, no,' Zak chides me. 'You were right to have a go. Weak heart, weak art. Who dares wins, big man.'

Who dares, in my experience, ends up very cold and uncomfortable. I met them once, in Afghanistan. Them. The Who Dares crew. I was filming a mass grave. Who were the dead? Who killed them? We never found out. But the two dozen were surely very dead. There's nothing like a fresh mass grave in high summer.

Semtex refused point blank. 'It's too much.' I couldn't really argue. This stuff isn't covered by a standard contract. It was the stench. We were hundreds of feet away and everyone was gagging, practically beaten to their knees by the rotting corpses, their faces covered with anything they could get. And there's the business of not asking a cameraman to do something you're not prepared to do

So I grabbed the camera. I didn't look. I really didn't want to. I let the hand do the filming. I waved the camera around in the right direction, although the footage was surprisingly sharp and composed. Or so I'm told. I never viewed it, and because of its nature it hasn't been widely viewed. It's not a Saturday-night date movie. I'm also told that three cameraman tried to shoot some footage first. Two fainted and one threw up before I grabbed the camera and did the business.

There are so many mes out there. So many of me out there, having their own adventures.

The stench didn't bother me because I had an appalling cold and I couldn't breathe through my nose, let alone smell anything, but I didn't tell anyone. As I walked back to the sanctuary of breathability, they were standing around next to one of their funny vehicles. Them. They, quite rightly, hate journalists and the Vizz. I know I do. 'Nails,' said one. That's probably the highest praise I've ever had and it's undeserved.

♏

'So I lost the house,' I explain.

'What was the doc about?' Zak asks.

'A French nobleman, Gilles de Rais, who liked to relax by killing children and summoning demons, some say. Others say not. He was one of the cleverest and toughest men of his century, the period of the Hundred Years War, and he was taken to the cleaners by an Italian con artist.'

'And you're surprised it went up in flames? Where're you staying?' asks Zak.

'A friend's lending me a place.'

'That's a good friend.'

Not really. Florian was, or maybe still is, a financial advisor. It's unaccountable because even I know he knows nothing about finance. But in a world where Johxn has a senior position in the Vizz, where Jack the List is regarded as a journalist, and I was Head of Textiles, why shouldn't someone whose financial knowledge is drawn from a quick read of the tabloids offer financial advice?

Florian advised a number of people who lost money in the crash. Their losses were more to do with the crash than any spectacular incompetence by Florian, or so Florian maintains.

178

But investors who lose money are unhappy. Investors who lose a lot of money are very unhappy. Florian was lucky that his investors weren't from the former Communist countries where money is the state religion. His investors were staid people who relaxed to jazz in the comfort of their comfortable homes. So they weren't going to risk that by having Florian killed. But having someone beaten up is easy on the wallet and the conscience, and offers almost zero prospect of jail time.

When I worked on a building site, with the last of the Irish navvies, you'd get someone skulking around asking: 'Do you lads want to earn some extra money?' Since Saturday night meant filling someone in anyway, there was usually an Irish volunteer. When I was young the labourers were Irish and the beggars were alkies from Glasgow. Now the labourers are Polish and the beggars are Romanians. Progress.

One night after Florian had been vigorously pummelled and told to stay still so his assailant could take a picture as proof, Florian realised there were at least half a dozen other investors who might take up the thumping method. He headed for the Orkneys and since property prices weren't right (and Florian would sooner lose a limb than a pound) he has offered us his place in Vauxhall on an almost house-sitting basis.

'You mustn't be too down,' urges Zak. Is there anything more annoying than someone telling you to cheer up? 'You will be up again soon. The see-saw of things.'

I like Zak's suggestion of the see-saw of things. That allows for a strong possibility of upward movement, but it is possible for a see-saw not to move. For one half to remain down permanently. I feel more like at the bottom of a long, greasy rope that I can't climb. When you're young, hope is the battery. Correction: your body is the battery, you've got millions of years of fine-tuning giving you the urge to roam the streets in the early morning seeking reproductive activities. But hope gives you some extra turbo-charging. As you get older it's different. Those awful moments of hope. That just cause distress. It's more comfortable to stay down, not to move.

'There is a lot of see-sawing,' I agree. I agree because I want the conversation to move on to the presentation of a kebab, and because I agree.

My most see-saw moment was probably in a kebab shop in Catford. The fight in a kebab shop is a rite of passage you have to have at least once when you grow up in South London. I'd just been to the most fashionable club (not that fashionable at all, but you have to take what you can get) in that neighbourhood. I was with the second hardest guy in our patch, called Weak, because he was like three Vikings sown together, so I felt I had insurance.

I'd just got the phone number of the most beautiful girl in the club, who'd actually danced with me when I asked her to dance. We were just tucking into our shish when these six guys came in, legless. One had this ridiculous embroidered shirt on (blame the dying days of disco). It was that classic 'what are you looking at?' moment. But when you're working with a classic, you don't change the text. To be honest, even if I had five mates, I wouldn't have said that to Weak. But booze. Drunken youths. Kebab shop. What are you looking at? You gotta do it once.

Weak always carried a pair of cyclist's gloves with him, solace for the knuckles, but they leave the fingers free for artistic gouging. He slipped them on and went to work. It was the only time I decked someone. My boxing came good. The guy went down like he was paid to. I was disappointed that there wasn't a larger and more appreciative audience. Weak threw the Shirt through the window. Then we were attacked by mops, as the staff piled in.

We ran off into the night, laughing. We'd trashed a kebab shop, floored six guys and Weak had grabbed a large jar of chillies on his way out. It couldn't get any better. I'd pulled a woman so beautiful I sensed it couldn't go anywhere, but I'd pulled.

'Did you see his face?' asked Weak, biting on a chilli. 'Fucking poetry.' That was the only time I heard Weak use the word poetry and that moment on a South London street might have been the high point of my life. I'd just been offered a job by Herbie. I was eighteen. I was going to Greece. I laughed, I laughed like the ruler of the world. But you know what they say about up.

'Where's your jacket?' asked Weak.

I had my money in my jacket. My credit card. My keys. My driving licence. For some reason my passport. The beautiful phone number.

'You can't go back,' said Weak, 'you'll get your head kicked in or arrested.' I did go back. I was beaten up *and* arrested. When I told my Uncle Joe he laughed the way he hadn't laughed since Nagasaki got nuked.

♏

'Isn't Johxn looking to spend big on some doc?' Zak asks. 'Everyone's talking about it.'

'Yes.' Johxn hasn't replied to the two proposals I've sent in. They weren't my best ideas, but I couldn't come up with anything better, and even if I had a killer idea, I wouldn't send it in straight away because I know he'll reject the first few ideas I send in, purely for laughs. But I know he hasn't replied to the proposals Zyklon Annie, Edison, Silly Milly, Jack the List et al. have sent in either. After all, you have to read at least the first paragraph.

'You have to be happy,' Zak insists firmly. I did sound especially glum. 'Don't be an ampallang, some ruminant, use tafakkur. I've lost much more than a house, and I can tell you, you can come back, you big crybaby.'

I remember there was some awful stuff in her past. A dead kid. It's quite galling how much more resilient women can be.

'So can I have my doner, then?' I indicate the wrapped doner next to Zak. The kebab aromas have got to me.

'You have to be happy,' says Zak. 'Look how that poor Mr Graham got killed? You should enjoy life and the gift of taffakur.'

I had heard that Gray Graham had been killed. I was slightly annoyed about it. He was stabbed. Of violent deaths, it's the most glam. It means something.

Some kid plays with a gun half a mile away and you're dead. Bullets go all over the place, they roam way beyond your eyesight. Most soldiers can barely see their targets or never do. Anyone can die in a car crash or get run over because someone's changing the music.

But stabbing is personal, it's never accidental, like a gun just going off; someone stabs you to death, and death typically requires a lot of stabbing, they mean it. And Graham was so boring. He never did or said anything interesting or funny in his whole life. He made tedious docs about tedious health issues because no one else wanted to. He didn't deserve to die that way, because he hadn't earned it.

If you gotta go, that's the way. The only thing cooler than being stabbed is an air force deciding to laser-drop a thousand-pound bomb right on you, personally, taking out two or three blocks, because they want to make abso-fucking-lutely sure you are gone. There is no higher praise.

Although once you find out it was Graham's neighbour, frothing about Graham's overgrown hedge, you feel better. A hedge dispute? But that follow-up info won't get far. He went out stabbed. Street. Edgy. Styl-ee.

I stretch out to take the doner.

'No,' says Zak.

'Sorry?'

'No, I don't think you're ready for it. I don't think you're really worthy of this doner. You need to change yourself. You need to be happy, Bax. If you're happy, you're beating the system. Promise me you'll be happy.'

'No.' It seems like selling out.

'Then you can't have your doner. Only happy people get my doners. Be happy, Bax.'

'You want me to go around with a spring in my step and a song on my lips?'

'Why not? Things will change, whether you want them to or not.'

'Anyone who smiles all day is not very observant.'

'What is history?' I sometimes wish Zak would limit the conversation to whether I want the extra chilli.

'I don't know.'

'Bax, tell me, what is history?'

'Man's desperate battle to get a doner?'

'You're not trying. No doner until you tell me, what is history?'

'I don't know. Mostly war. World war. Civil war. Uncivil war. Invasion. Assassinators. Strange laws about corn. Let's not forget the rape.'

'Not bad. But what are you missing?'

'My doner?'

'Bax, you've got the half that everyone notices, you've got the depressing half, you miserable bastard, but what's missing?'

'Please tell me and give me some food.'

'What's missing is the unknown tidiers. It's mess after mess, but what seems like an unrelenting tide of evil is matched by an unrelenting tide of good. Build. Debuild. Build. Debuild. Build. It's very tiring, all the to and fro, and that's why we have to die. The tidying doesn't get noticed, it's because the Baxters glamorise the dark.'

Me? I've made docs about bouncy castles and fun with spoons. That surely balances out the atrocity-specials, where I thought it was clear the message was that war is unpleasant.

'You're wrong. I'm too hungry to glamorise killing. And it's what the public want. They want violence. And animals. If I could make a series about time-travelling super-intelligent footballing Nazi sharks committing atrocities throughout the ages, I'd be the richest man on earth.'

'You're just obeying orders, eh?'

'It's strange that Mrs Average, who would get hysterical if her little Johnny grazed his knee, likes to relax in the evening with tales of nefarious poisonings, serial killing and big explosions, but I don't rule the world. Please, the doner?'

'No.'

'No?'

'How many chairs have you got through today, Bax?'

'Who told you that?'

'No one told me, Bax, it's tafakkur. And eyesight. Nabil,' she says addressing an old guy at a table, 'does he deserve a doner?' The old man shakes his head.

'I'm going to do you a favour. My doners only go to happy, slim homes. You should walk more, Bax, lose some pounds. Now I've got customers to attend to. You need to think more, you need tafakkur.'

She may be right. Tafakkur is a posh Arabic word for contemplation. But you can't think all the time, about everything you do. Because you just can't see that far down the road. No matter how much you want to. You fire a gun into the dark, you know there's a risk of someone getting hurt. But you say something, even that can do damage, way down the road.

It's the moments that are unimportant that often turn out to be important. It's the unthinking stuff, not washing-up properly, that kills you. Perhaps my greatest crime was getting Edison into the Vizz but that was a decision, however bad. I chose to open the door. Correction: it was a mistake, you have to have the *mens criminale* or whatever for it to be a crime. But you can be responsible for terrible things without knowing it, or only discovering the horror later.

Years ago, I had just left Wacky Towers when this breathless imbecile came up to me: 'I'm late for an interview, do you know where this is?' He showed me an address on a letter.

As a total Londoner, my tafakkur proceeded in the following order. First of all, we have maps, we've had them since the 1560s. Quite good ones. Secondly, as a total Londoner, I have contempt for those who are too stupid to realise that if you need to be somewhere for something important, you aim to get there early, very early, because the whole city can meltdown, any time.

Thirdly, as a total Londoner, I don't care about your problems and I have even more contempt for you thinking I might. Finally, as a total Londoner, I have contempt for you because you deserve contempt as you are, indisputably, a twat.

A few weeks later I met the twat again in Wacky Towers. It was Johxn.

'Oh, I gave you the directions,' I said.

'You did what?'

'I gave you directions, the other day, to get here.'

'No, you must be confusing me with someone else.' Of course Johxn probably would have found his way or got directions from someone else, but maybe not. Maybe not. I've never told anyone about that.

'Have you found Herbie's safe?' Zak asks as I move to the door.

'Shouldn't you know that?' I reply.

'I know that you will.' She smiles. That's nice. It's a generous thing to give encouragement, if not a doner. Encouragement is a great gift and it costs nothing. Herbie always encouraged me. When I thought I'd be stuck as an assistant cameraman for the rest of my life, he assured me I'd make docs one day. That one sentence, which for all I know he didn't even mean, kept me going, although Herbie probably didn't have bouncy castles in mind. That gave me a lot of fight.

'I won't find it, not now,' I reply. 'Unless you've got it stashed out back?' Why would I find Herbie's safe after all this time?

'I know you'll find it,' she says. Zak really is convincing. Sometimes, and this only happens every two or three years, people say something and you know it's true, it's like there's a drum-roll in your heart that goes with it, to signal it's not idle chatter, the way music in films tells you what to expect. 'It's more enjoyable when you have to work hard.'

That's not true. There's enough hardness as it is. 'Life is unimaginably hard. Fortunately,' was one of Herbie's jokes.

I resolve to go next door to get a bite to eat and then I shall munch it with gusto in front of Zak's shopfront.

Of course, any purchase is risky. Shopping can be more dangerous than you'd imagine. It too can provoke unforeseen misery.

The last time I worked with Herbie was in Japan. It's one of my favourite places, but it's so expensive it's unwise to do anything but breathe. At Narita airport, as we were leaving, Herbie spotted a bottle of eighteen-year-old Yamazaki whisky in the duty-free. It must have been a promotion or a mistake, because although it was still eye-wateringly pricey, it was relatively cheap. Mysteriously, we still had some money left on the budget, and let's face it, a Japanese receipt with Yama on it could be anything.

'Never come in under budget,' said Herbie. 'You'll bring the profession into disrepute and be hated unto the third generation.' I assumed the bottle was for his stash, but he gave it to Johxn. Herbie didn't do ingratiation, but he genuinely liked to get on with people, he disliked argy-bargy, and it is one of the oldest human traditions, a sweetener for the boss.

Some months ago, I noticed the bottle, along with a defunct espresso machine, in a box in Johxn's assistant's cubicle. The bottle was unopened.

'You're not a whisky drinker, then?' I asked Johxn.

'Not that Japanese paint-stripper. It's some cheap rubbish Herbie bought me. It's why I stopped working with him. I can't stand tight-fistedness. I thought I'd thrown it out.'

I did wonder if I should tell him that there are devotees of the water of life who consider Yamazaki the best in the world, but long experience has taught me that explaining to the ignorant that they're fucking ignorant never helps. There is no

187

thank-you. I took the bottle home, raised a glass to Herbie, and vowed yet again to destroy Johxn.

♏

'Peace be upon you,' says Zak. That's the trouble with a stock phrase – it loses meaning. Of course, when you're young you don't want peace, you want a bombardment of sex, drugs, cash and rock 'n' roll. Only later does the richness of peace become apparent. Herbie was big on peace.

'Peace is the greatest thing. Super-paradise,' he used to say to me. 'But you're too young to understand that. Indeed, you're too young to understand that you don't want to understand.'

As I cross the threshold out onto Brick Lane, Zak shouts after me: 'And money doesn't make you happy.'

'That's a wicked lie concocted by the poor,' I retort. My retorts aren't usually snappy, but I had that one on standby. Ellen always says that to me too.

GÖBEKLI TEPE
AUGUST

Libraries are important. I'm a big fan of the British Library. Every time I'm Euston way and I need a massive dump, I pop in. The toilets are great, and the café too, and it's a good place to have meetings and buy drugs. I got a reader's card years ago, so I could always claim I was doing research there, in case I needed to claim I was doing research somewhere.

Semtex is at a table in the café staring at some fruit concoction. I do find vegans laughable. It's wrong to harm animals, but it's not wrong to harm plants? Because they don't move around much? Plants, those sly seeders, they're just waiting to take over, I'm telling you. I filmed at Chernobyl and saw the plants punching through the cement. They're just waiting for us to slip up.

To live, you have to kill. I came across some research about how plants scream, in a plant-like manner, when they're uprooted. How they beg for mercy, how they suffer, how they natter with each other, in leafy repartee, proved by real scientists in white coats, but it's so easy to wind Semtex up, I can't be bothered.

'Have you had that Roger Crab reconsideration?' he asks.

'Yes, I have.' That's true. Yet again I've adjudged it a stupendously bad idea. 'I've been doing some research.' That's not true. I lay down my reader's card prominently. That's what it's for. Semtex is almost certain I'm conning him, but no one abandons their dream lightly.

'But nothing's happening, right?'

Things are certainly happening, but not for me and Semtex. The last year hasn't enhanced our value in the Vizz. It doesn't matter that most of the disaster was not down to me. Johxn still hasn't commissioned his Big Money Project, which has led some to question the existence of the money, but they don't understand Johxn. Why should he make one person happy (or as happy as you can be having to work under Johxn's guidance) when he can make everyone unhappy?

'There is Turkey,' I say.

'Z-work?'

'It's not Z-work. It's Turkey. I told you, it's that hand-me-down from Edison.'

Edison now regards work as beneath him. He was last seen in the basement of his large house in Richmond with a pneumatic drill, powering towards the earth's core. Some say he just wants to build a very large swimming pool, some say he's digging for buried treasure, some say he's just loco.

He phoned me the other week and offered me a proposition for a commission he'd got from Johxn; he'd get nearly all the money, and the credit; I wouldn't get a credit and I'd have to do all the work. I'd be a ghost director. I quite understand Edison: I'd like to be a famous director without having to do any work.

Which would you choose? If the Allower offered you a deal? To be feted as a genius but not to have done the work, to be a fraud, or to be a genius with great work but to die unknown?

'Turkey, right,' says Semtex. 'Not the bit of Turkey with the great beaches, but the bit that has a war on the go? What is it with you? You're like Dr Death, the atrocity merchant. You just can't get enough. Why can't we do Roger Crab?'

'If you want to get paid, you know, in money, rather than self-righteousness, we have to do Turkey. It's a simple in-and-out. It's not brain surgery.'

I can speak with authority about brain surgery because I've done some. Admittedly not the tricky bits, but when I was filming a neurosurgeon at work on a patient, he let me put the top back on.

'Every cameraman I know gets to do beaches or to cover porn shoots,' Semtex protests, 'or to hang out with Jack and the hyper-rich. Why do I have to risk my neck every time? Why didn't you get me to do the bouncy castles? That would have been a fun gig, with no one trying to kill me.'

'Why didn't I get you for the bouncy castles?'

'Yeah.'

'Because you were in jail.'

'You could have waited.'

I now have a powerful temptation to elaborate how many peace-loving bugs, friendly nematodes and happy-go-lucky bacteria were hideously mass murdered in the extraction of the spinach and baobab that have been blended into the smoothie Semtex is slurping. Just because you're small, don't you have a right to happiness? Listing the casualties involved in even eating a dockleaf worked wonders before. But business before pleasure. Having tried to avoid Semtex on my last two shoots, I'm trying the opposite tactic, to cheat fate by inviting him along.

'The fighting's in Syria. Not where we're going. We're not going to a zone.'

'Not a zone, but the border, where the lunatics and mortars play, and you can console yourself that you've not officially been blown up in an official war?'

Semtex didn't worry in the past about zone-work. That's what getting older is, you see how your luck stocks are running out, and caution is the drug of choice. Though, of course, there's often a final burst of why-not daredevilry when you get to the seventies.

'Think about it,' I say. If it gets ugly, I could use Semtex. Of course I don't want him to feel he's doing me a favour, I want him to feel I'm doing him a favour, although that's proved impossible in the past.

I leave Semtex to enjoy his self-pity and smoothie and go round the block to Granary Square for lunch with the Dutchman. My joyful anticipation of a free lunch is eroded by the ten-minute walk. London is a city of wrathfood. It's every six feet. The tourists with their suitcases. Their suitcases on wheels. Once upon a time bags were carried. Now everyone has the wobbly, screechy, wheelie features, so they take up twice or even three times the space, as they zigzag, flounder and bash into you, and generally have twice the opportunity to feed you wrathfood. Progress.

But let no one tell you there is no hope. There is. I've seen it. For some reason the word is written in large letters on a wall, opposite St Pancras. Nearby a lamp post boasts a photo of a goofy Alsatian. Above the photo the strapline: 'Stray Dog.' Below it: 'Man's best friend? Man's best meal!!!' The notice is laminated and tightly fixed with plastic clips to dissuade any reader from casually ripping it off, something a young woman is struggling to do as she expresses her disgust, while her friend is phoning the police.

I can't be sure Semtex is behind these provocations, but he has achieved nationwide outrage and far more attention than his camerawork got. Dozens of grief-stricken pet owners have blubbed to journos about their beloved moggy or pooch falling prey to London's now notorious pet-chef, Lord Yum-Yum. Budgies, hamsters and ponies have been added to the list by the imagination of distraught households, and the police have been inundated by denunciations, which all goes to show there's no need for the truth.

Crossing King's Cross reminds me it was the worst patch of London in my lifetime. Even most crackwhores shunned it. Islington, Notting Hill, Camberwell, all these places during my lifetime had poverty, mouldy flats, stabbings, shootings, lootings, shittiness galore, but they also had something else going on, some feeble art installation, urban guerillas, someone learning how to play guitar, wonderful pizza. Something.

King's Cross was mainline, uncut despair. The new buildings are on a par with the worst of East Berlin and there's the soullessness of the town planner everywhere, but it's still a vast improvement.

What's improved in London over the last four decades? Coffee and sushi. A good coffee or fresh sushi is available on any corner. It's scant compensation for the fact no one English can afford to live here, certainly in what's considered Central London. The Russians and Chinese are buying up the penthouses, the swish streets. I prefer the Russian mafia because they have a sense of humour; they'll tell you a joke or insist on showing you a hilarious tattoo on their dick before they shoot you. The Chinese are all business.

And at the other end, the distant bedsits, where the assistant cameramen of yore used to live, are now filled with six illegal Egyptians.

The streets are packed round the clock. You can't move because of suitcases and dimwits texting and everyone's grumpy because they have to eat wrathfood all day.

My lunch with the Dutchman at Granary Square, however, is probably the best lunch of my life. The food is great, pleasingly expensive, the service friendly and the Dutchman pays. He praises me so much it's embarrassing. I can take about three courses of praise, but by the time we get to coffee, even I'm glutted.

Even without the praise I like him. He's one of those rare, jolly people, a bit like Herbie. He goes on and on about how great my docs are, even the one about the bouncy castles. 'Hardly anyone seems to understand how clever that doc is. It's so clever. But you must look past the castles.'

He assures me he has money from a backer groaning under the weight of his riches and that I can do what I want. Any project I fancy, he can get the money. Like that. He gives me four phone numbers for contact, including his home number. 'Bax, if you need anything, anything, phone me, even at three in the morning.' He slips me two fat joints as we part.

Should I have another go at The Ray? Gilles de Rais? My *Magnum*? The Holy warrior? The Breton mujahid? One of the pioneers of the documentary? That's one of the reasons I find The Ray so interesting. Like me, he blew his wad mounting a spectacle. A real spectacle, a twenty-thousand-verse recreation of the battle of Orleans, in Orleans itself, in 1435, to celebrate the anniversary of Joan of Arc breaking the siege with her gang of homicidal maniacs, rapists and sadists.

The Ray assembled a huge cast, hundreds of extras and all the special effects the fifteenth century could muster, as well as innumerable references to The Ray's leading role in the fighting, which were all true. He was right up at the front, which makes you wonder whether he wasn't counting on dying gloriously. But the spectacle drained him, and like many a great visionary, The Ray had to skip town with unpaid bills.

On the one hand, I've done the research, I've already invested years, and having done the shoot once, I know exactly where to put the tripod. Arguably, doing it the second time round, it could be even better. Talk about dress rehearsals. The guy who played the judge was way too luvvy.

You work hard for something, when you succeed you get a strong sense of victory, a blast of I-told-you-so. On the other hand, you can work so hard, so long for something, you can't enjoy it when you get it. You've paid too much. You're too angry that you've paid too much when others have paid so little. The thought of the life lost in The Ray makes me ill. I fear The Ray is a devil too far.

And I can hear Herbie saying: 'Hard work? It's while you're working hard that you'll miss that opportunity to cheat or steal that will get you ahead.' The Allower has little time for dilly-dalliers, but equally doesn't approve of relentless labour.

It's a sunny afternoon, one of the three or four we get every year in London. I walk along the canal. Things couldn't be better. A blow-out the like of which I haven't had for years. Adoration. The promise of unlimited money. Sunshine. Unlimited money.

Yet my satisfaction is tinged with sadness. Because I know this won't happen. I don't worry this won't happen, I don't *suspect* it won't happen, I *know* it won't.

Why? I have no idea why, but you're not allowed anything this easy. You're just not. You're not allowed. It's not allowed. I don't know why it has to be this way, but it is. The Dutchman came out of the blue and he will return there.

When I get back home Luke is staring at the sleeve notes for Junior Murvin's 'Police and Thieves'. He tells me, 'Dad, we need a sit-down.' He's unhappy about the CDs I left for him to listen to. 'I don't like reggae,' he announces. What's going to happen to my vinyl collection, now gathering dust in storage? The rare stuff? The Bongo Herman collection?

Unless you're very dim you understand that, finally, material possessions don't matter, that you can't take it with you, but what else is there to play with while we're here? You want to simply hand over your tastes and attitudes to your kids, but you can't. And that is a good thing.

Luke will be okay, however, because he's got his mother's balance. That's the greatest gift. If you have calm, you've already won. When he was demoted from second archer to third archer in the school production of *Robin Hood*, I feared I'd have to give a pep talk about rollercoaster life, but he didn't mind.

I don't know whether the Dutchman will be kidnapped by aliens, or get hit by a bus crossing a road, or his backer will cop a catastrophe, but it won't happen. Nothing is that easy. It's not allowed. And you have no say. We're all bystanders. We have no power. Only luck. I've seen beautiful, shameless, well-educated whores fail just as certainly as if they were timid, ugly, illiterate saints. I've seen whores so beautiful, so ambitious, so shameless, you'd be certain they'd make it, but they've disappeared. Herbie was right.

Your doc is never as good as you'd like it to be, just as your life isn't. Herbie said that. It doesn't mean it's bad.

Turkey, on the other hand. Turkey, dodgy doings with Semtex, in a zone, an earthquake-prone, war-torn region, with cheeky water, swarming with homicidal maniacs and stray missiles; that, that might happen.

You can't win, but you can choose how you lose. Herbie said that.

♏

The best thing about going to a war or some dangerous zone where the Kalashnikovs and craziness roam freely is that you can get rid of those silly clothes your wife bought you. The terrible shirts, the ill-fitting pullovers, the ghastly scarf with reindeers, they go to war, they go to a coup, they go to the Z-work and they don't come back. Ellen has noticed the one-way traffic, but has come to accept that clothes are the first casualties of war.

I also have a special shitty wardrobe I take when I'm heading for a zone. A beaten old leather jacket, the tatty jeans, the cheap underwear, an old, scratched wristwatch. I leave the wedding ring behind. You aim to take nothing you can't cheerfully leave behind and if you take anything valuable, you make sure it's well hidden. I have lots of secret pockets and false-bottomed luggage. You have the dud wallet with expired credit cards and filled with colourful, expired, worthless banknotes (I like to use Soviet roubles) to hand over to some donkey-shagger if you're robbed. Give 'em what they want; it's such a basic lesson.

Anyone who's done Z-work knows two things. One, you can be perfectly safe in most zones. It's perspective. To viewers far away, it looks like you're close to the explosions, but you're not. Action is usually limited to certain well-marked areas, like some tourist attraction or nightclub, and if you stay away from them, you can even be bored. One of my best friends in Iraq, an American diplomat, spent two years in Baghdad during the height of the fighting. The worst thing that happened was bad sunburn when he fell asleep by the pool. Correction: and once being woken up at the dead of night by a very powerful truck bomb.

The second thing is no one gets unlimited safety. You're in a zone on tolerance. You're allowed a butcher's. But if you keep hanging around, you will be punished. You'll be shot, you'll be blown up, you'll lose a leg, you'll be killed.

A man is feeding his partridge outside my hotel in Gaziantep. Am I in a zone? It doesn't feel like it. Am I abusing my zone quota? It doesn't feel like it. It's hard to imagine a scene more tranquil than a man feeding his partridge. But of course wars don't look like wars all the time. No volcano erupts all the time. They can be very scenic in-between.

They like partridges in Turkey. I'm not quite sure why. It's like having an overweight budgie and it's not as if they can do tricks, but if that's your thing.

'It's a symbol of Kurdish independence,' a bellboy says to me. I can't quite see how keeping a tubby bird is going to bring down the state. I did a report once on how the Kurds were shafted in nineteen whatever, and I felt sorry for them being divided up. It seemed a simple story. But then I found out how the Kurds weren't one big oppressed family, but lots of different Kurds, with different dialects, different religious beliefs, and I thought, 'If you can't get your act together, why should I care?' Not to mention I had a Kurdish hairdresser who annoyed me and ruined my look, so my sympathy went.

You examine anything and the divisions go on and on, North England, South England, North London, South London, the divisions go on till it's you and your neighbour arguing over the fence. You just can't win. My friend who made it in LA had a house in Beverley Hills, next to a world famous rock star, though the rock star's property was obviously much larger.

As we were drinking on the terrace, my friend handed me a pair of binoculars. I could see the rock star smoking a cigar by the fence. It wasn't easy as there were half a dozen portable toilets lined up there too (he must have valued his own dumping facilities on tour). The star had an ashtray. How bizarrely tidy, I thought. He finished his cigar and then emptied the butt-full ashtray over the fence. And it was no accident. He had to walk a quarter of a mile to get to the fence. 'He always does that,' my friend commented. He'd retaliate by getting his gardener to hop over and shit wildly in the portables.

I pass a couple of hours in town, and when I get back to the hotel I find Semtex has arrived and is in the restaurant. We order *manti*, Turkish ravioli or dumplings, things in pasta. Who invented it? What exactly is the difference between pasta and noodles? Is ravioli really Italian *manti*?

'How was the research?' Semtex asks. I came out two days earlier. In my younger days I would have gone everywhere, I would have gone down the road to Göbekli Tepe, I would have gone clubbing. That's how you know you're getting old; I would now pay good money to be refused admission to any club. I went clubbing in places where you wouldn't have thought they had nightclubs. Tirana. Pyongyang. It's a testament to the human spirit that they have clubs everywhere. They may be small. They may be terrible, with one fatigued prostitute. They may overcharge. They may play music you can't believe. They may cause you enormous regret, but they're there.

'Nothing. Nothing at all,' I say. I'm meant to be investigating the smuggling of plundered antiquities from Syria that are shipped off to the art dealers in New York and London. I had a look at one local dealer this morning who had an incredible sarcophagus in his showroom. For some reason I suddenly wanted to have this sarcophagus as an over-the-top bathtub in a huge (also imagined) bathroom. Stone is so appealing, so

201

very much *there*, and there is something about something that old. It's important to have the shopping list ready in case things change. If I became Jack-rich I reckon I'd just spend a lot of time in the bath, laughing.

'It's not looted from Syria?' I asked, since the dealer had no minders and was small and old and not likely to attack me. He saw it as a legitimate provenance enquiry.

'Not at all. I can assure you it was stolen from a Turkish museum.' He politely offered me the catalogue. The dealer spoke excellent English; it's a pity he had nothing to say about treasures from Syria.

I know there are dealers selling stolen artworks from Syria and smuggling them out through Turkey. I know this because I'm smuggling some priceless bowl back to London in my luggage to some bloodsucker in Mayfair, but clearly it wouldn't be a good idea to interview my own dealer. I may have to arrange a faux dealer. Egemen will have to do. Blacked out.

Semtex stares sullenly at his *salgam*, with the eternal suspicion of the vegan, worried that this locally produced turnip juice, despite repeated assurances, might have been contaminated by some quadruped walking past and firing off a hair into the vat. Neither of us wants to be in this dining room.

Liliane swans in to the restaurant. 'What is this, a reunion?' Semtex asks.

'Ah, Bax and Tex, are you actually working, or are you on the run?' As we're sitting Liliane is just tall enough to look down on us. 'Either way, I have no doubt someone will arrive presently to arrest and strip search you.'

No question, Liliane is genuinely pleased to see us. Since she doesn't have to work with us, she's in a free-fire zone where she can insult us to her heart's content. The way she underlines strip search I wonder whether she's tipping off the local police about us as payback.

Her renunciation of the Vizz lasted six months. Just long enough to torpedo the Apocalypse. Just long enough to pat down the soil on the grave of my career.

She did actually go to a convent for several weeks, although one with excellent spa facilities and catering in the South of France. But you can imagine the chatter. My tongue-lashings about her pieces to camera were so severe she was batted out of the business. My threats to kill her were so ferocious she had to have plastic surgery, change her name and hide in a utility-free shack in the most inaccessible part of the Urals, etc.

When I discovered Liliane was here I was terrified she'd be doing Göbekli Tepe. I still want to do something about it and since it's just down the road I was going to get a taxi and have a butcher's. I would have done it yesterday but, what can I say? I'm too fat and lazy. I popped back to the hotel for a snooze. The Garden of Eden can wait. Liliane is lazy too, but she's clever and lucky. If she did something on Göbekli Tepe, it would probably be hard to beat. But Liliane's doing some big doc about the mosaics of the ancient world and the mosaic museum in Gaziantep.

She does have this hot chick, Nazli, working for her. She's the fixer everyone wants and everyone recommended. She's an astrophysicist in her main job. I was asking her what she did and she explained that she hunted supervoids.

'A lot of the universe is missing,' she elaborated.

'But isn't the deal with space that it's full of space?'

'You don't understand. These are big, huge gaps. Five thousand galaxies of gaps.'

'Maybe they moved to another universe?' I suggest. 'The quarks are always better in the other dimension.'

Nazli chuckles. I wasn't trying to be funny, but it's usually the case I get my biggest laughs when I'm serious, and making a beautiful woman laugh is always a triumph. I do love it when the experts, the rule-clutchers, are discomforted and the Allower makes them understand they barely know what goes on beyond their toes. Nazli is a shining example of how a doctorate is a vow of poverty, but knowing how to ask where the toilet is is always an earner. Since Nazli speaks every one of the five languages knocking around here, she freelances for all the big crews, fixing for extra cash.

Egemen is the fixer I got. Egemen seems to be the last fixer in the drawer. He's a student at what I've been told is an agricultural college, although that might just be a polite term for a farm. He's only worked for the Vizz a couple of times, so I persuade him that it'll be an education for him to work with me and that I won't pay him, I'll just cover some of his expenses.

As I watch Liliane tuck into her *pide*, the Turkish pizza, I consider whether I should denounce her to the police before she does it to us, but it seems weak playing the same gag twice.

What are the irritating people there for, I ask myself, as Liliane stashes it away. For introductions. It was Liliane who first mention Gilles de Rais to me way back in Greece. 'In England you have tea towels with the Queen. In France, we have had the coronation of thought. Should history be a matter of polemic games or reducing it to crude spectacle?' I hadn't a clue what she was talking about, but since she seemed to be against it, I had to be for.

'History should be spectacular.'

'Gilles de Rais is innocent,' she had said. She was joking, but it was what got me going, although it took me a while to ascertain the name wasn't Zil The Ray.

Considered by many experts as the most evil man who ever lived, what's attractive about his story is that all interpretations fit. Companion-in-arms to Joan of Arc, a homicidal maniac with his own beautifully dressed private army, in 1440 Gilles de Rais was found guilty, twice, of mass murder, paedophilia, sodomy, necrophilia, summoning demons and being a fashion victim, and was hanged.

Later referred to as Bluebeard for reasons no one knows, the evidence suggests The Ray was a devious, bad-to-the-bone paedo, who kept it under wraps by storming castles and doing a lot of charity work; or that he was a holy warrior, deeply disillusioned by the burning of Joan of Arc, who got into Satan because he felt let down by the other side; or that he was fitted up by his relatives after he blew his wad on good times, expensive manuscripts and pointy shoes (never mess with the money).

It should also be remembered that the French only won at Orleans because the English army drank itself to death and The Ray's household legion consisted of hardened Scots and German mercenaries.

Then, of course, there was the most important introduction of all. Many, many years ago an irritating nutter sat down on the train opposite to me, dressed in shorts that were too small. It was December. He had a Tyrolean hat with a broken feather. It was not a winning look in South London in the eighties. He was mumbling and twitching. This was the start of care in the community when the shrinks got tired of treating the nutters and released them into the wild.

We all understand that mental illness is an illness, but it's still irksome as fuck to have gibberers and jolters sitting opposite you, who might pull a knife on you, and I suspect there are some nutters who make the most of it, but I don't have the training or time to prove it.

I moved to the next carriage and sat down next to some scruffy, paunchy guy who reeked of dope: Herbie. Got chatting and I was launched into the Vizz.

♏

So far all I've achieved is to talk about partridges and fail to get to Göbekli Tepe. But we have our fixer, Egemen. You can be very dependent on your fixer, and the only way you can find out whether they're any good is to use them. Like a pair of shoes. There's the problem that just because someone is local doesn't mean they know the locality. And even if you have someone fundamentally good, they can still let you down because they're getting divorced or are moving house or their brother has cancer, and you get killed.

I ask Egemen if he knows anyone in the antiquities business. He doesn't. I ask if he has any contacts with local archaeologists. He doesn't. I ask if he has any contacts with the local police. He doesn't. I ask if he has any contacts with the local underworld. He doesn't. I ask if he knows of a place where we might find some shady characters. His face lights up.

'I can take you to a bar where there are many not-law-abiding people. But it is dangerous for you.'

'Let me worry about that.'

We all go to a bar called The Soldier of Fortune. The exterior couldn't be more drab and distressed, brickwork pock-marked as if by bullets. A large painting of a happy skeleton with a bandana, wielding a rocket launcher, looms over the battered door. Semtex grabs me by the arm.

206

'Do you think this is a good idea?'

'What else can we do?'

'Okay. We're going in. We're having one drink. One drink. You're paying. You're paying and if there's any trouble, any trouble at all, you're on your own, star. I'm not backing you up.'

Inside, far from the scarred, one-legged veterans of countless wars staring bitterly into their beer, we find a well-lit, well-furnished club with well-dressed teenagers gazing into their phones. Some webbing and camouflage are strewn about, with pictures of tanks and helicopters, to give some credence to the military theme. They have an impressive cocktail list, with apt names: Bayonet Charge, Ataturk's Machine Gun. If any of this clientele are scoffing at the law, it's down to poor bookkeeping for tax.

'Where are the bad people?' I ask Egemen.

'They are not here.'

Almost as a joke, we ask a couple of drinkers if they could sell us some hot artefacts. They actually call the police, who actually question us.

You can't claim to be a real docker, a hardcore current affairist, unless you've been deported. And getting deported from, say, North Korea doesn't count. Or Saudi Arabia. Anyone can get deported from North Korea; in fact, it's hard *not* to get deported. Getting deported from Finland, for example, now that's something. Edison managed that.

I wonder whether this trip will be cut short or whether I have to bribe someone, but the police are very friendly. I predict the result of the Fenerbahçe–Galatasaray match, which is being shown live, and I receive an admiring slap on the back for forecasting the injury-time goal. The top cop says, as he leaves, that he shouldn't be doing this, but there is one dealer he can tell us about, off the record, hush-hush, as we're now mates.

Egemen looks more perplexed than he normally does. 'He says this man is . . . It's hard to translate.'

It's true, interpreting is hard, even if everyone is speaking the same language. One evening I had the rare experience of getting the beautiful girl in the club to dance with me. She had fantastic legs and was laughing at my jokes. It looked like it was going to be a long night, but then she walked off with a curt goodbye. Weak, who had piled into her stubby friend, told me later: 'Her friend said you were onto a sure thing there until you told her she had legs like a sweaty East German shot-putter. You never get it right, do you?'

I was puzzled because I hadn't said anything like that. Why would I? Then it occurred to me I had praised her legs as athletic, in my dictionary: shapely, healthy, desirable. I say 'good', you hear 'bad'.

Egemen is looking around the bar as if hoping someone will hold up a sign with the answer. 'He says . . . he says this man makes the devil wear funny trousers.'

'What, he's a comedian?'

'No, he is more devil than the devil.'

'I don't see how that's devilish.'

'He is more clever than the devil.'

'I don't want cunning devils, I want devils who are evil.'

The cop adds something.

'He says this man is a son of wrong.'

'Now that sounds right.' I end with: 'Chalky.'

Chalky is apparently the Turkish word for 'good'. I throw it in to show how much I love other languages, and how much I appreciate Turkish culture and how deeply I'm immersed in it. We shake hands and all go our ways satisfied.

The name I've been given, Cenk, of course, is the dealer I'm smuggling for, so we're back to square one. I am tempted to use him, but that would really be asking for trouble.

'Aren't we going to this man?' asks Egemen.

'That's a beginner's mistake, Egemen, to believe anything the police say. You should really be paying me for the training you're getting here. It's a trap.'

We go to a nearby bar and sit down. A guy at the next table hears us speaking English and asks us where we're from.

'London? I am going there,' he says. 'I take some treasures from Syria to sell. They are . . .?' He performs a mime of picking something up and putting it inside his jacket. 'Raided?'

I get Egemen to confirm that he is taking looted goods to London. He is. He is also willing to give an interview. He has two cuneiform seals on him that he shows us. I don't think he's aware that this activity might incur disapproval. There is of course a catch. In half an hour he is leaving town.

I beg and offer the prospect of a small fee if he stays longer. He says he'd love to but he can't as he has an appointment at some exclusive brothel and it's very difficult to get one these days as the British intelligence services are booking up everything. We rush to our hotel, and get our gear. On our way back, our taxi breaks down. By the time we get another and return, our smuggler has, of course, departed.

Back at our hotel, we have the traditional one-last-drink drink. The restaurant is busy.

On his own at one table sits Sir Shot-a-lot, an Irish guy whose name I can't remember, I doubt if anyone can remember his real name. He's a freelance who's never managed to do any journalism as every time he turns up at a zone, he gets shot. Normally, if you see him at your hotel, you move out, because you know it's going to happen. Then there's one

Somali guy I recognise as a failed rapper from Battersea, MC Cool Hot Shit or something. I doubt if he's in town to check out the mosaics.

A hysterical fit is thrown by a bug-eyed weirdo when his order is delivered. The waiter explains it is a vegetarian dish. 'But it looks like meat,' the weirdo froths. 'It looks like meat. I'm not eating anything that looks like meat.' The waiter covers his real opinion by apologising. The weirdo then demands to see the manager because he feels the waiter's apology isn't sincere enough.

I nudge Semtex. 'Now you can see what you look like.' Most of the trouble in the world comes from men, and most of it comes from men who aren't getting laid. It's the most destabilising force on the planet. You can't be furiously angry if you're getting your pleasure events; dejected, sullen, peeved, irked, angry, yes, you can't avoid rage, but not going-mad-with-an-axe furious. Instead of spree-killing you go grumbling home for some doggy action.

I don't know much German, but I can tell the guy in the corner is reading an S&M classic, so I can safely assume he's the man from MI6, tagging the loopy as they go over the border into Syria and the madness bonanza. MI6 and their huge rooftop dishes have completely ruined my phone reception in Vauxhall, so I can't resist going over.

'I'm told you can buy looted artwork dirt cheap around here. You don't have any idea where, do you?'

He puts down his spanking handbook and gives me firm eye contact. 'No idea at all. But do let me know if you find any.' He returns to his reading. The right-back-atcha makes me think he's military rather than a wire-tapper.

I return to my seat. The chair crumbles underneath me. Semtex is crying with laughter. Time to call it a night.

'You can't go yet,' says Semtex.

'Why not?'

'Because I haven't finished laughing at you.' He starts waltzing around holding a chair. We're asked to leave.

In my room, I have a trawl on the Wi-Fi before turning in. It occurs to me, rather than doing the old-fashioned thing of walking around, talking to locals here in Turkey and asking probing questions, I can just check if someone in London or New York has done the work and posted it, so I can pinch it. But all the references to plundering are woefully vague. Why are journalists so lazy? I'm going to be forced to do some work. I switch to the bitching pages and regret it.

Lovable Psycho: *Reunited at last, the Prince of Darkness and the Comtesse de Foufounette, out in the wilds of Turkey. They're doing a series about great floors of the world. The Prince never aimed high.*

At moments like this I think of my Uncle Joe. The sharks. The nukes. I should be able to take a few weeks of this.

♏

The whole atmosphere here in Gaziantep is relaxed and friendly, but then of course that's an inevitable consequence of leaving London. Everywhere is relaxed and friendly after London, even Pyongyang.

But I don't feel lucky, I just don't, and if there's one lesson I've learned, it's trust your instincts. I want to go right down to the border and see if we can get some smugglers to talk, and as there's a war raging across the road in Syria, we're not going without some bodyguards. Insurance, insurance and insurance.

Egemen arranges for bodyguards. The two smallest body-guards I've ever seen report for duty, one carrying what looks like an eighteenth-century musket. It's never how you want it.

'I didn't hire them because they are my cousins,' says Egemen.

I've brought the body armour. Do I wear it? There's a curious thing about body armour: in my experience, bullets flock to it. It's like a gilt-edged invitation to get mortared, shot or peppered with shrapnel. So unless we're in very heavy weather, I don't want to put it on.

The other thing is that unless you're in a situation where you're likely to get mortared, you look a bit craven in body armour. I go for my Kevlar-weave undershirt, good up to three, although you sweat like a pig. They cost a fortune, but when you've done favours for Colombians that's what you get.

Wearing something that has PRESS on it in big letters poses the same dilemma. It can work to your advantage. Being a journalist gets people to open up, to air their most disgusting secrets, or to help you, but sometimes it gets you shot at. Or gets you kidnapped, because you have value, or it's thought that you have value.

As we drive off from the hotel, I spot a small shop selling trophies. There's something reassuring about a trophy shop. It's reassuringly ordinary. It reminds you that most of us just want a little recognition, a bronze figurine for scoring a hat-trick or running a hundred metres, a medal for some classy spelling.

ᛗ

That's the great blessing of big cities, you blend in easily. You're another face in the crowd. It's hard to be anonymous in a zone where there are only five houses and two trees and everyone knows what everyone else's grandfather did in 1930. Even if you look the part perfectly – clothes, beard, hat, the right brand of cigarettes, the right drink – they know you're not from around here, because they know everyone from around here.

'Where is the border?' I ask Egemen.

'The border is everywhere,' he says. I can't figure out whether it's a problem of language or whether Egemen is just the local stoner who's unable to answer any question other than: are you Egemen? A small, elderly, obviously poor man walks past and greets us with the politeness you encounter only in out-of-the way places.

'He is a hitman at the university,' says Egemen. I have no idea what he means and I'm not wasting my time water-boarding him to find out.

I gaze in the direction of Syria. It's peaceful as far as I can see. Here at least, there's nothing to stop you walking over. We film one dealer who is happy to show us his goods but not his face. Even criminals can be quite proud of what they do and don't want to pass up a slot in the Vizz.

But I need a classy talking head. This is the sort of situation where you'd call in a professional head, like Tycho. You've probably seen Tycho a hundred times because he's one of the foot-soldiers of the Vizz. He does a lot of contesting on quiz shows, but he's most useful in the profession because he'll say anything you want.

It's a form of acting or improvisation, I suppose. Tycho's great talent is that he's totally average. Height. Build. Hair colour. There's nothing memorable about him. So you give Tycho some spectacles, a wig, a beard, or some stick-on tattoos and he'll be a floating voter, a marine biologist, a disenchanted croquet fan, an exhaust pipe fetishist, a recovering alcoholic. When you're having trouble getting the right interview, you give Tycho a call.

So I make do with Egemen, blacken him up and give him a list of things I want him to say on camera. 'Isn't this wrong?' he asks.

'It's standard industry practice. It simplifies things. It's to make it easier for the audience,' I clarify with my best director voice. He is reassured, but his remaining uncertainty actually adds to the authenticity of a shifty dealer.

℩

My Uncle Joe wasn't a great talker, but he did give me some advice. 'When you're captured, you've got to try and escape straight away. The longer you're a prisoner the weaker you get. Early on, that's your best chance.' I guess I was ten at the time. For a long time I thought it was strange he told me that, but in the end, he was right. You have to wait twenty, thirty, forty years sometimes to fully appreciate what has been said. 'Eat when you can,' he said to me. 'Sometimes you won't feel like it, sometimes you won't want the food, but eat. You need the energy.' I've kept that in mind.

℩

You always need the mood shots, the cutaways, to give yourself some insurance in editing. Semtex is getting some shots of kids playing football, when Egemen says: 'They want to buy some honey.'

For a moment I wonder if this is a mistranslation or code for some filth, but no, our bodyguards want to buy honey from a local little old lady who is famous for her bees. 'This is the best honey in the world,' Egemen says. It occurs to me it would be a nice present for Luke, even if Egemen is overselling the product.

'We will only be gone five minutes,' says Egemen, getting in the minivan.

'You're all going?' I ask.

'It's fine,' says Semtex. 'We need another ten minutes or so here. Off you go.' I slip Egemen some money for honey. They drive off with Egemen holding up his hand, the fingers extended to emphasise the 'only five minutes' assurance.

Semtex is now shooting the sunset.

You can't reinvent the wheel every week. It's good to have some stock shots. I've done some bad things over the years, but I draw the line at sunset and sunrise. They can look stunning, I concede, if well done, but they've been done to death. I'm lazy in many matters, and cheat in some, but I have a blanket ban on the sun. It's like shooting in a hospital – it's too easy. It shouldn't be allowed. I could go to the best run, best financed hospital in the world, find a waif with tubes and break your heart without a problem.

'Have you gone soft?' I remonstrate.

'You're *jiben* irritating. Go and find a bouncy castle.'

It's also ridiculous because Semtex isn't great on colour. Movement, crowds, composition, something complicated, moving parts, yes. The kids nearby playing football, for instance, he'll make a minor masterpiece out of.

Semtex is absorbed in the sunset, so he doesn't see them approach. Right on time. Four guys, late teens, are definitely walking towards us. The lead guy, wearing a Real Madrid strip, is now pulling out a handgun from the back of his trousers, a stupid place to keep a firearm, but blame the Vizz.

'Hostiles,' I say. This is the benefit of having worked together for so long. Semtex responds instantly, without question. In a second, we're definitely walking too. Away.

If we had had wheels, I would have considered just getting in and driving off. I'm not convinced they're up to pulling a trigger, or that the gun is loaded.

'Hey, we need to talk,' Mr Real shouts in passable English.

If you act aggressively, shout or fight, you'll probably get it back, but if you simply ignore people, it can confuse them. Herbie told me how he had shaken off a gun-toting mugger in Brazil merely by acting as if he didn't hear what he was saying, by using his mantra: 'The pea-green thirteen machine.'

We're walking with a will. The four are now running. The gun is fired in the air. Semtex is sprayed in the face with some chemical. He clutches his face and curls up. One of the reasons I've kept up the running, wheezing around parks and being humiliated by housewives, was precisely for this sort of situation, so I'd have some oomph for emergencies, so I could do a bunk. Just run. But I can't leave Semtex. It would be nice to be robbed, but we are being abducted.

A car pulls up and we are bundled in. They put blankets over our heads and we are driven around. It's hard to say for how long. Five minutes? Ten? Twenty?

We then walk off-road for another fifteen or so. We're taking the back route into some village. It's got dark. I can just make out one woman nearby squatting down doing something to vegetables. I stumble and trip on some rutty field. Worse, I have no sense of direction. I don't know which way Gaziantep or our hotel is. They know this patch, but the stumbling and tripping in the dark is making me more angry than being abducted. I look in vain for someone to take an interest in us, but no one's around.

Our kidnappers aren't very professional. There's the fact that they're about eighteen for a start. They're disappointed we're not American. Mr Real asks me for the address of the British government. I'm told to write a ransom note. They ask for a million dollars. Why not?

I'm tempted to put in a sentence or two about how our kidnappers are morons, using slang, but with access to the web, you can look up any word now and they might get angry, and secondly I don't want to indicate that our captors are cowboys because it might encourage the authorities to do nothing. They take our shoes as if this will somehow stifle escape. Semtex and I are locked in a small room.

Mr Real says, with a big grin to show how much he appreciates his own joke, 'You are our guests.' He translates for his circle. The three others laugh. No matter how small the group you always get a leader.

'This is your fault,' Semtex says. I repeat to myself that there's no gain in getting angry when things go pear-shaped. You need to get to the other side. That's all that matters. I can argue with Semtex, insult him and indeed punch him hard in the mouth back home, with a proper pair of gloves. I make a vow never to think about why I didn't ask one of the bodyguards to stay. Or why I didn't just leg it and leave Semtex. I then take a vow that this is the last time I work with Semtex and it's the last time I'm a zonary.

I consider our options. Who are these people, apart from being clowns, and what do they want? I can't work out what they're speaking. Bad Turkish? Good Kurdish? Where are we, which side of the border? Did anyone see us get abducted and will they care enough to report it? The kids playing football? This lot strike me as old-fashioned bandits, not political, not religious. Will anyone come looking for us? Possible but unlikely. An image of Liliane getting into a foam bath at the hotel comes to mind.

They've emptied our pockets, but haven't spotted I have a money belt, which is old and shitty and so doesn't look like a money belt. You have money, you can always negotiate. Over the years it has truly shocked me what even a twenty-dollar bill can achieve. If there's only one guard, maybe we can pay him off. Keeping the belt is a minor triumph and makes me feel less disappointed in myself.

In the other room Mr Real is playing with my phone. I hear various tracks, including Bongo Herman's 'Bongo Riot'. Bongo Herman gets a number of replays. I'm surprised because it's not one of his strongest tracks. I try to draw strength from Bongo Herman's battles with Bongo Les and Bongo Pat but it doesn't work.

The door opens. Mr Real is there. 'You are a Bongo Herman supporter?'

'Yes. My name's Bax, by the way.' Lesson number one: make friends with your kidnappers.

'For years I have searched for "Bongo Riot". It is crucial. Ital vital.'

This is very annoying. I am now obliged to give him some respect. His admiration for Bongo Herman shows some discrimination. Many seasoned reggaeheads don't know about Bongo Herman, and Turkey is not a reggae stronghold like Europe or the US. Secondly, Mr Real can't be more than twenty and his generation listen to rubbish and have no taste. It's natural each generation want their own thing but even if you're into the current Jamaican scene, you shouldn't be, it's dross, poncey gunmen cutting a track to some crappy computer.

'Which is your Bongo Herman top track?' I don't like this question. Your tastes are always shifting. But I don't say it's an idiotic question. We're bonding. And he has his gun.

'"Freedom Fighters".'

'Based on the Jack Ruby "Long Story" riddim?' This is outrageous trainspotting. Is he going to give me the matrix

218

number or break out a Nyabinghi drum? Have I come all this way to meet a Bobo Dread?

Mr Real rubs the back of his head with his gun, in that way when you're mulling things over. That gun is his proudest possession – he must sleep with it. 'I love "Freedom Fighters" too. You are a Bongo Herman supporter, I must let you go.' He points his gun at Semtex. 'But you must stay.'

Semtex looks at me: 'Go.'

He's being practical, if I leave I can do something to help or at least identify his murderers. I don't know what comes over me.

'I'm not leaving him,' I say. 'He's a Bongo Herman fan, too. He gave me that track.'

'You are not leaving definitely. No money, no leaving.' Mr Real says something local to his circle. They chuckle. It's evident we're not going anywhere, however much we groove on Bongo Herman.

A shake-up is good for you, I tell myself. So many things don't matter now. The bills. That I don't have a proper smart pair of trousers (because I hate to shop). That I didn't get invited to Silly Milly's party this year. Milly has a big bash for the Vizz every year. Being there doesn't help, but not being there hurts. I consoled myself that the invitation got lost in the post, because Silly Milly always constructs some weird invitation on nachos or fabric and actually posts them. These concerns shrink away to nothing.

I knew a reformed pickpocket. If he saw someone on the bus who looked really down, he'd often steal their purse or wallet and then run up to them and tell them he'd found it. 'It cheered people up. Mostly.' The escape from misfortune. The revelation that decency is out there. That it's not all bad. I had that last month: a girl came up to me and gave me a ten-pound note that had wormed out of my pocket. It was touching until it occurred to me that maybe the charm of being a person who returns a ten-pound note was worth more to her than a ten-pound note. London.

There's something about my face that causes members of the public to say 'cheer up'. It's annoying because I'm not asking anyone to intervene and if I was miserable, which most of the time I wasn't, it's my business. Last time someone barked at me like a sergeant-major to cheer up I told him that my wife had just died. I regretted it because he spent the next twenty minutes assuring me how sorry he was and that he knew an undertaker who could do me a deal.

Stay out of my life, and I'll stay out of yours. Otanes. Like the great Otanes in Herodotus, you want to sidestep it all. He didn't want to be the King of Persia, he didn't want to rule. Even executing your enemies is quite time-consuming. However, Otanes didn't want to be ruled either. He wanted to sidestep it all, but *with* the goodies and the glory. It's quite easy to sidestep the drudgery of others if you're willing to live in a hovel in the Orkneys, but not if you like some goodies and glory.

ɱ

The next day it's quiet. 'It's quiet, isn't it?' Semtex remarks.

The quiet becomes thicker. There's no Bongo Herman, no music, no gloating, no chatter. Mr Real hasn't shown us his gun for hours. We can sense that no one's there. They've been gone for a long time. We can just peer under the rickety door: no sound, no movement, no shadows, no feet.

'They're not around,' Semtex concludes. 'Time to antler up.'

'They can't have just left?'

'They're probably outside somewhere. They can't be relying on this nonsense door to hold us. But let's antler up and charge. I know you're good with chairs,' Semtex says. 'Let's see you do the door.' There are times when it helps to have weight.

We wait to see if the door smashing has produced a response. My shoulder hurts. A rickety door still hurts. Nothing. The house is empty, seriously bare. It doesn't look as if anyone lives here in a regular way. There are two rickety chairs and a very worn table. All our stuff is gone. On the table is a red double-ended dildo.

This trip certainly can't get any crazier. Their disappearance is particularly odd since they enjoyed abducting us so much.

I take down the front door, which is also locked, by giving it a couple of kicks and using my weight. My shoulder now really hurts. Outside it's quiet. One of the problems of escaping is that we have no idea where to escape to. I've always been good on direction and again that's why I've kept up the running. I like the possibility of being able to turn and run. Cars break down. There's quite a lot of terrain even a Range Rover can't take. Your legs. Your pins, they'll take you anywhere. They're a truly great invention.

But what we need is a car or a taxi. To drive us to comfort and safety.

Around the corner, we see an old man puffing on a cigarette. Since I only know five words in Turkish, I don't know why but I give him a go in Arabic, as if anyone who speaks Arabic or has eyesight couldn't tell I'm an overweight director from London.

'Where are the bad men?' I ask. It's one of the twelve phrases I know.

'You are the bad men,' he says. I think.

I change to airport-speak. 'Taxi?'

He looks at me in that special way you reserve for backward children. He points and sure enough, down the road, a hundred metres on the right, is a taxi, with a taxi sign, with the driver pulling on a cigarette. I'm already looking forward to telling dinner parties how we escaped from our captors, the red dildo gang: 'We called a taxi.' Fuck me, what a line. Correction: 'The best thing to do when you're abducted is call a taxi.' It such a good anecdote that I feel glad we were snatched.

I should know better. Never think you've reached bottom; you haven't. There's always more bottom. As we hobble to the taxi, a pick-up truck zooms in front of us. Four men get out.

'Why are you here?' That's a good question, but they don't wait for the answer. 'Who are you?' These men are serious. They have big guns. They have quotations in Arabic wrapped around their heads and beards.

It's one of those moments when I wish I'd taken that regular evening class in Arabic. Three of them have big, bushy, pushy beards. In-your-face beards. The fourth guy, who evidently was aiming for major beard, only has a few lonely wisps of hair dangling from his chin.

We have just met a whole new class of kidnapper. Your friendly local militia. One prods me in the stomach with his rifle: 'Peace be upon you.' He has an oddly high-pitched voice, like a squeaky toy.

'Taffakur,' I say. I don't think there's anything to lose.

♏

It's hard to go through the mental toughening a second time, especially when it's failed. Or did it? We did actually get out. The mental toughness worked. It wasn't, ultimately, the fault of the toughness that we were abducted again immediately.

222

'We are all people of the book,' I say, referring to the section in the Quran that talks of brotherhood. This is phrase two that I know. 'My name is Bax, by the way.'

'You are shit,' Squeaky Toy says. He's not especially angry. He's doing his job. They're a bit confused about us wandering around without papers or phones, money or shoes. They haven't spotted my money belt, which gives me a sense of superiority. They find our abduction and robbery story hard to believe, we appear too benighted to be spies (spy-hunting is a real mania in zones), but on the other hand they're not going to accept we're wandering Sufi scholars.

'Where are we?' I ask.

'You are where you need to be.' Squeaky Toy is a bit of a philosopher.

♏

'We've got to do something,' says Semtex. We're in what I presume is a *sardab*. It's nice to know the correct local term for a hole in the ground or cellar. That you have a rapport with the local culture. There's a funny smell, but I can't figure out what it is they used to store down here.

'I'm open to suggestions.'

'You're the brains of the operation.'

If we're in Syria, I wonder whether invoking Jack's name will be any use. No one could object to his doc on Miss Syria, but his one on Assad means execution all round.

'We're going to have to do them,' says Semtex. 'It's the only way out.'

'Easier said than done.'

We're summoned out of the hole. They have a video camera, which they can't operate. They argue, presumably complaining about the manual being missing or that it isn't clear enough or

223

that Failed Beard hasn't read it properly. They then tell Semtex to set the camera up.

'I can't use it,' he says. 'I've never used one of those.' It would be funny, but our current captors have the eyes of total nutters. None of this lot is likely to die serenely in bed at the age of eighty.

'You said you are cameraman; do it,' says Squeaky Toy, who is obviously the top nutter. 'It is time to make history.'

After some deliberation and fiddling, Semtex gets the camera working, films me introducing myself and some declaration in Arabic from Squeaky Toy. I'm not sure about this, but what can we do? It feels a little bit like digging your grave.

'Your government is evil,' Squeaky tells us.

'Why are you telling us this? I know my government's evil. I really, personally, do know the government's evil. I know it better than you.'

'You are responsible.'

'No I'm not,' I insist. 'Tell you what, come to London and I'll help you kill them. With pleasure. Any taxpayer would.'

I wonder if I should claim that Zyklon Annie is the head of British intelligence and that I can provide Squeaky Toy with her home address? Offer to help kidnap her? When they check up on her and say she's an old bag who makes boring docs about health care, I can say, yes, it's the perfect cover. However, I hold back because if I give that up straight away it might look unconvincing. I'll wait a day.

Yet again I bury the thought that this all Semtex's fault. That's not going anywhere. If I get out, I promise myself, as a treat, I'll strangle him with my bare hands. Anger, despair,

224

these are your adversaries. Your own self is what you have to beat, that's why it's so tiring because it's always there.

Make the list. At the top of the list: get out of here. Again, I think of my Uncle Joe, how he made it through the worst of one of the worst wars. So far, apart from the humiliation, which is not much worse than being in Johxn's office, the worst thing that's happened is being prodded in the stomach with a muzzle.

We are shepherded back into the hole. 'You are thirsty,' Squeaky Toy says. He looks very frightening and I find him frightening, but he has this high voice. Both Semtex and I now refer to him as Squeaky Toy. It's probably the absurdity of his high-pitched voice that makes him so stroppy. Squeaky Toy takes a piss into a jar. And leaves the jar. 'If you are thirsty just ask for something to drink.'

Our first group were dangerous, in a reckless, drunk-on-Saturday-night, kebab-shop way, but not that frightening. They wanted money or a laugh. This bunch scare me. I'm thirsty but I can hang on a little bit longer. A few hours later, just as I'm pondering how bad it could be to drink the piss, they give us water; the piss is a practical joke.

'We are proud of our hospitality,' says Squeaky Toy. Everyone is proud of their hospitality, no matter where you go. Everyone can rule the world.

They throw in in some hard sweets past their expiry date. This might actually be hospitality. To me they look like shitty old sweets that no one else wanted, but who knows? They might be highly valued local delicacies.

I remember what Uncle Joe said and suck on a sweet that has a fruity but undefinable taste. I wonder if Semtex is going to ask whether the sweets have been produced using animal products, but he pops one in his mouth. Is this going to be our staple fare? One journalist who was kidnapped in Iraq was fed bread for months. He finally successfully argued with his captors that if they were as upright and principled as they claimed to be, couldn't they get him a decent meal? So they ordered a *masgouf* from a fancy restaurant nearby. He died of food poisoning the next day. There was a lot of recrimination as to whose fault it was and whether it should affect the ransom.

Bad behaviour is often because of boredom. It's the same for delinquents on street corners or jihadis; you start cooking up new ways of killing because there's nothing good at the cinema and anyway if you're a true blue jihadi you're not allowed to go to the cinema. How many times can you read the Quran? There are no car chases in it. There's no beginning, middle or end. Just advice about what to do with your third wife. It's like a compendium of agony auntery. Nothing happens. Shall I sum up the Quran? I can do it in under five words. One God. Be nice.

I read it once when I was stuck in a hotel room in Baghdad, waiting. The Jews have better stories. Perhaps that's why they run Hollywood. And the Bible has sex and violence. The smiting. Jesus giving it to the money-changers.

Kids on street corners in London now, of course, are less of a problem because they have unlimited gaming and unlimited wanking to unlimited hi-def porn.

♏

His banana-clip gun in front of him, Squeaky Toy is sitting at a small table. I try not to read too much into this; in many parts of the world, Dallas, Waziristan, carrying a gun for a man is as normal as wearing a pair of trousers. There are two chairs. Semtex and I are instructed to sit down.

226

Squeaky Toy produces a deck of cards. Does a fancy shuffle to demonstrate he knows his cards. 'We will now play poker. We will play poker for your lives.'

'Okay,' says Semtex. He's up for this, the mad fucker. I know he fancies himself as a poker player.

Squeaky Toy almost falls off his chair laughing. His boys are doubling up, Failed Beard hooting hardest because he has to make up for the lack of chin splendour. They're laughing so hard I consider making a break for it. By their reaction we're the best ha-ha in these parts for a hundred years.

'What sort of idiots are you?' Squeaky Toy has to wipe away a tear. 'How dare you insult us by thinking we would play poker for a human life? Haram. Haram. You have insulted us by drinking my urine. Do you really think we make our guests drink urine?'

'I didn't drink any of it.'

'You drank some of it.'

'No, I didn't.'

'You drank from it,' he insists and there's no upside to disputing this further. He wants to tell the story of how the dopey foreigners guzzled the piss while their attentive hosts were pouring out some chilled mineral water with lemon slices for them. 'We are famous for our hospitality. What would you like to eat?' Is he going to dump into a bucket now?

'Baba ganoush,' I say, another one of my twelve phrases. It's one of my favourites. I might as well ask.

'Me too,' says Semtex.

Squeaky snaps his fingers, doubtless something he's seen in a film somewhere. Predictably, Failed Beard scuttles off.

Squeaky holds out the deck.

'Now,' he says. 'Pick a card, any card.'

He does a number of tricks with the cards even I know how to do, plus the disappearing coin. He does some stuff with matches I hadn't seen before, but who cares about matches?

We get the food.

♏

I would have died in Afghanistan if it hadn't been for my son. We had a three-day walk to get out. We were being chased. It was that genuine march-or-die thing. Either you kept going or you'd die, one way or another. I kept thinking would it do any good to say to our pursuers, 'I almost interviewed Osama bin Laden before he was really famous, you know.' After the first day I realised I couldn't make it. I was in good shape, younger, fitter, slimmer, but that didn't mean I could do twelve-hour days uphill, with strange contests going on in my guts, without food or water. I started to cry because it wasn't that I didn't want to walk, but it was too much. I was exhausted; my feet were a mess of blisters. It was too much.

Luckily, I was at the back of the group because I was fading, so no one could see me blubbing. I would have given up then, if it had just been me, I would have cashed in my chips, said enough's enough, but for my son.

I will never go back there. Not for any amount of money, Correction: well, all right for an implausible amount of money, but it would have to be three big yachts' worth at least. And then only for a short visit, and I would feel unwell the whole time.

The thought of Luke gees me up. There is a slab, a flagstone on the floor. Does it cover a drain? Whatever it is, it'd be too small for me but Semtex is almost wire. If it weren't for his head, he could probably get under most doors. We spend hours digging it up with our fingers, till they bleed, when we

228

lift it up, there is nothing underneath but good old-fashioned earth.

'At least we know Herbie's safe isn't there,' says Semtex. 'We've got to rush them. I doubt there's more than two or three around. I'm not going out like a fucking potato, in a hole in the ground.'

'Potatoes have feelings, you know.'

It's true. I reflect if I have to rush someone, I'd sooner rush someone with a rifle, than a pistol or knife, because if you make a grab for it, you have more chance of grabbing something. But I don't fancy it. Because I don't want to die. Up close, I suppose I'd have a chance against Squeaky Toy, because he's not big, and I've got the weight. If I push him against a wall or throw him to the ground, he's got a broken rib or intense pain.

'Do you think the outside world's going to do something?' Semtex asks.

'No would be my guess.'

I don't feel any confidence that London will send a rescue team or do anything constructive. If they even know we're in hot water. Do we wait? See if the cavalry arrive? No one invited us here. I know abductees who spent more than a year in misery while money or a deal was sorted out, or indeed while a ransom note failed to be delivered. I'm not built for that.

To get out, by ourselves, we've got do some major damage to someone and then the courtesy, however thin and well-hidden it may be, will definitely go.

'We're getting out of this, we're definitely getting out of this,' says Semtex firmly. He sounds as if he's been listening to some self-help tape where you're instructed to repeat your goal decisively until it arrives.

'How?'

'I'm trying to cheer you up.'

'You're not doing a very good job.'

The trap door opens and Squeaky Toy peers down on us. It's the perspective that makes it so attractive for him. Is he going to do another one of his magic tricks? I can't explain why but there's always something dodgy about aficionados of magic tricks. I'm not talking about amateur magicians who are trying to be professional, or are putting on a full amateur show. No, it's the pub magicians. The ones who fiddle with coins and cards, the barely legerdemain.

'Do you think about death?' Squeaky Toy asks. He's wrong-footed me here. I can't think of a good answer. Go witty? Go thoughtful? Go grovelly? I recite the Islamic profession of faith. It's one of the twelve phrases I know in Arabic. I had memorised it for precisely a situation such as this. When I was in Iraq I had it on a loop on the car stereo so it would sink in. Deep.

When someone says something to you, at that moment, you can't be sure whether they're half-hearted or lying or they'll change their mind. You'll probably find out later, but at that moment, you can't know, for sure. The credibility conundrum can work to your advantage.

'I had someone at school like you,' Squeaky Toy addresses me. 'He was an asshead.' My preparations for a situation precisely like this have fallen short. 'He looked like you. Fat. Stupid. He made everyone laugh he was so ass.'

Are we getting somewhere? I suppose Squeaky had to do tricks at school to avoid getting beaten up. I hope he was beaten up a lot. And he's definitely not getting laid. What's behind this bulletin?

'I liked him a lot,' Squeaky continues. 'That's why we shoot you last. Thin people are not funny.'

I remind myself that death threats and mock executions are standard in these situations, basically a requirement. But it doesn't do much good. Squeaky's brandishing his rifle. I have the feeling he's on his own. If it weren't for the rifle and being on the wrong side of the law of gravity, I'd have to consider rushing him. I'm glad I don't really have a choice.

'I don't want to worry you, but I love killing,' he announces. I believe him.

He watches us as if expecting a reply.

'It's not good. You should be sorry for me.'

♏

You can't be terrified for long. Eventually you cope or maybe, like everything else, you simply get bored with terror. I've probably lost several pounds or more through fear, but after a day of gasping and sweating, I'm focused. I'm thinking how to get out.

In case we're here for a long time I resolve to find something to do mentally. That's the advice I heard from everyone's who been through it. Stay tough, have something to do. One American spook told me he spent his captivity planning how he would hunt down his captors, their families, their friends and their livestock and kill them all, and how he coined new ways of expressing the concept of 'fucking killing them all', such as 'render them respiratorially inactive' or 'abrupt metabolic cessation'. He had a list of over two hundred phrases by the end.

Why me? Why me? That's a very common question that has never had a satisfactory answer. We live in an environment of cause and effect, so we see that everywhere, or try to see it everywhere. Why am I stuck here, while Liliane is in a foam bath? What is the cause? What have I done? Cause and effect have let me down.

♏

231

'I blame you,' says Semtex. I remind myself I would feel worse if I were on my own. Misery is one of the few things you want to share. 'This is your fault.'

'You've mentioned that. If it makes you feel better, it's my fault.'

Of course, it's not my fault in the way Semtex means it. But it is my fault. I didn't have to be here. We didn't have to be here. I've never understood why most people find it so hard to say they're wrong or that they've made a mistake. Of course, there are circumstances in which an admission of bad judgement can get you punished: 'I was wrong to kill everyone in the house.'

But in many situations, it's just easier and less ridiculous to fess up. 'I forgot to buy the turbot.' Just say that instead of getting into scenarios where you were never asked to buy a turbot, you were prevented from buying the turbot because of alien abduction, or there was a global backlash against turbot that meant turbot had disappeared from all retail outlets.

And complete surrender can be an effective weapon. Semtex is now annoyed that I haven't offered a denial allowing him to go off on one, with a carefully prepared list itemising my culpability. So he goes off on a different path.

'You just attract this stuff. Why couldn't you be more positive? Why couldn't you have made a doc about Roger Crab, someone who wanted to make the world better, instead of a child murderer? Of all the personalities, in all of history, in all the countries, why did you choose someone that off?'

'First of all, The Ray was probably fitted up. Secondly I never got to finish it, but as you know, it ended in disaster. I did make a doc about bouncy castles. That's about as uplifting as it gets. And another one about a very happy man with a spoon in his ear. The whole thing was about happiness cheaply obtained, with a spoon.'

'I have a bad feeling about this,' says Semtex. I'm glad he can't see my face.

'Aren't you meant to say that before we get kidnapped?'

'No one's stumping up big money to get us back.'

'We have to figure a way out.' I'm surprised by how confident I sound.

'I'll tell you something I've never told anyone.'

This worries me because although being in this position makes you very broad-minded, I don't want to hear something sordid that will make me think less of Semtex. I'm not in the mood.

'Is this about the sandwiches?'

'I shot some people once.'

'That's not much of a surprise.'

'That's not the story. These black guys were running a crack house next door to me. I wouldn't have minded if it had been quietly run, if they'd cracked in the privacy of their abode as it were, but it wasn't. It was the neighbours from hell deluxe edition, losers who like to do their screaming at three in the morning.'

'Didn't you call the police?'

'Do you want to listen? I'm telling you something important. And have you ever called the police? I called them fucking day and night. Part of the problem was that one of the dealers was the local community rep dealing with the problem of crack so they couldn't arrest him. I was younger and hot-headed.'

'And you shot them?'

'No, I moved. The best way to deal with a problem is not to deal with it. Just skip it, star. But having had a number of

233

full and frank exchanges with these arseholes, I had to settle up. So one dark night I went back for them and knee-capped them, big time. As a committed vegan and Buddhist I felt I couldn't go any further.'

'You're not a Buddhist.'

'I never claimed to be a model Buddhist. Who is? Apart from Buddha, of course.'

'They didn't recognise you?'

'I don't think crack landlords are at the top of the game when it comes to memory. I was balaclava'd up and wearing eight layers of clothes so I looked about twice my size, and I said, 'That'll teach you, Tony,' as I left, because neither of them was called Tony, so in the unlikely event of them going to the police, they'd think it was some other crackhead who was the target.'

'You got away with it then. The perfect crime.'

'It wasn't a crime, but a rightful expression of . . . rightfulness on my part. And it depends what you mean by got away with it.'

'You're in a hole, not in jail, so you dodged that one.'

'Like anyone who's watched television, I knew I had to not only get rid of my clothing, but the gun. And having done a number of crime progs I was always puzzled why criminals dump the whole gun, because a distinguishing feature of a gun is it's gun-shaped and it's a fair size, and if you come across it in the mud at the bottom of a lake, it feels like a gun. I stripped down the gun into small bits, which to an unfirearm-appreciating man in the street don't look like a gun and are harder to find because they're smaller. So I took the barrel to Epping Forest, the slide out to Richmond, the firing pin to Catford, I scattered a dozen bits over fifty fucking square miles.'

'Where's the punchline?'

'A week later, I'm pleased with myself. No sign of the law. Pleased with my payback. It's a glorious day, I open the front door and the gun parts are in a small pile on my doorstep.'

'That's unforeseeable.'

'Now I can't be definite it was my gun, but it was Glock parts, heaped up, on my doorstep. A few screws were missing but it was a complete gun. That was . . . ten years ago? While we're stuck here, I'd like to hear if you can think of an explanation, because I can't. If someone was following me around for some reason, they'd either keep quiet about it, or keep the evidence, or they'd shop me. I just can't come up with an explanation, that's what weirds me out.'

'What did you do?'

'After all that trouble it didn't seem worth getting rid of the gun again, but I took it to Eel Pie Island and deep-sixed it. What's the point if it's a homing handgun and it's just coming back again? For a long time I hated opening my front door. This may sound ridiculous but it was like the universe vomited up the parts to say, "We run things and don't you forget it. Don't get above your station." Some of those parts were well underwater, even if you knew where they were they were almost impossible to retrieve. So, Mr Smartarse, what's your explanation? Anything as mad as that happened to you?'

'No.' I'm not telling Semtex.

'You know, we have to do something radical to get out of here. We're going to have to do them. The funny thing about you, Bax, is that there are a lot of folk in the industry who are terrified of you. They don't know you're as soft as fucking whipped cream. They don't know the only things you've trashed are chairs.'

Failed Beard interrupts us. He wants to talk to us again about urban planning in Denmark. We've explained before, several times, that we have no knowledge or interest in urban planning anywhere, let alone Denmark, but he doesn't believe us. He thinks we're holding out on him.

♏

They give us water and some dry bread. The baba ganoush was clearly meant as a special treat. They have plans for us. They check up on us a lot at the beginning. It's like getting a new pet, I suppose, or receiving a big cheque. You can't stop looking and relooking. They're pleased with themselves because they've moved up in some league table. Who else has pet Brits?

I think about my wife. She'll be all right if I don't get back. Ellen has a secure job and it's completely, completely predictable. She can always organise her holidays six months in advance. The dullness of her job looks much better from a hole in the ground but I couldn't live like that. It's unfortunate, but I need chaos. I like a bumpy ride, but not this much.

I think of my son. I don't understand parents who aren't willing to die for their children, who wouldn't do anything to help them. Of course, the deep blindness of parental love can be as horrific as neglect when you have to listen to someone's ten-year-old murdering a piano.

'What do you want on your gravestone?' Semtex asks.

'Aren't I the designated pessimist in this cellar? How about "He hoped and he hoped and he hoped and . . ."?' I don't ask Semtex what he wants. But after a while, I'm so bored.

'What about you? What would you like? "Dun Biting"?'

'"I'm not here".'

I watch a bug processing on the wall. For some reason an article I read on the plane comes to mind. I'd estimate there are no more than forty basic news stories, so once you've lived a while they get very familiar. Eat insects is one. Every so often there's a piece on how we should be noshing on grubs and locusts because there are so many of them, they're healthy to eat and the world would be a much fairer place if we just reached for a grasshopper.

Saving money tips is another. There's always something about how changing your bank account or utility supplier can make a difference. That's one that makes me angry. It's the dishonesty; the suggestion that snipping off a few quid will make a difference. No it won't. There's one grim truth, the only way to make money is to make money. Putting money in a different savings account or switching supermarket is as much use as stirring a cup of tea. You want big money, you need a big money maker. I'm getting so angry about this, when I should be angry about other things, that it makes me realise that I'm getting nutty.

'Do you think people can change?' asks Semtex.

'Not really.'

'There's no hope, then.'

'Okay, they can change.'

'Because that's the only real question,' says Semtex. 'If we can't change, if it's just a matter of hiding a bit of yourself, or revealing another bit, if that's the best you can do. We're stuck. We're stuck in ruts. We're just stuck in ourselves. And everything is preordained.'

Squeaky Toy opens the hatch.

'I hope you feel safe,' he says, 'because you are very safe.' He throws in some more bread. I'm hit in the face by a crust. 'We are famous for our hospitality.'

'I wonder whether some people are people,' says Semtex.

'What do you mean?'

'It's like Squeaky Toy, how do you know he's a person? He looks human, acts human, but maybe he isn't.'

'I don't understand.'

'He has no soul. He's here to make up the numbers. An extra. A puppet.'

'You need a steak, pal.'

'Maybe the whole problem of evil isn't a problem. Maybe there isn't any suffering, only the appearance of suffering. All the wars are just special effects. Maybe it's just there as a test.'

You can never outrun your hippy parents.

'Speak for yourself, I'm suffering.'

'Are we? This is unpleasant, it's frightening, is it real suffering?'

Why can't I be locked up with someone with a good supply of 'a man walks into a bar' jokes?

'So how do we pass the test?' I enquire.

I don't find out. First we hear people above us. Someone's arrived. Lots of voices. Are these negotiations about us? The shouting is very loud and angry. Most insults the world over revolve around genitalia. Where would we be without them? I hear another one of the twelve phrases I know; it's a very personal dispute. It's also interesting that in the Middle East, it's not fuck you, as in much of the world, but I, personally, will fuck you. They're big on the bum. Then gunfire. The gunfire is terrifying loud. Those are two things that reporting fails to convey well. How astonishingly loud war is (and how bad it smells).

I almost vomit with fear. This is getting beyond my self-control. The gunfire is loud and in an enclosed space, painfully loud, and bullets at this range aren't going to wound you, they're going to cut you in half. I'm panting and sweating like some marathon runner. The smell of cordite reaches us.

There is silence. Silence for a long time.

'I don't think there's anyone out there,' Semtex says eventually. We shout for food and water. No reply. Semtex shouts some abuse. Mothers are always mentioned. Nothing.

'Let's go for it. The door, Immenso.' It takes both of us hours of battering and thumping to get out. I'm a mass of bruises. The room is empty, apart from a lot of blood. An extraordinary amount. At least one person didn't make it, because there's more than a body load dispersed everywhere.

'Fuck,' Semtex comments.

It looks like our kidnappers were ... kidnapped. Why didn't we get drawn in? Did our kidnappers keep quiet about us out of some code of honour? Did they keep quiet because they hoped to come back? Did they keep quiet the way I kept quiet about my money belt?

'No one's going to believe this.'

'If you get the chance to tell them.'

'It doesn't make sense.'

'Believing in sanity is insanity, star. That much I know.'

We peer outside. We don't have much choice about what to do. We can't stay here. Best foot forward. We leave a trail of bloody footprints. I wish I had a camera it's such a powerful image. Down the road a woman is hanging out laundry.

'Taxi?' asks Semtex.

♏

'You still looking for Herbie's safe?' Semtex asks me as we ride back to our hotel in Gaziantep.

'Not really. I gave it a go at the time, I did everything I could. Talked to all the villains I could talk to. Put up notices, rewards. I don't see how I can find it now, five years on?'

'Why are you so keen on it?'

239

'Herbie had all sorts of ideas. Maybe he had some research hidden in it. He certainly didn't have money. Why else have a safe? And I was hoping I could catch the burglar somehow. It was horrible, just after the funeral, and there were other things taken his son might have wanted, apart from the safe.'

'It might have been disappointing. Just his favourite porn.'

He's right. What I'd have found might have been disappointing or it might have made me think less of Herbie.

'We'll never know.'

Semtex looks out at the passing streets for a few minutes. 'Are you positive you want to know?'

His tone tells me he knows something.

'What?'

'I didn't say I knew anything."

'No, no. If you know something you can say nothing. Nothing at all. But if you start the do-you-want-to-know game, you have to say.'

'Do you want to know?'

'I've got no choice now, have I?'

'All right.'

'You didn't find the safe?'

'Of course not. But I found the guy who stole it.'

'How?'

'By not looking for him. I did an interview a few weeks ago with this former burglar-junkie who was responsible for three hundred burglaries in Hendon, right next to the Police College. He was known as the Hand of Hendon before he reformed and got into the security and meditation business.'

The only thing I hate more than a junkie who'll steal anything is an ex-junkie who'll bore you with how his life has changed.

240

'Herbie being a Hendonian, I asked him if he had lifted any safes.'

'Why would he remember?' I say. 'And how can we know it was Herbie's?'

'Because, among other things, the safe contained a massive inflatable penis.'

When I did the bouncy castles I brought back a big bag of giant blow-up phalluses for everyone, including Semtex and Herbie. Not Johxn.

'He also had a vivid memory of the safe because he had so much trouble carrying it off, and he nearly lost a finger getting it open, so he did his nut when he got inside.'

Semtex pauses.

'Come on. What else was in it?' I have to admit I never thought I'd have to tour Turkey to find Herbie's safe.

'You won't like this. The safe contained two whiskey bottles filled with piss. But you'll like this. There was also a note: "You're not as clever as you think you are."'

That sounds right. I hadn't believed Semtex was on to something. But the note is classic Herbie. Plus the two bottles of piss to make the safe even heavier. I should have known Herbie wouldn't have been foolish enough to keep anything valuable in a safe. I should have guessed that. Just as I carry around a sucker wallet.

So where's the unseen footage of the Loch Ness Monster? The map to find Excalibur? The letter that confirms Elizabeth I was a man? The trick for anti-gravity? What the Russians did on the moon? If Herbie had a stash for his secrets I'm unlikely to find it now. Nor am I ever going to find out what Johxn was worried about.

'What did you think was so important there?' asks Semtex, as if he hadn't asked me this a dozen times.

'Herbie had so many ideas and contacts, I expected . . . something. And Johxn is very jumpy about it.'

'He is. I told him you had a lead when I bumped into him the other day. He danced around like his feet were on fire. He's got a bad conscience about something.'

'Well, we're not going to find out.' The last time I heard from Herbie was voicemail. A short message: 'I need to talk to you.' He sounded like his old self. Upbeat. Brimming. With something to divulge. But I was busy that evening and the next morning I got the news Herbie was dead. Had he found something to compromise Johxn? Did he have him bang to rights?

'You're not a good poker player, are you?' says Semtex.

'I don't play poker. Or any card game. I'd sooner be fucking.'

'Let me put something in your suggestion box, Bax. Why don't you tell Johxn you've found it? Use the Occult Canaanite art of lying. And then ask about a big fat juicy commission. See what his guilt will cough up? Watch his smugness collapse, like a chair sat on by you. There's no need to thank me. Although a two-hour special on Roger Crab would be about right.'

This is possibly the first sensible thing Semtex has ever said to me. It's been a long wait. Johxn still hasn't made his mind up about his Big Money deal. Should I go for Göbekli Tepe, the Garden of Eden or The Ray? Or maybe something else, because I don't want to leave home for a long time.

'I can't do that; that would be wrong.'

We get back to our hotel. We have no rooms. A large party from Sudan has got them. The receptionist gives us her best 'but we thought you were dead' look.

I phone Ellen. She launches into a tirade about the washing-machine acting up, which tells me that she hasn't been at all worried about me being non-there for four days. We weren't missed. My hostage video didn't air. It's probably better that way. The whole episode would only reinforce her view that she married an imbecile.

The next day an invoice from our bodyguards turns up. It's printed, but they drew a smiley face at the bottom of the page with a couple of exclamation marks.

I almost buy a jar of honey at the airport for Luke. Then I put it back on the shelf. I'm not buying honey any more.

♏

At Heathrow, as the cold whistles around us, Semtex turns to me in goodbye mode. 'We won't forget that trip in a hurry. Bax, you're a true mate, a cellmate, maybe even a soulmate. I'll give you that. But I can't work with you any more. Don't take it personally. You're the original disaster-magnet.'

We shake hands and he walks off. Then stops. 'Yes, one more thing, Bax. I almost forgot. I'll tell everyone, everyone and particularly Johxn, off the record, in a shaky, confidential voice, having made them swear to secrecy, like I absolutely shouldn't be telling them this, that you busted us out. How you killed them all. How you gave Squeaky Toy and his boys a big dose of trigger time. Because I'm not sure you didn't. In case Herbie's safe isn't enough. They will bow down to the Prince of Darkness.'

Who knows? Who knows how things will change? I'm thinking when I've had a good rest I'll find that knuckleduster I have in a box somewhere. Then I'll find the Hand of Hendon, and I'll say to him, 'Don't you remember me?'